THE BOY WHO STEALS HOUSES

Also by C.G. Drews

A Thousand Perfect Notes

THE
BOY
WHO
STEALS
HOUSES

C.G. DREWS

ORCHARD

ORCHARD BOOKS

First published in Great Britain in 2019 by The Watts Publishing Group

1 3 5 7 9 8 6 4 2

Text copyright © C.G. Drews, 2019

The moral rights of the author have been asserted.

A CIP catalogue record for this book is available from the British Library.

ISBN 978 1 40834 992 2

Typeset in Sabon by Avon DataSet Ltd, Bidford-on-Avon,
Warwickshire

Printed and bound in Great Britain by Clays Ltd, Elcograf S.p.A.

The paper and board used in this book are made from wood
from responsible sources.

MIX
Paper from
responsible sources
FSC® C104740

Orchard Books
An imprint of Hachette Children's Group
Part of The Watts Publishing Group Limited
Carmelite House
50 Victoria Embankment
London EC4Y 0DZ

An Hachette UK Company
www.hachette.co.uk

www.hachettechildrens.co.uk

If lost, please return to the De Laineys.

CHAPTER 1

If it hadn't been so dark and if his fingers hadn't been so stiff with dried blood, he could've picked the lock in thirty-eight seconds.

Sammy Lou takes pride in that record. It's one of the few things he *can* take pride in, considering his life consists of charming locks, pockets full of stolen coins, broken shoelaces, and an ache in his stomach that could be hunger or loneliness.

Probably hunger.

He should be used to being alone by now.

He just needs to crack this freaking lock before someone sees and calls the cops. The house has been empty for days – so says the mouldering newspaper on the driveway, the closed curtains, the lack of lights at night. He knows. He's watched.

And now he's been at this lock for over two minutes. His palms go slick with sweat and the dried blood dampens and slips between his knuckles. His lock picks, a gift from his brother and usually an extension of Sam's thin and nimble fingers, feel too thick. Too slow.

He can't get caught.

He's been breaking into houses for a year now.

He *can't* get caught.

One of his lock picks gets jammed and he whispers a curse. He wriggles it free, but his heart thunders and seconds tick by too fast, so he abandons the lock and melts back into the shadows. There's always another way.

He slips around the house, undone shoelaces slapping his ankles. The house is old bricks, the windows cloistered with drawn blinds. It's harder to see back here, with a tall fence blocking the moonlight. But a woodpile sits under a small window and it whispers welcome.

Sam dumps his backpack on the grass and scales the woodpile, placing each foot and hand gingerly so he doesn't end up underneath an avalanche of split logs. He's sore enough as is, thanks. His hands trace the small bathroom window, and for once he's pleased he skipped out on the growth spurts regular fifteen-year-old boys encounter. He's a year off for his age. Maybe two. Looking small and pathetic usually works to his advantage, plus it turns tight windows and poky corners into opportunities.

Half balancing, half hugging the wall, Sam fiddles with the lock while the woodpile gives an ominous groan and shifts beneath him.

Things this family is good at: locking their house.

Things they suck at: stacking wood into a sturdy pile.

If this doesn't work, he'll have to—

'You could always break it.'

Sam's heart leaps about fifteen metres in the air – and unfortunately his feet follow. For a second he scrabbles to grip the wall, bricks ripping fingertips, and then he loses balance and tumbles backwards. The lock picks go flying into the darkness.

At least there's not far to fall.

At least the woodpile doesn't tip over too.

At least, Sam thinks, still on his back and staring up at a silhouette smudged against the stars, it's only his brother.

For a second Sam just lies there while the dewy grass soaks his shirt and his heart migrates back down his throat.

'Dammit, Avery,' Sam says.

'I didn't bring a hammer.' Avery pulls his phone out of his pocket, flips on the torch app and shines it straight in Sam's eyes. 'But we could use a rock or, like, your head since it's hard and ugly enough.' He gives the tiniest breath of a laugh, but follows quickly with, 'That was a joke. I was joking. You can tell it's a joke, right?'

Sam wasn't prepared for this tonight. Interruptions and complications and—

Avery.

And Avery wouldn't show up unless—

'Is something wrong?' Sam shields his eyes from the glare. 'Are you hurt or in trouble or ...' His pulse quickens. 'You're OK?'

'What?' Avery blinks, confused. 'Yeah, I'm fine.'

Sam didn't realise, until the *I'm fine* comes, how tight his chest is. How shaky his hands suddenly are. He has to close his eyes a minute and fumble for a thin grip on calm. It's fine. Avery's fine.

Sam scrambles up and snaps, 'Turn that light off.'

He doesn't mean to snap. It's just that rush of panic for nothing.

'You're mad?' Avery tucks the phone to his chest, as if that could stop Sam taking it off him if Sam really wanted to. Avery's all elbows and sharp jawlines, with a scar at the corner of his mouth, and a pointy elfish face that says he skipped the effort of growing too.

'I'm about to be mad.' Sam's teeth clench. 'Turn it *off* or I'll smack you into the middle of next week.'

Avery frowns but turns the light off.

Sam's lost his night vision now. His ears strain, but he doesn't catch any movement or whispers. Or sirens. He's not caught.

'I could get you a phone.' Avery rocks on his heels. 'That would fix everything.'

Of course it would, Avery. A phone would fix the fact that Sam is a house thief in clothes he stole from a second-hand store, who needed a haircut months ago, with skin tight against his ribs like a tally of all the meals he's missed.

His fingers curl into fists. Sticky with blood. It's all bluff anyway, because he'd never hit Avery. In fact, it's the opposite. Sam spends his life hitting the world and smoothing over the rusty corners so Avery won't fall and hurt himself.

'I wouldn't need you to fix stuff,' Sam says, the barest frustrated tremble in his voice, 'if you'd stop ruining everything.'

The result is instant.

Avery wilts, shoulders hunched to make himself a smaller target. Sam is stupid, *stupid*. He shouldn't have said that.

'I didn't mean it.' He shuffles his hands in the grass in vain hopes he'll find the lock picks. Maybe he'll find a hundred dollars and a five-course meal down here too. But Avery's already started flapping, hands moving anxiously against his thighs in one of his endless tics. His thin lips have folded into their signature downturned pout, all poor waif and damp eyes that remind you that you're a complete asshole for being angry with him.

'Why didn't you hear me coming?' Avery says. 'You're supposed to be a burglar.' He glances around, hand-flapping escalating to a fist beating his own leg. 'We need to break in before we get caught and—'

'OK, OK, calm down.' Sam rubs his temples. 'What do you mean *we*?'

Avery touches the tips of his fingers to Sam's chest. 'You. And me. We.'

Sam opens his mouth to argue, but why bother? Avery isn't supposed to be here, even if Sam did off-handedly tell him what house he was breaking into tonight. But if Avery decides he's coming in – he's coming in. Sam's never said no to him in his life. Plus he's not wrong about how loud they're being. Sam's truly lost it this evening. Two failed break-in attempts and now he's arguing in a stranger's backyard with his brother who can ruin everything and then tear up and make Sam feel like the monster.

Not that it's an untrue feeling. Not when he has blood on his knuckles.

He suddenly feels very tired. It has nothing to do with his aching cheekbone or bruised chest or two locks that defeated him.

It's just this.

All of it.

Standing between puddles of moonlight to steal into a house that isn't and will never be his, just so he has a place to sleep tonight.

'Just shut up and follow me,' Sam says, grabbing his backpack. 'Quietly. And don't – don't *break* anything. I want to stay here for a few days. You know that's how I work.'

Avery starts humming, which could be agreement or mean he's not listening. Sam smothers his annoyance. Breathe. Just breathe.

Sam moves towards the back door, the last hope, and Avery follows, flapping his hands distractedly.

The back of the house presents a patio crammed with too much furniture and barely enough space to squeeze through to the door. Sam inspects the lock and then slips paperclips out of his pocket. He keeps them for emergencies. The job is hard without a sturdy hook to keep the pressure on the lock. His fingers shake.

'Are you screwing up?' Avery says in a conversational tone.

Sam stabs harder at the lock. 'How about you just tell me why you're here?' He is relieved Avery's here, of course – safe and right where Sam can watch him – but a dark, selfish corner of Sam's heart was looking forward to sleeping tonight without *worrying*. Well, Sam always worries about Avery, whether he's in sight or not. But a night alone would be a quiet break.

Seriously, Sam? This is your brother. You don't need a break. You shouldn't want one.

'I just missed you,' Avery says.

'Sure,' Sam says, knowing Avery won't notice the sarcasm. 'You're definitely not here because you want something.'

Once they stole houses together, but it quickly fell apart because Avery needs sameness and moving around so much had him in endless fretful meltdowns that even Sam couldn't soothe. Now? Avery rotates between sleeping in the back of the mechanic's shop, hoping his boss doesn't catch him, and hanging around a group of twenty-year-olds who have him run bad jobs and tell him he's cute while he smiles like an excited puppy and doesn't freaking *get* that they're using him. They let him sleep on their broken sofa. And that sameness? Only having to rotate between two places that don't change? Avery will take that instead of staying with Sam, waiting for him to *maybe* find a new place to sleep every night. Now he tells Sam that he's *got friends* and he's *got a job*, and he *can take care of himself.*

And then, when he inevitably still falls apart, he reappears and Sam has to fix everything.

Always.

That's why Sam's bloody and bruised tonight, isn't it? Fixing things for Avery. But if Avery knows what Sam did tonight, why he just beat someone up, he'll freak out. So, simple: he doesn't get to know.

There's also this small vicious corner of Sam's heart that wonders if Avery chooses to stay away because of how often Sam hits things. How much it scares him. But Sam does this for Avery, so it's not fair for him to judge—

Just don't … don't think about it.

Sam wriggles the paperclip and the lock gives a satisfying click. Finally.

Avery chews his lip. 'Don't you get lonely living like this?'

Sam's always alone, even when Avery is only a whisper behind him. He doesn't feel like explaining, because Avery won't get it, so he just slides the door open and lets Avery go in first while his own pulse evens out with relief. Now to wash off the blood. Now to curl up in a soft chair. Now to be still.

Except Avery is here and Avery is never still.

He tumbles inside and flips on a light switch and the *supposedly empty house* floods with hues of orange and gold.

Sam flies across the room and slaps the switch off. 'Are you trying to get me caught?'

'But why—'

'No, stop, just … just stop.' Muted anger crunches between Sam's teeth. 'Close the blinds. Actually, don't. I'll do it and you be quiet.'

Avery's already wandered off, absently raking apart the house with his eyes and calculating the worth. That leaves Sam to fix the blinds while smothering the nervous hitch in his chest because this isn't how his break-ins work. Avery really is ruining it. Sam has his methods, his routine, and afterwards he gets to feel safe and calm. He gets to snatch a few hours where his pulse isn't hammering a tattoo against his skull. Where he can breathe. An invisible boy living in an empty house.

Avery is anything but invisible.

Now he's trawling through the house, flipping light switches and touching everything and giving a running commentary on prices they could fetch at the pawnshop.

It's a comfortable home, the kind for people who can afford holidays. Small bedrooms, soft rugs on the floors, walls with framed photos of awkward teens and golden retrievers, and a large TV with an admirable gaming collection. Avery pets it excitedly. Sam says no way in hell.

Sam leaves his backpack on the kitchen table and moves through the house. He flicks through calendars and notes on a desk, searching for evidence of how long this family will be gone. When they'll come back. He finds a flight itinerary in the rubbish.

A week.

He could have a week in this house.

But just to be sure, he checks: pet food dishes? None. Evidence of a house sitter? None. Food in the fridge? Nothing fresh.

The house is his.

His shoulders relax a fraction.

Avery sprawls on a recliner in the lounge, hitting a lever that snaps the footrest up and down with loud clacks. Sam leaves him to it while he decides what to steal.

He didn't always rob the houses. Back when he was fourteen and so desperate for a house again, a *home*, he just broke in to sleep in the beds. Eat the food. Pretended he could keep this. Pathetic idiot.

Then he started taking keys. To remember each house by.

Then he started taking money. Then jewellery. Laptops. Cameras. Phones. Hidden credit cards.

Avery gets rid of the stuff, courtesy of his shifty friends, but he balks at coming along. Except tonight, apparently.

What did you do now, Avery?

Sam just fixed Avery's last screw-up. He's not ready for another.

Sam reaches for his backpack (the collection of keys is one odd habit he keeps to himself because Avery would touch everything and the keys are special, OK? They're his) but Avery appears from behind the pantry door. He holds up a packet and a distinct look of horror crosses his face. 'What the hell,' he says, 'are *seaweed crackers*?'

Sam sighs. 'Are you staying all night?'

Avery busts the packet and peers inside. 'These are diseased. Anyway, I want to—' He looks up. 'Oh. Your face.'

Sam should've gone straight to a mirror to inspect the damage. He needs to soak his knuckles and put antiseptic on the cuts, but he forgot since he's used to feeling like a rug with the dust beaten out.

Avery pulls himself up to sit on the bench top next to an empty fruit bowl and crushes crackers between his fingertips instead of eating them. 'You said you were going to stop beating people up.' The accusatory edge is there.

Something in Sam's chest tugs, like he's a boy made out of paper and string and the threads have been pulled too tight. 'Leave it.' His voice stays low.

Avery doesn't notice Sam's tone, he hardly ever does. His legs swing, pace growing frantic. Sam needs to intervene before agitation turns to panic and Avery spins out.

'You said you'd stop hitting,' Avery says, 'and I'd promise to keep my job at the mechanic's. Those are the rules.' Crackers crunch. Packet rustles. Heels drum on the bench.

'I guess we both broke the rules,' Sam says quietly.

Avery's eyes widen. 'But I—'

'Save it. I know you drove a car into the wall at the mechanic's shop.'

'I didn't—'

'Were you drunk?' Sam's scowl is all flint, but wasted on Avery because he's looking anywhere but Sam's face.

Avery snaps his fingers by his ears and doesn't answer.

This is all so unfair.

Sam can still see the other apprentice mechanic in oily coveralls splayed out on the cement behind the shop, holding his broken hand and whimpering. Sam didn't mean to take it so far, but does he ever? He went there to beat up the guy, make him unable to work for a day or two so the boss wouldn't fire Avery. He'd need him. Avery would have a chance to redeem himself. It was *simple* – until bone snapped and Sam got a split lip and a boot imprint on his chest and limped off into the dark before the apprentice could see his face or call for help.

The guy was big, but Sam's good at fighting. Practice.

It scares Avery, the way Sam hits. It scares Sam too. But what's he supposed to *do*? He's got nothing else. He doesn't get to spin into a screaming heap when it gets too much like Avery does – Avery who's wired a little different, Avery who acts like he's younger instead of two years older than Sam.

'I'm probably going to get fired.' Avery throws the crumpled packet in the sink and swings his legs viciously. 'But I had this genius idea.' His voice lightens, a good indication the idea is terrible. 'See, there's this super sweet sedan in the shop right now. We'll have hours before anyone knows we took it.'

'Took it where?' Sam's voice is tight.

And Avery says, 'We could leave town,' like it's the easiest thing in the world.

'In a stolen car? Are you *insane*?'

'We'd ditch it tomorrow. Get another. I know cars. No big deal.'

'That's not part of our plan,' Sam says.

'Our plan sucks.' Avery rocks on the bench. 'It's impossible. Let's just drive away. You. And me. We.' He smiles then, small but unguarded, like he really thinks Sam is going to go for this.

Doesn't he know Sam at all?

Sam looks down at his hands, fisted and trembling. He's furious at the hot tears pricking the back of his nose. He wills himself to be still, find that pocket of calm. 'We made a plan.' His voice shakes in an effort to stay level. 'We're going to earn money, get a house, fix ourselves up—'

'I'm not even eighteen. And you're a *wanted*

criminal. There's no way we'll ever steal enough for a house of our own.'

This is not what they talked about. This is not what they spent countless hours planning last year, lying on the trampoline in their aunt's backyard because she'd locked them outside again.

We're going to live in our own house. We're going to be OK.

'No.' But there are too many cracks in Sam's voice. 'No, we're not stealing some car and we're not leaving town and—' He stops because it's all crashing into him. How unrealistic his wishes are. How naive he's being. He's supposed to be the one with his head screwed on, but he'll chase this dream until it cuts him to ribbons.

It's hard to breathe, but he's not sure if that's his bruised ribs or the agony of fighting with his brother.

Avery's voice grows shrill. 'But if we stay the police will catch you! I can't let them catch you. They'll put you in p-prison and then – I can't ... you *can't*—' It ends in a frantic cry and Avery's fingers rip at his hair and then suddenly he's off the bench, knocking the fruit bowl as he goes.

It splinters against the tiles like a gunshot.

Someone's going to hear.

The shouts.

The crashes.

The brothers.

Avery flinches away, knocking into a chair so

hard it flies backwards and hits the wall, leaves an indent in the plaster. This is Avery. Unintentional chaos.

Sam just watches, frozen, while Avery recoils from the mess, his tics exploding until he punches his own leg and gasps furiously for air. Sam tries to reach out, catch his brother's arm and stroke it until he stops hurting himself and swaps to a calmer tic – like he did when they were kids – but Avery snaps away.

'I'll leave then.' His thin chest moves in and out, too fast. 'I'll steal a car and drive away by myself. You c-can get caught if you want. I don't care. I don't care!' He shoves Sam then, and Sam sucks in a sharp breath.

'Don't say that.' Sam's voice is barely a whisper.

Avery storms towards the door, his limbs jerking like a puppet. He turns back with one last vicious glare – except there are tears in his eyes and his lip trembles. 'I'll leave you.'

Don't ever, ever say that.

He slams the door on his way out.

Sam stares at the chaos, the broken dish and the dent in the wall. The family will come back and never understand what happened here.

Sam doesn't understand.

But he can't stay here now.

He's already shouldering his backpack, the weight of a hundred stolen keys clinking their comforting song. He should run after Avery. Make him calm down, make sure he doesn't hurt himself – make sure he doesn't do anything stupid like try to leave. He didn't mean it, right? They're all each other has. Avery's the only who sees Sammy Lou, the forgotten boy.

I'll leave you.

Sam doesn't take anything on his way out.

That's his secret failure.

He doesn't break into houses because he enjoys stealing. He stalks vacant windows and tricks locks and sleeps in stolen beds because he just wants to be home.

CHAPTER 2

Sam puts half a city's distance between him and that house. He'd like to outrun the angry words cutting their displeasure into his back too, but those are harder to shake. And as if the night needs to get worse, the sky joins in the contest of Who Can Make Sammy Lou Cry The Most and rolls in fat clouds to pour on his shoulders.

Sam gets soaked as the temperature plummets and the world forgets it's on the cusp of summer. No, let's have a winter rerun. Won't that be fun?

He ends up at a playground near the beachfront and climbs a kiddie-sized rope ladder to huddle under a plastic roof. It keeps most of the rain off. He wraps his arms over his head and shivers violently enough to rattle his teeth and send spasms of pain through his bruised chest.

He should be in a house right now, warm and dry.

He should not be envisioning Avery driving a thousand kilometres away.

Avery will go back to his shifty friends' house. Probably? No, no he will. Stop panicking. Stop sitting here feeling sick about not knowing if

Avery's in the rain or stealing a car or curled on someone's battered sofa. It was a stupid threat. He could never just go.

Sam rests his cheek on his scrunched-up knees and maybe he dozes or maybe he just crouches there in a chilled daze until the showers stop and dawn traces fingers through the sky. It'll be a nice day – Saturday, right? That means homes will be full of people spending lazy mornings amongst their quilts, with promises of coffee and honeyed crumpets and a stroll on the beach. At least that's what he pretends normal people do.

Sam's shirt clings to his skin like a damp hug and it's an effort to uncurl himself and plan his next move. He tries to order his thoughts as he flexes his dead fingers. He could:

(1) find a new house

(2) steal clothes

(3) get food, because when did he even eat last?

(4) go find Avery and please please please make him understand he can't really be alone.

He's a mess, is Avery Lou, and Sam's the only one who knows him. Who cares. But looking for him will mean facing that he beat someone up so Avery wouldn't lose his job and Avery *hates violence* and Sam should be in jail already and and and—

Sam holds his head. His thoughts spin, dizzying. He feels genuinely ill right now. His nose won't stop running.

OK, focus. There is another option:

(5) go back to Aunt Karen's house. She might be in a good mood. It's been a year since he ran away, and seeing Sam all ill and pathetic might melt her cold heart and she'll take him back.

Or she'll call the police.

Who is he kidding? This is Aunt Karen. If she sees him, she'll go straight to the phone.

So Sam picks the brave option: avoid everyone and find a new house. Which means walking the sodden streets as the sun rises and his nose impersonates a waterfall and his head fills with cotton wool. It's hard enough to *think* let alone figure out which houses are empty. Stealing houses is an art. You don't just blunder into the first one that looks quiet. He should have this part perfected, but this morning he feels so off.

He looks for the dead giveaways: overflowing mailboxes; front lawns with tipped-over bins that have clearly been there for a while; uncut grass; overgrown flowerbeds; empty driveways; drawn curtains; spiderwebs clawing across doors; and that slick quietness that coats an empty house and whispers it's OK to enter. The stillness is the hardest to explain, but he can feel it.

Except right now all he feels are aching bones – bruises and fevers.

He needs to get off the streets and lie down.

He tries two houses.

For the first, the back door is disagreeable to his

makeshift lock picks, since, thanks to Avery, he's still using paperclips – but he finds fresh milk in the fridge and the garage still smells of car fumes.

The second house is definitely a victim of longer-term abandonment. But a sticky note on the fridge reads 'BUY PRESENT FOR PARTY ON SATURDAY' in purple glitter pen. He can't risk staying here.

He could find a payphone and call Avery. Maybe they'll just agree to forget how Avery thinks he doesn't need Sam because it's not true and it stings and—

Embarrassingly, he thinks he might cry, so he forces himself to walk further, faster, his feet tapping out *screw my life* with every step. At least his clothes dry in the warm midday sun. Positives, right?

He sneezes then and has to sit down in the gutter because he thinks he just dislocated a rib.

Wow, he's so healthy.

A car trundles past while he waits for the dizzy spell to pass and, as his eyes follow it, he finds himself looking across the road at a house the colour of butter and sunflowers and summer days. It has a tired picket fence and rose bushes that resemble an angry jungle and the front lawn is full of kids' toys and bikes and an upturned wading pool. The letterbox overflows with junk mail and the open-air carport is empty.

Promising.

Sam checks the street.

Quiet.

He peels himself out of the gutter and strolls into the yard like it's the most natural thing in the world to break into a house in the middle of the day.

He listens at the doors but it's silent. Peering through the curtains shows a very lived-in house – he's never seen so much washing piled on a sofa – but no sign of life. Well, the day can't get any worse, so he picks the lock with a vague sense of desperation.

Please be empty, please please please.

The lock pops and Sam shuts the door and leans heavily on it, thinking of finding flu meds. He's in a laundry with an industrial-sized washing machine and yet more clothes spilling from baskets. He picks his way to the doorframe and into a sprawling living area. It's an open-plan room, with support poles instead of walls. The kitchen, dining area, and lounge are tangled together and swamped with a tornado of toys and clothes, books and chairs, Monopoly pieces and pencil cases, a broken science project and far too many left shoes. A sewing table sits near the front windows, bright fabric spilled on to the floor and boxes of lace and bobbins tumbled together.

'Not at all overwhelming,' Sam whispers, surveying macaroni crafts plastered over the fridge.

He has to blink a few times just to figure out where to focus. He has no idea how to tell if *this* sort of house is inhabited. Check for fresh food?

The fridge is empty except for a dubious-looking Tupperware container and a toy train.

OK then.

Still … that's promising.

He picks his way across the room and notices the front curtains are drawn. Another sign that the occupants are away.

Then he sees a huge whiteboard hanging in the kitchen, horribly decorated with dolphin glitter stickers, and sporting messages like:

DENTIST @ 3:40 JACK – DO !! NOT !! SKIP !! AGAIN !!

PLS BUY MILK

JACK NEVER CLEANS THE BATHROOM

GRADY HAS CAR THURSDAYS

US TEENS COME BACK FROM CAMPING ON SUNDAY (DON'T SAY WE DIDN'T GIVE YOU DETAILS, DAD)

Sam shoulders sag with relief.

Back on Sunday.

The house is his.

He rummages through a medicine kit in one of the cramped cupboards and helps himself to flu meds. Take that, you freaking streaming nose. He swallows the tablets dry and vaguely wonders if they're drowsy-inducing.

He takes his slow, aching bones upstairs to a second floor that is as chaotic as the first. But through the mess of art projects, bags, and enough

Lego on the floor to be considered warfare – the house feels warm. Cosy. Lived in. Sam's favourite type of house.

By the way, Sam, you are a freak.

He feels feverishly warm.

A brief tour of the bedrooms concludes that this house is mainly populated by boys. Only one bedroom looks remotely feminine, with two identical white beds with floral bedspreads. A piece of duct tape runs down the middle of the floor to separate one side's haphazard piles of books and swords made from sticks – from the other of pincushions and fabric and boxes of buttons.

OK, so these people don't believe in cupboards. They believe in obstacle courses.

He has a new appreciation for only having one brother. Imagine a dozen Averys? No thank you.

He picks through a closet and finds a fresh T-shirt, since he's been using his to mop his streaming eyes and nose, and then he wanders into an office. He could pick any bed, obviously, but it's tidier in here and somehow he ends up in a comfy armchair in a pool of sunshine. Once he's curled up in a shirt that smells of eucalyptus washing powder, with his backpack dumped on the floor and the sun petting his hair, Sam finds he can't get back up.

He is so very, very tired.

He curls into a ball as the flu meds kick in.

Side effects probably ... definitely ... include ... drowsiness.

The sun is so warm on his cheek.

He'll just sit here for a minute and then—

BEFORE

He's seven years old, seatbelt cutting into his chest as the car speeds across the dark city.

The strap is broken so his dad tied it down – tight, too tight. But if Sammy complains he'll just get another slap. Instead, he chews his lip as they pull into a car park in front of a club that pulses a kaleidoscope of coloured lights and thundering beats.

Avery hums softly to himself in the seat beside Sammy. He runs his favourite toy car over his face, eyes closed in a momentary bliss of sensation. He reaches over to run the car on Sammy's face too, but Sammy shoves him back with a scowl.

He knows Avery's just sharing, but Sammy's hungry. He hurts. He's tired of being stuck in a car for days and days with Avery and his stupid toys.

Sammy says, 'Dad, he won't stop *touching* me,' before he really thinks about it. Then he goes still. Scared of a slap. Scared, even more, that Avery will get it.

He should've stayed quiet.

His dad shuts off the car and is on his phone, craning his neck to see the club. People stream out and in, wearing silly dresses. They must be cold. Sam's cold. He can't ask for his jacket because Avery was shivering earlier and Sam let him wear it.

His dad half turns in the front seat, his eyes molasses pits in the dark car. He reaches back and snatches the toy off Avery.

Avery gives a surprised yelp.

A sick hole gnaws at Sam's stomach. He didn't mean ... he just ... He doesn't want Avery to cry.

'Grow up, Avery,' their dad snaps. 'You're too old for this rubbish.'

Avery's mouth makes a perfect O and he flaps his hands in front of his face. Another thing he's *too old to be doing* that makes their dad so annoyed.

Their dad gives a disgusted growl and shoves open his door. He gets out, breathing smoke in the frosty night air, and then leans back in to look at his sons again.

His voice is a warning growl. 'I'll be a few minutes. Sit here while I pick something up. If I hear a peep, you get hell, understand?' He glances at his phone again. 'After this we drive to your aunt's and see if your mother has run off there.'

Avery lurches half out of his seat, hands flapping wildly. 'My car!'

Their dad smacks his hand against the roof of the car and Avery shrinks back. 'You get the toy back when you stop being such a brat.' He slams the door, swearing.

They watch him stride across the car park,

shoving Avery's toy car into his pocket and putting his phone back to his ear.

Sammy glances sideways at Avery. He watches his brother's chest going in and out so so fast.

'I n-n-need need need—' Avery breaks off, looking at Sammy with wild, wet eyes.

He needs his car. It's his special car. He always has it.

Fix this, Sammy.

'He'll give it back,' says Sammy. 'Just be good. Just wait.' *Please please please.*

They've been driving for ever, since their mother took a packet of cigarettes and their dad's wallet and stormed out of the caravan they were borrowing and didn't come back.

His dad has been angry ever since.

Well, he's always angry.

'Just be good, Avery,' Sammy repeats, desperate now – but Avery's already popped open his door and slid out.

This is not good.

Sammy grabs for his own seatbelt, but it's tied so tight. He can't move. 'Avery, *don't.*'

But Avery's already trotting towards the pulsing lights and music, his tongue sticking out in determination. He hates loud things. Why's he going in there? He doesn't need his car that much, does he?

Sammy doesn't want to get hell when their dad comes back.

He tugs harder at his belt and then kicks his legs, but he's stuck.

He sits there, handfuls of wild butterflies in his belly. He wants his mum and some honeyed toast and Avery snuggled up next to him in their trundle bed in the caravan, humming a little song and breaking off to kiss Sammy's elbow because he hasn't figured out brothers are supposed to fight and bite now that they're seven and nine. Avery never figures anything out.

But maybe it'll be OK?

Sammy's trying to wriggle sideways out of the seatbelt straps when he hears the scream.

Avery's scream.

He knows it anywhere because sometimes all Avery does is scream. Because his shirt itches, because his food is different, because something is *wrong wrong wrong* but he lost his words to explain.

Sammy twists to stare out of his window at the club. His dad bursts out, followed by men in coloured shirts and gold chains and shiny shoes. Are they all laughing? Avery's in a ball in the middle, rocking with his hands over his ears. No no no no – you don't laugh when Avery's like that. You have to hold him. You have to take him away till he calms down. Even Sammy knows this and he's only seven.

But the men shove his dad and sneer and laugh and one nudges Avery with his shoe and Avery screams again.

Then their dad, all hunched over and flushed, picks Avery up and throws him over his shoulder. Hard to do because Avery writhes and kicks. Then his dad fairly bolts for the car while the mean men laugh and vanish back into their club.

Sammy holds his breath. As soon as his dad opens the door, he'll ask him to give Avery back the car. It'll fix *everything*. It doesn't matter if Avery's too old. It makes him feel better.

The words are lined up in Sammy's mouth, all ready – but his dad doesn't open the door. Instead, he throws Avery down on the gravel between parked cars.

And he hits him.

Avery's screams turn to sobs.

Sammy fights with his seatbelt now. Really fights. Avery didn't mean it – he didn't try to be bad – he just—

no no no no no no no

This is Sammy's fault.

His chest burns and the butterflies explode out, scared and twisted and sick. He slaps his palms against the glass, but his dad is *bringing hell*.

Avery's screams cut in half between the damp *thwack thwack*—

Sammy slaps at the window. He cries out, but there's no one else in the car park. No one to hear over the thunder of the club. No mother. No teacher. No one who cares that his dad's molasses eyes are burnt out and his teeth white shark lines in the moonlight as he bites out, 'You *lost* my only chance working with them – you – stupid – little – *shit*.'

Avery's voice cuts off into something garbled and sick and then his screams

c

r

a

c

k

and stop.

Silence.

Sammy's beaten his knuckles bloody on the window. His chest burns with something like tar and *rage* and he doesn't shy back when his dad wrenches the car door opens and dumps Avery on the seat. His dad slams the door, kicks it viciously, and then gets in the driver's side.

Sammy can't breathe. He is red fire and he is burning. You're not allowed to hit Avery like that. *You're not allowed.* He stretches shivering fingers to his brother. His brother who is finally still and quiet.

He's being good.

Avery is a paper doll all in ribbons, hair flopped over closed eyes. His lips are bloody and his thin jacket has ridden up to show darkening bruises.

The car rips out of the car park and takes a corner so fast Sammy's head hits the window. His cry cuts off and he jerks at his seatbelt again and *finally, finally* it comes loose. He wriggles free and crawls across the seat to Avery.

His dad slams the radio on, turning it up to blast. But his eyes find the rearview mirror and meet Sammy's.

His dad's eyes are furious.

Sammy hates him. His lips peel back like he is now a tiger and he would *bite* his father if he was closer. Sammy, strong and fierce, crouches over his brother. Protects him. The car skids over frosty roads while Sammy rubs circles on Avery's palms and kisses his bloody cheek and wants and wants Avery's eyes to open.

'It's OK,' Sammy whispers. 'I'm here. Avery? It's OK.'

He repeats it a hundred thousand times as the radio blares and his dad punches the steering wheel.

Sammy's voice is trembly but fierce. 'If anyone hurts you again, I'll kill them.' He wipes blood from Avery's lips. 'I'll kill them.'

CHAPTER 3

Deep in the house, Avery is shouting.

Sam shifts, fingers still desperately knotted around sleep because he doesn't want to let go. He's warm and dry and, well, OK, not *entirely* comfortable since there's a crick in his neck from sleeping awkwardly in a chair. But he hasn't slept this well in a long time. Probably because he drugged himself. Whatever. Just … just a few more minutes …

Thumps follow the shouts, and then a clatter of dishes.

Sam frowns in his sleep.

Wait: if Avery is shouting he's probably seconds away from melting to the floor and losing it. Sam needs to get up and—

Sam tries to roll over but his legs get caught between the armchair and a bookshelf. And it's that moment when he remembers he's not in a house with Avery.

He's in an empty house.

That's not …

empty.

Sam sits bolt upright, catching himself before he pitches off the armchair. *Holy shit*. He's in a house that's *not empty*. The cosy warmness of the room has dissolved in sparks of flames. He's not even sure what time it is. Did he sleep all night? He couldn't. He wouldn't.

He scrabbles off the armchair and over to the desk. Shoving aside a few folders and tins of pens reveals a sad-looking clock that *must* be wrong because it reads eleven forty-five.

Sam's slept for a whole day.

His heart chooses this moment to rabbit out of his chest. This can't be happening. Not hearing Avery sneak up on him is one thing. But sleeping through a family returning? He's losing his touch.

He's losing his mind.

He can't be here—

What if they walk in—

They'll call the cops—

He can't be arrested, he can't can't can't—

Footsteps pound past the office and the closed door rattles a little. Sam's heart vaults into his throat and he stumbles backwards, trips on his own backpack, and ends up sitting hard on the armchair. *Think*. They haven't come in here yet, so that's good.

Good? Nothing is good.

He's in a house full of people. He's upstairs. He can't get out.

'DAD!' a girl's voice hollers right outside the

office door. 'TELL YOUR SON TO SET THE TABLE.'

The voice is close, *so close*.

'Which one?' someone else yells, softer and distant.

'THE ANNOYING ONE.'

'Like I said, which one?'

Sam envisions how being found would go down. Screaming. Hands scrabbling for a phone. A frantic, startled fist shooting out and catching Sam in the mouth so his teeth cut into his tongue and he tastes his own bloody sins.

Then the office door shudders again, like someone kicked it as they walked past.

He has to hide.

Sam dives for the cupboards, yanking open a door and looking in dismay at a mess of paperwork, a vacuum cleaner, and piles of board games. Terrified, he glances at the door only to see the doorknob half turn and then pause as someone yells down the stairs again.

No choice.

Sam folds himself into a thin groove in the cupboard, crushed between the vacuum cleaner and Cluedo. He drags the cupboard door shut by the tips of his fingers, but doesn't quite get it closed.

Then the door opens and he forgets how to breathe.

A girl storms in.

Sam only sees a sliver through the crack – just an edge of a purple sundress and an olive-skinned ankle, long fingers scurrying about the desk until they snatch something.

Sam's knees are at his throat. His heart punches new bruises into his ribs.

'I found your charger, Dad!' she calls, then her voice lowers, 'Seriously, how does he manage to lose it so much?' She turns – and trips over Sam's backpack.

You're such an idiot, Sammy Lou.

Sam stuffs knuckles into his mouth and bites. Just hold on, just wait.

But that backpack is full of keys, full of stolen ridiculous keys, that one glance at would reveal something is terribly off. And, pathetically, it's special to him. It's the only thing he owns.

'Ugh, Jack,' she mutters, and steps over it.

She steps over it!

Sam remembers oxygen.

She plugs the charger and a phone into the wall and then stomps out of the room like the backpack meant nothing. And in this mess, that's probably likely. Whoever 'Jack' is, he can happily take the blame. Sam is fine with that. He is also fine with never ever coming out of this cupboard. Even though she's slammed the door on her way out and he's in the clear again.

Please don't come back.

He closes his eyes and focuses on not dying as his legs lose feeling and the house rumbles and shakes with the cacophony of a Sunday lunch downstairs. There has to be a small army of people down there. A loud, noisy, violently laughing army that will be his—

Saving?

Because what if, and from the sounds of it this is likely, there are dozens of people downstairs? What if he just loses himself in the crowd and – sneaks out?

He has to do something, because being folded like a pretzel can't be the way he dies.

He vaguely imagines Avery's reaction to this story – a worried frown and then a burst of laughter, which Sam should be annoyed at but also stupidly pleased because amusing Avery is worth everything.

After a few deep gulps, he crawls out.

He grabs his backpack and opens the door a crack. The hall is empty. Unfortunately downstairs has no walls to hide behind.

When did he get so careless?

Go.

Just go.

Don't put it off.

Go.

He slips out of the warm office, his false safety. His chest hurts, his head is still completely scrambled from the meds, which is probably why he's making this stupid bid for freedom instead of waiting. He's doing this.

He gets to the top of the stairs and ducks

down, peering through the banister rails to survey the damage.

The damage is immense.

There truly are half a million people down there. Bodies twist and tangle in a dance of musical chairs and potato salad as they pile the long table with a feast. Toddlers sprawl on the floor or twirl round and round the haphazardly placed furniture on a trike that someone yells at them to take outside. A baby cries. A plate breaks. The TV booms the theme song of a car racing game that a group of wild-haired kids cluster around. Someone yells for them to turn it down. No, turn it *off*. No, get ready for lunch. Get the baby. Wash your hands. Stop eating all the corn chips.

Conversations mix. Explode.

People laugh. Faces light up.

They are all hopelessly consumed with each other. Drunk on *people* and *noise* and *food*. Sam can do this. He can just walk down those stairs and out the door and no one will think to stop him. They'll see him, sure, but he's forgettable enough to be invisible.

Isn't that his entire life?

Sam moves for the stairs, hand on the rail. Blood pulses in his ears. The noise is deafening, not unhappy, but it seems everyone has something to say and they try to say it the loudest.

There's a flash of purple amongst the masses – that girl from the office. At this higher vantage point Sam can make out a twisted bun of unruly chocolate hair and sharp elbows. He has a feeling that if he's caught, it'll be her shrewd eyes picking him out as the impostor.

Do not look at her at all. Just don't.

Sam's whitened knuckles are just about to release the rail so he can sprint, when air brushes behind him. A boy, taller than Sam and with the tiniest spiky ponytail and hands full of batteries, clatters down the stairs past Sam without even looking at him.

Sam nearly hopes, nearly breathes—

The boy hesitates on the last step and then swivels back to look at Sam. His eyebrows are angry forests.

'Dude, I don't even recognise you,' he says. 'Jeremy's friend? He cycles through them so fast I never know anyone any more. Don't you know how Sundays work? Get a plate or you'll end up on the floor with the brat brigade.'

Sam manages to sweep the panic off his face and he nods quickly.

The boy shrugs and heads towards the TV and the teens bickering amiably over chip packets and remotes.

The exit is officially an ocean away.

Sam just stands there, swaying slightly in the middle of the stairs. The flu still clings to the corners of his tired eyes, his numb brain, and he trembles with indecision.

One step.

The next.

They could all see him if only they looked up.

Next step.

Several kids tumble past in a shower of crumbs and sauce and Sam lurches back on instinct. They're shooed along by another boy. He's tall and neat, with glasses and a disapproving older brother aura. When this boy's eyes fall on him, Sam's mouth opens to blurt something like, *I'm Jeremy's friend?* But the boy beats him to it.

'I'm thirty per cent sure Jeremy has a Twice Burgundy shirt like that.'

For a second, Sam hasn't a clue what he's talking about. But – oh wait. He stole a shirt. Sam glances down and realises with horror that it's some band shirt. It's probably unique. It's probably special.

In his defence though, he didn't mean for these people to see him in it.

He didn't mean to be here.

'Jeremy's friend?' The boy sighs. 'He has so many I can't keep up.'

'Yeah.' At least words, and not an unholy sob, come out of Sam's mouth.

'I swear,' the boy says, rubbing his eyes, 'he's building an army. Did he even tell you how Sundays work? You grab a plate and a chair straight away or you end up on the floor with the kids.'

Apparently being 'on the floor with the kids' is synonymous with 'hell' and Sam can see why.

There's a picnic blanket spread on the polished floorboards and piles of children are face-painting with tomato sauce and stepping in each other's potatoes.

'You look shell-shocked. Here.'

And before Sam can protest, he's suddenly taken by the shoulder and pulled the rest of the way downstairs and towards the table. Towards people.

Run.

Hit him and run.

He nearly does.

But then he trips on a pile of Lego and his kidnapper keeps him upright as he propels them towards the enormous table, laden with more food than Sam's seen in his life. A small space on the bench suddenly opens up and his backpack is jerked from his shoulders and tossed against the wall with a muttered '*What are you carrying? Rocks?*' Then Sam is squeezed between arms and shoulders and a plate appears in his hands.

'Just stab someone with a fork if you can't get what you need,' the boy says. Then he's gone.

Sam might be having a panic attack.

He tries to get up but the person next to him thinks he's reaching for the potato salad. So now he has a bowl of salad in his hands.

Then his plate grows a hot buttered bun and two people are asking if he needs onions? Sauce? Oh, you must be one of Jeremy's friends, right?

And he's nodding.

What is he supposed to do?

Sit down?

Eat?

Sam sits there for a moment, heart sped up so fast he can scarcely see straight. But as the noise washes over him and no one's eyes catch his and no one shouts how he's an impostor – he relaxes. Just a little. Most of the teens are as dishevelled and crumpled as he is too, probably from their camping trip, so he doesn't stick out.

Well, what the hell, right?

Sam eats.

He's officially taken house burglary to the next level. Forget stealing a bed, a key, a home for the night. He's stealing families and their Sunday lunches.

CHAPTER 4

Sam attempts to eat his body weight in potatoes and bloody beetroot sandwiches while rowdy conversations wash over him. Faces blur together. No one pays him any attention except to pass food, and you know what? He's totally fine with that.

But he won't press his luck.

As plates empty and dishes disappear and conversation turns to coffee and trying to pry sticky children off the floor for naps, Sam slips from the table. He sneaks towards his backpack only to have his way blocked by the girl in the purple dress. Her hair sticks up in an unapologetic frizz and her lips flatten at the sight of Sam.

His pulse stutters.

Well, he knew he'd get caught, didn't he? This is the stupidest and most insane thing he's ever done – inviting himself to a stranger's lunch. He deserves the shriek of *intruder*.

Except it doesn't come.

Sam finds his arms piled with dishes and the girl points to the kitchen with a vicious jab.

'I was just leaving—' Sam says.

'To walk to the kitchen and become an honorary dishwasher,' the girl finishes. 'And don't give me any lines about being *Jeremy's guest* because as soon as I find him, I'm stuffing his ugly face into the dishwater too. You can't invite a million people over and –' her voice rises '– NOT HELP WITH THE DISHES, JEREMY.'

Sam stares.

'Kitchen.' She claps her hands together briskly. 'Sink. Scrub. Dishwasher is already full. Move it.'

Considering she's made of sharp corners and fierce eyes, and Sam doesn't want to get on the bad side of any of that, he goes. After all, he did eat their food. And you wouldn't call the cops on someone washing your dishes, right?

Right?

This entire day is doing his head in.

He gets lost behind a mountain of dishes and empty bowls and abused blackened frying pans and soapsuds in a house he fully intended to rob a few hours ago.

Plates keep coming.

This is some cruel sort of karma for his thieving ways.

He's just trying to balance a pot on top of a precarious stack of cups, when a man enters with a toddler on one hip and a plate of brownies perched on his fingertips. He swings the plate towards Sam, who really feels like he deserves this. He wipes his sodden hands on his shirt. He takes one.

'Take two,' says the man. 'Caramel brownies. Did they leave you with the dishes? You must be new here, son, I don't even recognise you. Although that's pretty normal with how many friends Jeremy has.' He smiles ruefully. 'So the trick is to disappear before dessert comes out.'

Sure enough, the calamity of bodies has thinned out drastically. They're now playing cricket on the street.

'Although it means more cake for the dishwashers,' the man adds. 'I'll leave the plate here. But don't advertise it or you'll have Moxie all over you. I swear she has a sixth sense just for caramel.'

'I heard that.'

Sam spins to see the girl reappearing in a swirl of purple and scowls. 'I will not be all over *anyone*, thank you very much, Dad.' She peers at Sam. 'You're still here?'

'Yeah?' The word pulls from Sam's lips, cautious, because any second now one of them is going to notice he doesn't fit.

'Feel free to stay for ever if you do the dishes,' the father of this overcrowded house says, moving off while the toddler fusses in his arms.

Obviously he didn't *mean* that, but still – the words stick to Sam's ribs as his heart speeds up. People don't usually toss words his way that aren't punctured with anger. He's so pathetic, right? That he'd lap this up.

The girl still looks at Sam.

Moxie.

He stuffs the brownie in his mouth and turns back to the dishes, anxious to keep his hands busy. She pulls herself up on to the bench top and, legs swinging, sets to work on the plate.

'So,' says the girl.

Startled, Sam drops the pot he's scrubbing into the water with a splash. Wait. She's going to *talk* to him? He hasn't … he can't … he hasn't really talked to anyone except Avery in months.

Maybe years.

'You're not whining about being lumped with the dishes.' She holds up fingers to tick off a list. 'You're quiet. You're kind of small compared to Jeremy's usual strays. And my dad waved a plate of brownies under your nose and you didn't eat the whole lot.' She punctuates that by helping herself to another piece. 'I don't trust you.'

Sam's throat is dry. 'Well, I don't trust whoever killed this pot. Did they cook potatoes or souls of the damned?'

'Ah.' Moxie peers at the blackened base. 'That was me.'

Oh.

Any minute now Sam is going to melt into the floor.

This is why it's better to shut up – you don't accidentally insult the prettiest girl in the room.

And she is pretty, in a frazzled but fierce kind of way. She swings her legs, toenails painted the same purple as her dress. He notices there's hand-sewn embroidery all over the skirt. So she's the seamstress.

Sam realises he's been staring and not answering, so he lets out the weakest laugh in the world and promptly wishes to die.

'So how was your trip?' he hears himself saying, while three-quarters of his brain shouts *what are you doing!* The boys seem to have been camping and the others ... he's not sure. He would like to know how his house stealing went so wrong.

'Well,' Moxie says, 'it sucked. You try being trapped in a car for four hours with preschoolers who either scream or want to sing *Jingle Bells* for the forty thousandth time.' She rolls her eyes to the ceiling. 'The things you do to visit grandparents.'

'True,' Sam says, and hopes he doesn't sound like someone who's never visited grandparents in his life.

'How was your trip?' Moxie says.

Sam must hesitate too long, because Moxie shakes a brownie at him impatiently. 'The *camping* trip you boys all went on? I mean, Jeremy said it was just "a few of the guys" but I'm guessing the fifty billion people here are all casualties of eating baked beans in the scrub for two days. You all need to shower, by the way. For hours.'

Sam can play along, right? He's got this. 'Oh, well ... it was great. Good, um, weather.' What do you even say about camping? He's never *been* camping. Unless you count sleeping on the veranda

of his aunt's house because locking the Lou brothers
out was her go-to when they pissed her off.

Sometimes he thinks she's the reason they both
started taking apart locks.

'Chatty, aren't you?' Moxie licks brownie off
her thumb. 'Ah, caramel,' she says, the lemon in
her voice exchanged to sugar for just a second.
'Only the best thing in life.'

'Except for honey,' Sam says.

Why is he still talking?

Why, Sam.

Why.

'Excuse you,' Moxie says. 'You're here to wash,
not disagree.'

He's here to steal, actually. But somehow he's
stolen dishwater and a T-shirt soaked with
soapsuds.

'Speaking of being disagreeable,' she says. 'Why
hasn't Jeremy come to rescue you anyway? I keep
forgetting you're his since you're in here and not
out there.'

I'm not really Jeremy's, he wants to say.
Technically now I'm yours.

Sam opens his mouth to spin a floppy lie, but
he's saved by the stream of sweaty teenage boys
tramping inside with volume set to maximum. Half
of them bolt upstairs and the others rummage in
cupboards for towels.

'Hey, we're going to the beach,' a boy tells
Moxie. Her brother? They share the same olive

skin, although he has a buzz cut and the softest brown eyes.

'I'll go tell Dad.' She slides off the bench and runs upstairs.

The boy taps his fingers on the bench and notices Sam.

'Hi,' he says. 'Are you Moxie's friend? She doesn't usually invite people over.' He smiles. 'I'm Jeremy.'

No, I'm supposed to be your friend.

'Ah, yeah, Moxie's friend,' Sam says. 'I'm Sammy – um, Sam.'

'And she ditched you with the dishes? Typical. Get out of there, man. We're going to the beach. I'll get you a towel.'

Sam tries to protest, except exactly no one cares. He gets the impression that this family is exceptionally bad at listening.

He's not going to the *beach* with them. Come on.

Sam finds himself sitting on the bottom step with a beach towel in his arms while watching a dozen boys slamming in and out of the downstairs bathroom and changing into swimmers and eating. Again. Because why not.

Just don't ask me who I am.

Please.

Jeremy reappears, eating leftover potato salad with a soup ladle. 'Ready?' he says to no one in particular. 'Jack? Is Moxie back yet? What's she doing up there?' He raises his voice. 'How long does it take to put swimmers on, Moxie! We need to go!'

The one who possibly is Jack – and who Sam remembers as the boy from the stairs with the spiky ponytail – appears in board shorts with a towel slung over his shoulder.

'Girls,' he says. 'You know how they are.'

Moxie materialises behind him and executes a swift elbow jab to his ribs.

Jack yelps and grabs his side like he's been shot. 'The hell, Moxie?'

'If something even remotely sexist comes out of your mouth again,' Moxie says, her eyes glinting, 'I will take a pound of flesh per word.'

Jack swears again and checks his ribs for damage.

'And for your information,' Moxie says, 'I was asking Dad if any of us are supposed to be babysitting. But we're clear.'

'We're clear!' Jeremy raises his towel like a conqueror before battle and a cheer goes up.

The hordes pour towards the door. Sam's piecing together a hazy sketch of this family of the butter-yellow house – which ones are family, which ones are friends. Jack and Jeremy appear to share a face, so definitely twins. And Moxie is nearly a head shorter than everyone else. He wonders if she's his age.

He shouldn't even care, even though his soul aches to go with them, to be part of this collision of fun and laughter. Instead, he has to melt back into being nothing, invisible, alone. He wants this. He absolutely can't have it.

She swishes around the room, collecting shoes and a towel, adjusting bikini straps peeking out from under her purple sundress.

She catches his eye and he looks away.

'Coming, dishwasher boy?'

CHAPTER 5

It's because they don't know him.

He can trail behind a group of jostling boys as they throw sunscreen and jump on each other's backs while the sun bakes their shoulders and tugs at freckles, and he can be perfectly unknowable. He's absolutely mad, of course, to follow them. He left his backpack inside, so he can't just vanish now. But there's something intoxicatingly alluring about people who smile, who are caught up in salty air and jokes and everyday adventures, who don't stop to look at him with shocked eyes that say, *How could you do that, Sammy Lou? How could you?*

They don't know him. They don't know the reason he ran away from home a year ago. Why the police want him. Why his aunt won't even look at him.

And it feels good.

He walks next to Moxie, because the others' wildness is equal parts fascinating and terrifying. Plus Moxie moves with a grim, no-nonsense look on her face, like getting to the beach is a mission and she'll achieve it no matter what.

It's comforting to be near someone who knows how to get what they want.

The party cuts through a caravan park, which involves scaling a chain-link fence. Sam climbs it too easily, too fast, and feels Moxie watching him. Maybe try to look less like a criminal who knows how to escape, OK, Sammy Lou?

The shortcut takes them down a sandy track and then bushes fold back to reveal the sparkling sea, blue enough to make your eyes ache.

The boys take off towards the cliffs and tumbled rocks, throwing towels and shirts. Moxie rolls her eyes and keeps her towel rolled up and sand-free.

She glances sideways at Sam. 'Are you swimming in jeans? Because if you drown, guess who's not rescuing you.'

Sam shrugs in what he hopes is a nonchalant and convincing matter like *yeah, sure, this isn't so weird*.

Jeremy, still struggling out of his shirt, wads up the fabric and throws it at Moxie's head. She bats it off and glares.

'Eh, just swim in your boxers,' Jeremy says lightly.

'And there he goes,' Moxie says, 'trying to get everyone out of their pants.'

'I'm fine.' Sam reaches to pull his stolen T-shirt off and then remembers the boot-print bruise. He jerks the hem down quickly. Jeremy doesn't seem to notice, but a quick glance at Moxie shows she saw.

She purses her lips together, like she'll ask.

Please don't ask.

'Just in case you haven't been here before,' Jeremy is saying, 'we all jump off the rocks like brainless maniacs. It's deep enough. We threw Jack in headfirst to test it once. No broken neck.'

'Pity,' mutters Moxie.

'Just don't do anything I wouldn't do.' Jeremy claps Sam on the shoulder and grins broadly and Sam doesn't break it to him that he has no idea what Jeremy would or would not do. 'And definitely don't do anything Jack wouldn't do. Actually, don't do anything Jack *would* do. Just when it comes to Jack, don't.'

Sam opens his mouth to answer, but Moxie chooses that moment to shrug out of her sundress. Sam finds himself looking anywhere but at her indigo bikini. And then realises how conspicuous that is. And then realises he's blushing. And then decides he needs to go drown.

Moxie catches her frizzy hair into a knot and then storms off to the rocks where the others are jumping. Moxie never so much walks as marches with angry intensity. Sam wonders if it's because she has to hold her own amongst so many brothers.

Jeremy pats Sam on the shoulder. 'You look nervous. Never fear! I'll haul you out by your ankles if you start drowning.' He gives Sam a cheerful shove and then jogs towards the others.

Sam considers just sitting by the towels, but that would draw more attention, wouldn't it? He rolls up his jean cuffs and trails down to the water.

White foam waves break along the beach line, but this close to the cliffs, the ocean has carved out deep pools between rocks. It's probably not the safest thing in the world to climb on them and vault off – but that's exactly what everyone's doing. The water seems deep. The rocks are hot. It's impossible not to yield to their salty lure and climb from one to the other while all round him people push each other into the bright blue sea.

He finds himself following Moxie, as she hops nimbly to one of the highest peaks. Jack is already up there, peering over the edge, wet hair plastered about his ears.

'Don't you jump from up here, you moron.' Moxie's tone is warning.

Jack ignores her, eyes lighting on Sam. 'Dude, you have five seconds to get wet or I'm throwing you in headfirst.'

'Not from up here,' Moxie says again. 'This is a new level of dangerous.'

'Yes, Grandma.'

'Oh well, by all means go split your head open,' Moxie says. 'I've always wanted to see if there are brains in that skull of yours or just handfuls of stupid.'

Jack grabs her and she shrieks and beats at him

with bunched fists. She's laughing though, and Jack shoves her around without letting her get too close to the edge. Sam's heart still crawls into his mouth. His eyes say *they're just playing* but his brain trips back to memories of Avery being slammed to the ground by their dad, getting up with a bloody mouth and terrified eyes.

He looks away. He can't imagine Avery enjoying this day. He tries, but he just can't. Avery would watch with slitted eyes, fail to figure out why this is supposed to be fun, and leave.

Jack and Moxie start to climb down, bickering about how many 'handfuls of stupid' a skull could hold, when Sam backs up until he's got no room left – and then he runs.

'Hey!' someone says, a note of panic in their voice.

Moxie? Jack? Does it matter?

Wind batters their words away and then Sam leaps, toes pushing off the rough rock and then tucking into his chest as he curves into a somersault.

And for a moment he's

f

  l   g

    y   n

      i

He hits the sea.

And the sea hits him.

Water rushes up his nose and smashes into his ears and buries him in writhing white foam. It's shockingly cool. His legs and arms kick out like lanky spider limbs and he surges back up. It's so beautiful underwater, so quiet, so peaceful, he almost wants to stay down.

Then his head splits the surface.

He's got so much water in his ears it takes him a moment to realise everyone is cheering.

For him?

Jack appears to be punching the air and yelling something about *that's how it's done* and Sam realises that no one else is backflipping off rocks. Where was the part where he stayed *low profile*? Seriously, Sam.

Jack cups hands around his mouth to shout, 'That was badass!'

Moxie stands with her toes on the edge of a rock, her eyes traced with something like worry. Something like anger.

But Sam's attention is snagged from her as someone else hollers, 'Again!' followed by more cheers.

'But show me.' Jack is already clambering back up to the higher ledge.

Jeremy treads water and then splashes water into Sam's face. 'Maniac.' But he's smiling. 'Where'd you learn to do flips?'

'Trampoline.' His words taste of sand and salt. What are you supposed to do when you're twelve and stuck bored in a backyard? He and Avery used to sketch house plans on their homework and practise flips and pretend they weren't hungry. 'It's not hard.'

'Oi! What's your name again, blondie?' Jack shouts from somewhere above them.

'Sam?' But he says it like a question.

'Well, get up here. Where'd you even find this kid, Jeremy?' Jack peers over the cliff edge, throwing pebbles at their heads.

Jeremy dodges and gets a mouthful of ocean. He goes under garbling.

Sam's heart gives a catastrophic lurch and he waits for Jeremy to come back up and say *I didn't find him*, followed by Moxie saying she's never seen him until today, followed by them all realising he has stolen their lunch, their beach, their attention.

But Jeremy comes up with a handful of sand and strikes out for the rocks. 'I'm about to grind this up your nose.' His brother's question is forgotten.

Jack shoots him a crude gesture and then waves fiercely at Sam. 'Get up here, kid. I'm keeping you till you teach me that.'

Sam stops his frenetically moving arms and legs and lets himself sink under the waves for a second.

I'm keeping you.

Underwater, no one but the ocean sees him smile.

BEFORE

Sammy is seven and maybe Avery is dead.

Spiderweb lines of frost crinkle over their car windows, turning pink as the sun rises. They drove all night. Sammy needs to pee so badly and he wants Avery to wake up. *Please please please.* Avery's chest moves in ragged little gasps in his sleep, a broken birdcage of tears.

The car pulls into a driveway, the engine rattles off. Sammy, now with Avery's head in his lap, goes stiff. He doesn't recognise this place, this street, this boxy white house with pea-green curtains. His dad goes to the boot and gets out Sammy's backpack. Then he hammers the front door.

'Karen? Karen, open up.'

A dog across the street barks.

A slow car rumbles past.

Avery shifts in his arms.

Sammy's heart bounces and he knots fingers in Avery's shirt as a whimper escapes his brother. Avery looks up and Sammy strokes his cheek and mumbles *it's OK* even though that's a lie. There's something wrong with Avery's eyes.

They're dull and broken and hollow.

There's a whining screech as their car door is ripped open and their dad reaches in. Sammy snatches at Avery – but their dad is big and strong, bristles and wire. He drags Avery out.

Avery doesn't even whimper.

Sammy scrambles after them, ready to scream and *scream* if he has to – but his dad is holding Avery like a baby, not like a naughty boy he'll start hitting again. 'Be on your best behaviour.' His voice is raw.

Sammy follows him up the driveway where the front door has opened and a lady as tall as a ladder stands wrapped in a dressing gown patterned with tulips. Her lips are a line. Her brow furrows.

'What's going on, Clay?' she snaps. 'I just told you, Jen isn't here. Why would she be here?'

But Sammy's dad just shoves past her and takes Avery into the house.

Sammy hesitates on the step, shivering and so desperate to pee he thinks he might wet himself. His aunt stares.

'Are you the autistic one?' Her voice is a rubber band snap. 'I haven't seen you kids in four years. No, six.'

'I'm Sammy,' he whispers. He doesn't remember her.

'God, you're the baby?' She puts fingertips on his shoulder and pushes him inside, voice rising. 'You need to explain what happened, Clay.'

The house is cold, the curtains thin; the lounge holds just a tiny TV and two wicker chairs. Avery sits in one now, hands curled over his head while he rocks.

His dad dumps their backpack on the floor and digs fingers through his hair. 'They need to stay for a while, Karen.'

Aunt Karen's jaw drops. 'I'm not looking after your kids.'

'Yeah, well I can't— I just— I can't deal with *that*.' Their dad stabs a finger at Avery, who shrinks, like he's being slapped again.

Like, in his head, their dad hasn't stopped hitting him.

Then his dad yells. Then Aunt Karen yells. They shake fingers and point at doors and their dad hits the wall and Aunt Karen says she's calling the police if he doesn't calm down.

Sammy wants to cover Avery's ears. His eyes. His whole trembling body.

Someone has to protect him. It's supposed to be the big brother protecting the little brother, but for them it's swapped, isn't it? It crushes his ribs a little, knowing no one's going to look out for him. But he can do this.

He shivers and watches Aunt Karen storm out and their dad roar that she's *keeping these goddamn kids for a while*. Then he turns on his boys, eyes molten pools. He pulls something out of his pocket and moves towards Avery.

Sammy's chest tightens. He throws himself between them, skinny arms raised to take the slap, the curse.

But his dad just holds out the toy car.

Sammy's chest tightens, a fist on his lungs. Then he snatches the car. He turns icy eyes on his dad – and then as quick as a whip, he smashes the toy over his dad's knuckles.

His dad gives a surprised grunt and looks down at the small cut on his hand.

Sammy knots his fingers around the car, ready *ready* to do it again.

'You start hitting things,' his dad says, voice low, 'then you never stop and you end up like me.' His laugh is cut glass. 'Because that's where it ends, Sammy boy. Blood and jail.'

Sammy's bottom lip trembles, but he lost his words. He wouldn't give them to his dad anyway. His dad is a monster in the dark and Sammy will never be like him.

Aunt Karen reappears and they yell some more and then his dad slams out of the house, while Aunt Karen screams down the driveway that she *doesn't want these kids.*

Sammy very slowly, very carefully, pries open Avery's fingers and tucks the car in. There's a smear of blood on it, but that's OK because it's the baddie's blood and Sammy is the superhero.

Aunt Karen comes back inside, rewrapping her tulip dressing gown.

'Is he coming back soon?' Sam says.

Aunt Karen closes her eyes. 'You're staying with me for a while. Did your father do that to Avery?'

Sammy nods, because in the light you can see Avery's swollen cheek, his broken lip, the bruises blossoming on his back where his shirt is hitched up.

Aunt Karen sighs and reaches for Avery. She tries to pull off his shirt but he gives a mangled growl and kicks wildly.

'Avery,' she snaps. 'Let me help. God, you're not even all there, are you?'

He's fine, Sammy wants to say. To shout. To stand on top of the wicker chair and scream. Avery is good and he laughs like chipped pieces of fairy magic and he knows a million facts about cars and there's nothing *wrong with him*.

Aunt Karen snatches at Avery's wrist, the one that holds the car, and Avery freezes, his gaze flicking from the car, to his aunt, to Sammy. His eyes are burned out blue.

'Don't take his—' Sammy says, but it's too late.

Avery starts screaming.

And he just

doesn't

stop.

CHAPTER 6

They arrive back at the yellow house behind the wild rose bushes at dusk. The air cools, crickets pick up their song, and the night sighs under suddenly weary eyelids.

Sam's salt-crusted jeans have stiffened against his legs and sand rubs every crevice of his skin. Every time he tilts his head, more sand rains down his cheeks. He's exhausted. Too much sun and throwing himself off rocky outcrops when the flu still has fingerprints on his bones. His eyes are a little blurry and he's starving and

yet

he's not felt this happy in forever.

He nearly forgets that he's the thief as he trails up the short garden path to the veranda where everyone slings towels over rails and dusts sand out of hair. A few of Jeremy's friends give backslapping farewells and leave, but the rest just topple back into the house.

Sam hesitates on the stairs. He has to get his backpack, obviously, but then he needs to leave for—

nowhere.

Moxie brushes past him, her skin cool and damp against his for a single heart-pounding moment.

'You might as well stay for dinner,' she says. 'Sunday night is waffles.'

Sam stays.

The house has emptied considerably. A lone preschooler rides a trike around and around the sofa. Several girls (around ten or eleven, which is the most terrifying age, in Sam's opinion) are at the kitchen table surrounded by mounds of waffles and blueberries and maple syrup. Sam feels vulnerable without a thousand bodies packed in to cover his tracks.

Moxie's dad waves from the kitchen. He's got a spatula in one hand and his apron says: LEAVE WHILE YOU STILL CAN – DAD IS COOKING. Hopefully that's a joke.

'How many are staying, Jeremy?' he says. 'I've got two waffle makers going, but do I need another batch of batter?'

'Dad, what kind of question is that?' Jack says. 'We're teenage boys.'

Jeremy smacks him playfully on the head. 'Only six of us guys left. And Moxie obviously.'

Moxie pulls a face like an unimpressed frog. 'Gee, Jeremy. Thanks for remembering me. Don't forget Jack's new adopted hatchling Sam.'

Sam shrinks. He can't help it. Being pointed out to adults is never good in his experience.

'Nice of you to stay, Sam.' Their father piles waffles on a plate. 'Did you swim in your clothes? Jeremy, lend him a shirt.'

Sam is, in fact, already wearing Jeremy's shirt but no one seems to have registered that fact. Jack argues with the others about who's showering first and Jeremy strides in and out of the laundry with armfuls of towels like he's used to tackling the washing machine. Their father wisely makes more waffles.

It's then, with the room not so loud or overcrowded and with everyone busy with food or washing or ramming a trike into the wall, that Sam realises they're missing someone.

A mother?

'I can get your clothes washed and dried in a few hours,' Jeremy says. 'You can wear my shirt, but pants are going to be a problem.'

Sam blinks, still registering the fact that they're now going to *clean his clothes* for him.

'Everything of mine will end up around your ankles,' he goes on. 'Dude, don't you ever eat? Please consume at least nineteen waffles tonight. For the greater good of humanity and pants.'

Their father takes a fresh plate of waffles to the table. 'He could wear a towel?'

Sam feels a little panicky.

'Dad,' Jeremy says, patient, 'would you wear a towel in a house where Jack would find it super amusing to step on a corner?'

His father shuffles around some jam pots to make room for the plate. 'I see your point.'

Jeremy and their father turn to look very hard at Moxie who's wringing her hair out in the kitchen sink. She still has the frog-shaped frown on and doesn't see the fixed looks until she flicks her hair back so it stands up like a salt-encrusted shark fin.

Then she notices. 'What?' She looks at them and then at Sam. 'Oh, haha. No.'

'Come on, he's your height,' Jeremy says. 'I'll clean his clothes super fast. After all, you invit—'

Sam's super considerate body chooses that moment to execute an organ-rattling sneeze.

He looks up to three concerned faces.

'Look, he's gone and caught cold,' Jeremy says reproachfully.

'I had the flu already,' Sam says. 'It's fine. It's nothing.'

The father turns back to the griddle. 'Wet clothes aren't helping. Moxie ...' He casts her a meaningful look.

Moxie throws her hands in the air. 'Oh, *fine*.' She stabs a finger at him. 'You. Follow me.'

She stomps up the stairs, like the whole world has offended her. Sam follows, acutely aware of the fact he just avoided being thrown out on his ear.

Or would he be?

He's not exactly a stranger any more. He showed Jack how to do a backflip. Someone tipped sand down his shirt. He gave Moxie a leg up over the chain fence on the way home. He's eaten their potato salad and worn their clothes.

The trouble is he *stole* it all, every moment. And that's the part people don't overlook. They feel betrayed. Betrayed people have the hardest fists.

By the time Sam's dragged his stiff legs up the stairs, Moxie has gone into both her room and the twins' and returned with an armful of clothes. She shoves them at him and propels him towards the bathroom. This whole family is really forceful.

'But these are girls' jeans ...' Sam starts.

Moxie abruptly releases him and narrows her eyes. 'And? Will they puncture your fragile masculinity for the evening?'

'Um.' He remembers her telling Jack she'll take a pound of flesh and he can imagine it.

'If they don't fit, then we'll discuss,' Moxie says. 'But they're big on me anyway. Now go. Use soap. Towels under the sink. And throw your clothes out the door straight away so I can take them to the washerwoman.'

Sam blinks.

'Jeremy,' she clarifies. 'Jeremy does laundry. Jack does yard work. Grady is supposed to houseclean, but he whinges about allergies. I look after the babies *way* too much. And we all cook, which sucks.'

'And you don't ... have a mum?' Sam says.

Moxie's inconvenienced look fades for a second and sadness shadows her eyes. 'No.' She turns to go, but her fingers catch on the doorframe and she spins back. 'That bruise looked pretty vicious. What happened?'

Lies run through Sam's head. None tumble out of his mouth.

'Hmm,' Moxie says. 'Jeremy's mysterious, silent adoptee.' With that she turns and Sam is alone and can breathe again.

CHAPTER 7

He gets a real hot shower. With real soap. And puts on fresh clothes that smell of soft cotton and cupboards. Moxie's jeans fit, which *is* a stab at his ego, but it's a relief not to be carrying half the ocean in his pockets.

He comes downstairs all self-conscious with damp hair and a shirt with a huge yellow smiley face on it which seems to go against his entire personality. He feels like Moxie chose it on purpose.

The tone downstairs is as worn out as he feels. Everyone seems contentedly sunburnt and sleepy and the boys have video games going in the lounge room while they eat waffles and scoop ice cream straight from the tub. Sam slips on to a bench at the table and watches as Moxie artistically arranges waffles with raspberries and maple syrup. A thumbprint of berry juice stains the corner of her mouth.

Not having had such options with waffles before and feeling overwhelmed, Sam just progresses through three types of jam in orderly succession. He's content with this until Moxie groans, leans across the table and slides his plate away.

'That is the most boring way to eat waffles I have ever seen in my life.' She snatches a jar of chocolate spread and gets to work. 'It's actually hurting my soul.' She sprinkles slices of banana on top, then a generous scoop of vanilla ice cream. She tops it with chopped nuts and a twist of caramel syrup. Then she slides it back to him. 'The De Lainey special. Eat and be educated.'

He does and, when he's halfway through the explosion of flavours, realises he didn't even thank her because he's so used to being silent. Seriously? He's embarrassing.

'So,' he says, coming up for air and tapping his spoon in what he hopes is a casual way, 'where did everyone else go?'

'They don't all live here, obviously.' Moxie fixes herself a similar waffle catastrophe, going heavy on the caramel. 'Most of them were Jeremy's herd, plus the kids next door, and a few people stopped by from church. The rest of the little kids were my Uncle Robin's. He's trying to catch up to Dad, apparently.' Her tone is flat. 'Six hellion cousins there. Obviously there's seven of us De Laineys.'

Oh, that's good to know.

'Jeremy isn't, erm, the oldest, right?'

Moxie looks faintly curious as she licks her spoon. She's probably registering the fact that he's at the table again, and the rest of the guys are sprawled in front of the TV.

Maybe she won't think too hard about it?

Which is a huge joke, because Moxie has furrow lines on her brow – likely from a constant state of thinking too hard.

'No, Grady's the oldest,' Moxie says. 'The nerd over there.' She points with her spoon to the taller boy who first forcibly shoved Sam into the lunch fray to begin with, and is now eating blueberries with his nose deep in a book. 'He's nineteen. Jeremy and Jack are next. Then me.' She swivels the spoon towards the conglomeration of smaller girls who seem to be arguing passionately over a board game while getting syrup everywhere. 'Then Dash, who's ten, and is obsessed with elves and trolls and her stupid homemade sword.'

A head snaps up from the end of the table, all frizzed braids and dirt-stained cheeks.

'I heard that,' Dash says. 'There is nothing stupid about the Thirteen Elven Kingdoms of War.'

'It's a book series,' Moxie says to Sam.

'It's our *life*!' one of the other girls says while the others nod in fierce agreement.

Moxie rolls her eyes. 'And lastly there are the babies.' She tips her head towards the kitchen where her father is wiping the sticky hands of a toddler and a small boy. 'Toby is three and … well, we just call the other the Baby. There are too many names around here as is.'

She goes back to attacking her waffle, the family tour finished. So he's left to slide a tentative question at her. Not that he has any right to ask. Not that he should be drawing attention to himself.

'And you ... sew?'

'And I design.' Her mouth is full of ice cream. 'I'll be a famous upcycling fashion designer someday.' Her smile is slightly self-satisfied and more than a little beautiful. 'And before you ask why I'm not drowned in friends too, it's because, unlike the twins, I don't need an audience twenty-four-seven. And,' her lips tip down, 'my best friend is away for the summer. Which means I'm facing the most dull holiday of my life.'

Sam's absently fixing himself another waffle, although he's getting full. But he's been too hungry too long not to stuff himself when the opportunity presents.

'And you?' Moxie says. 'How'd you and Jeremy meet?'

As Sam's flu-numbed brain scrabbles for a lie, the De Lainey father walks in and taps his mug on the back of a chair. He clears his throat several times until one of the boys scrabbles to pause the TV and dozens of eyes peer over chairs at him.

'Small announcement that concerns De Laineys.' He indicates with his mug for the twins to come over.

They extricate themselves from the others and flop at the table while the TV blares back on. Grady uses a spoon as a bookmark and looks up.

Moxie keeps adding more and more caramel sauce to her plate.

Sam should leave before Moxie asks more questions. Before her dad talks to him which – no, just no. Sam feels sick around adults.

But there are still waffles left and ... well, waffles.

'I want Monday's schedule organised,' their father says, 'so I might as well give you the summer plans as well.'

'Lie about in the sun and exist on watermelon and corn chips?' Jack says.

'Wishful,' their father says, 'but no. I already told you boys that you're apprenticed to me for the summer.'

There are collective groans and one, '*I thought you were joking.*'

'But then who's looking after the babies?' Moxie asks, but the words are barely out before horror dawns across her face. 'Oh *no*. Nope. Absolutely not, Dad.'

'I'll take the weekends,' their father says. 'You're wonderful with the babies and—'

'I'm not their replacement mother!' Moxie bursts out.

Sam slides another waffle on to his plate and tries to look like he's not listening. Except that he is. He feels a twinge of sympathy for Moxie's rapidly reddening face.

Her father's voice stays unfailingly mild.

'Sweetie, I'm not trying to make it that way. But I need the boys to build houses with me.'

Sam's fork pauses, half stabbed in the bowl of blueberries. Mr De Lainey builds houses? His heart beats a little faster.

Moxie drops her head to the table, hair tumbling over her ears like a chocolate waterfall.

'I'm sorry, kids, but this is the summer.'

Jeremy and Jack are already getting antsy, glancing back at their friends.

'Right, so we're sorted?' Jack says. 'No fun for us to prepare for the shitty world that is adulthood. Gotcha.'

Their father's lips thin. In that moment, he looks like Moxie – barely masked displeasure. 'Language, Jack. And we talked about this. You need work experience and I took on that house project that's a lot larger than I anticipated. And there are ...' His voice thickens. 'There are those hospital bills.'

It's like a magic phrase that suddenly has all four De Lainey teenagers looking anywhere but at their father. Grady immediately gathers plates and mumbles something about loving building. Jack slinks back to the sofa and only Jeremy pauses for a moment to rest his head briefly on his dad's shoulder.

'You can knock off at three,' his dad says. 'You know I hate putting this on you kids and ruining your holidays, but—'

'It's OK, Dad,' Jeremy says. 'We're just whining.'

His dad brushes affectionate knuckles over Jeremy's head and then Jeremy slips back off to his friends. 'Don't make tonight too late.'

Moxie is still face down on the table.

'Moxie.' Their father gently nudges her shoulder.

'Murmph.'

'Look, it's just the babies. Dash will be next door most of the summer, I assume.'

Dash, who's obviously winning the elven board game and raking in piles of fake dragon coins while the others look peevish, waves a hand. 'We're going to make a film! Esther has a camera!'

Their father smiles but Moxie finally peels off the table with a ferocious look in her eyes. 'And *I* was going to work on my design portfolio. You realise I don't even have Kirby to come over and make it more tolerable, right? I'm *alone* and broken.'

Her father starts clearing up plates. 'You can still sew. I'll take over as soon as I get home. And when school starts, we'll get the babies in daycare. Please, sweetie? This deadline is a beast.'

'Fine. *Fine*. Just. Argh.' She snatches her plate and stomps off to the kitchen.

Their father sinks down in the vacated spot and looks wryly at Sam. 'I'm sure your folks aren't spoiling your summer plans, eh? I feel like the worst dad.'

Sam's mouth opens and closes because he can't think of anything past *'you're basically the best father in the world compared to mine who I haven't even seen in eight years after he beat my brother unconscious'* or *'my folks would love to spoil my summer plans with a ride in the back of a police car after what I did at my old school, so you're doing fine.'* But he doesn't. And the De Lainey father doesn't seem put out by Sam's silence. He just gathers dishes while telling the girls to finish up their game, and then he disappears to put babies to bed.

Moxie reappears with a bowl of microwaved popcorn and instructs Sam to take it into the lounge. He does, unthinking, because Moxie is a force to be obeyed, and he finds himself swallowed by a sofa and a movie as everyone settles down for the evening. Younger guests disappear back next door and Dash is forced off to bed, while the teens are told to keep the sound low and have every non-De-Lainey out by eleven. The lights flick off. As soon as their dad leaves, Jack changes the film to a horror.

Moxie flops on the sofa next to Sam. It was the only available seat, he tells himself. That's why she sat next to him.

He's forgotten. And accepted. All at once.

And he's so hungry for it, so wildly and madly hungry, that he stays.

Even though the movie seriously freaks him out.

He's not a big fan of bodies going through wood chippers and blood splattering, but then one character gets possessed by a demon and attacks the others. With fists. And the more Sam watches, the tighter his muscles wind and the harder he finds it is to breathe.

Ridiculous. There's plenty of air.

But his lungs don't
  quite work
  any more.

He feels Moxie watching him out of the corner of her eye so he focuses on the screen, focuses on being still. Stop twitching your fingers. One character crushes the other to the floor with a boot and then punches them with a fist. Again. Again – *againagainagain—*

Then the walls in the creepy asylum explode with monsters so fast, so violently, that Sam's flimsy grip on calm shatters. He gives a strangled cry and jumps so high that he falls backwards off the sofa.

He hits the ground on his back, legs in the air like a dead bug.

Several heads peer over the back of the sofa at him. Like they're seeing him, *really* seeing him.

Oh no.

Behind them, the TV blazes red and black as blood sprays.

Sam opens his mouth – to defend himself? Explain? Say watching this movie is like shoving a knife beneath his ribs because of *all the things he's done*?

Then the weird silence is broken by Jack's bark of laughter. 'Did you see his *face*? Holy shit, kid, have you not seen this movie before?'

Footsteps pad upstairs and the De Lainey father's voice trails down, softly warning. 'Jack. If I have to pull up your language one more time tonight, you're losing your phone.'

'Child abuse,' Jack mutters. 'How is his hearing so good?'

Jeremy pats his shoulder. 'Only for you and your swearing, buddy. If we're asking to use the car, he can't hear a thing.'

Sam picks himself up, wondering if he should bolt for the door to get away from this suffocating humiliation. His face is so hot, his clothes so tight.

Moxie's shoulders shake softly and it takes Sam a long, blurred moment to realise she's laughing.

'This one,' she says, gasping, 'is precious.'

'I think he's actually scared, guys.' Jeremy half rises off the chair, like he's going to – what? Pat Sam's back and tell him *it's just all fake, Sammy boy. Fake blood! Fake demons! You're OK!*

Sam wants to bury himself. He avoids everyone's eyes as he slowly climbs back over the sofa and sits.

'I'm not ... scared.' Sam picks up a pillow and tries to dissolve behind it.

'You nearly pissed yourself,' Jack says.

Jeremy hits him.

Moxie is still laughing silently, a hand over her mouth.

The room hushes again as they watch the last

minutes of the film where everyone predictably dies or turns into a monster and it's so depressing that Sam keeps his face in the pillow.

Suddenly Moxie's mouth is very close to Sam's ear and he stops breathing.

'I'm sorry.' Her voice is soft as sand and sea. 'I shouldn't have laughed. Are you OK?'

The question beats against his ribs and he wants to hold it for ever. Pathetic, pathetic Sam.

'I'm fine.' Is his voice really that high or is he just hyper aware of his body right now?

He pretends to watch again, but Moxie is still looking at him as credits roll and guests peel themselves up and look for car keys and shoes.

'There's still part two,' Jack says.

Sam might be sick.

'It's past eleven.' Moxie licks popcorn salt off her thumb. 'So you guys better get out of my house.'

'Hey, I live here,' Jack says.

Moxie sighs. 'To my permanent annoyance.'

Boys head for the door, fake tackling and joking about the movie as they leave. This is the part where Sam slips away. Which means this day, this perfect and unprecedented day, is over. He'll never have this again.

He has to leave.

No one notices as he slips from the darkened room, nimbly circuiting toys and highchairs, while his fingers catch up his backpack straps.

The front door hangs open, night air and

stars and long empty streets at his fingertips. The twins hang off the veranda rails, waving goodbye to friends. Friends that Sam's supposed to be leaving with.

Sam looks at the stairs.

He wouldn't dare.

The De Lainey father appears then, scrubbing a hand through his shock of dark hair. Most of his attention is on counting the bodies still downstairs. His eyes rest on Sam.

Sam hates being looked at – not hard, not closely, not by adults. Adults either don't see him or use slaps to get answers.

'Thanks for coming, Sam,' says Mr De Lainey.

He remembers Sam's name?

'Hope you had a good camping trip with the boys.'

'Yeah,' Sam says. 'I m-mean, it was great.'

'Good, good.' The smile is warm. It's real. Mr De Lainey looks tired, but soft happiness rests behind his eyes. 'See you again soon, son. Have a safe trip home.'

'I will – I mean, yes sir.' Sam's eyes flick to the stairs.

You wouldn't dare—

Sam's throat is tight. 'I just have to get something from upstairs?'

Mr De Lainey smiles and waves for him to go. He reaches for the kettle and a mug.

Sam bolts for the stairs.

He takes them two at a time, his backpack jingling with a hundred stolen sins.

No one will notice if he doesn't come back downstairs.

No one will go into that office this late.

No one will see a homeless boy curled in an overstuffed chair under the window.

Sam closes the office door behind him and lowers himself into the armchair, his heavy backpack pressed tight to his chest. The room still smells of summer days and toast crumbs and ... safety. He'll leave tomorrow. First chance. This is stupid, reckless, but it's just one night and then he's gone for ever.

One last night that feels strangely like ... home.

BEFORE

Sammy is eight and it's war at the kitchen table.

Dinner was technically two hours ago, but they still sit there, listening to Aunt Karen in the next room yelling on the phone. Sammy swings his legs, loose shoelaces clacking against the plastic chair as he alternates between his and Avery's homework. Avery's is harder, being a year ahead at school, and he works fine in class – but at home? He gets overwhelmed and cries. He gets that way about a lot of things.

Like the broccoli and bean casserole on his plate right now.

Avery's face is damp and red, his hair plastered to his face with sweat. He had a meltdown for the first hour, while Aunt Karen shouted that he was *too old for this* and kept shoving him back in the chair. Then he changed to screaming, then to high-pitched keening, and now he's quiet – exhausted and slowly beating his forearms against the table till they bruise purple.

He's ten. He's getting too much for Aunt Karen to pin down.

That's why she's on the phone.

'—complete rubbish, Clay. They're not my kids!'

Avery flicks his fingers in front of his eyes between beating his arms.

flick

thump

flick

thump

Sammy scrawls answers into homework he doesn't understand. The phone call, however, he understands just fine.

'—foster home. I do not want these goddamn boys. I warn you—'

Sammy glances at Avery, who's now blinking slowly like he might fall asleep in his plate. It's been a year since their dad beat the hell out of him, but there's a small scar in the left corner of his mouth. A forever scar.

To remind Sammy he has to always, always protect his brother.

Their aunt gives a frustrated shout and then goes silent. Call over. She strides into the kitchen, all hard edges and splinters. She wears bright chunky jewellery and her cheeks are sunken and her lips know only frowns.

'Well, the police finally caught up with your father,' she says. 'Theft, drugs, assault – he's in prison for a while.'

Sammy thought she'd be smug about it. But the dark circles under her eyes and the twitchy way she reaches for another cigarette says it doesn't cancel out the fact she has two nephews at her table that she couldn't want less.

'Which means you're still staying with me, because who knows where your mother is.' Her eyes cut to Avery and the cold plate before him. Untouched except for the bit Sammy tried to eat to cover for him when Aunt Karen's back was turned. His ear still smarts from being caught and slapped too. 'But if I don't see some attitude adjustments ...' She breaks off, taking a savage drag of the cigarette.

Sammy's legs freeze, mid-swing, shoelaces making a final *clack*. 'You'll send us to a foster home?'

'Avery, for certain.' Her lips twist, angry and bitter. 'Someone can look after him who specialises in naughty little boys with *special needs*.'

She says that like it's fake. Like Avery is trying to be difficult.

Frantic fluttering crawls up Sammy's throat. Leaving Aunt Karen doesn't worry him, but they'd separate him and Avery, wouldn't they? That can't happen. He's Avery's protector, his everything. He looks wildly at Avery, but Avery's popped his hands in his pockets – where he keeps his toy car, secret so no one can take it. He's not listening.

Sammy's words come choked. 'But, please, you c-can't. We have to be together—'

Aunt Karen slaps a hand in front of Avery's plate and he jumps. 'Then eat your dinner, *right now*.'

'He can't—' Sammy starts, but Aunt Karen cuts him off with an impatient gesture.

'He can and *will* do as he's told.'

Avery growls at her.

'Fine.' She stomps to the kitchen. 'You're getting the wooden spoon and some consequences.'

Sammy's out of his chair, blood flooding his face in hot waves. He trips on his shoelaces while the world presses granite fists against his chest, a suffocating weight that whispers *save him save him that's your job*.

Why can't she just let him eat fish fingers every day? He loves those. Avery doesn't *like* how casserole tastes or how it feels in his mouth or how it's mixed together or how his plate is so full it scares him to start. It hurts him. Sammy could tell her this if she listened.

If anyone listened.

But he is the invisible boy and no one cares.

Aunt Karen marches back, a wooden spoon in hand, but Sammy snatches the plate full of sticky, congealed casserole and flies across the room with it. He throws it in the bin – plate, bean sludge, fork and all.

Avery's eyes widen.

Aunt Karen spins on Sammy. 'How dare you—'

And then Sammy grabs Avery's hand, pulling him from the table and the tear stains and the oncoming smacks from an aunt who *doesn't want these goddamn boys*.

They're out the front door while Aunt Karen is still yelling. 'Stay out there like animals then!'

The door slams. The lock clicks.

Night air kisses Avery's wet cheeks and frolics fingers through Sammy's curls. They're used to this, but it's *cold* tonight.

Avery's hands flutter. 'I c-c-can't—'

'I know.' Sammy pets his arm. 'Just let me think. I could ...' He glances across the street at Mr Shepherd's garage, which is *always* open, showing his pack rat collection of boxes and junk and rusted-out machines. 'I could steal some tools.' Excitement flickers in his voice. 'I could undo the window locks and we can go to bed.'

Avery pulls his car out of his pocket and runs it over his face.

'I could steal some biscuits too. You like biscuits.' He strokes Avery's arm, anxious again, because Avery's so thin, and even though he's playing with his car, there's no flood of babyish calm in his eyes like there used to be.

His eyes are just sad.

'If Aunt Karen doesn't want us, we can find *our* own house.' Sammy takes Avery's hand to cross the road.

'Can you do that?' Avery whispers. 'Steal houses?'

'Yeah,' Sammy says. 'Yeah, of course I can.'

CHAPTER 8

Sam goes through the desk drawers in the De Lainey office, listening to the family stomp through a Monday morning. It sounds very traumatic. The two little kids are tag-team crying. Jack and Moxie lock in a shouting match. No one can find car keys. They're out of groceries and their dad confesses there's no money today, but tomorrow he'll fix it. Dash says she's leaving home. For ever.

'You'll be fine with the kids, Moxie!' Mr De Lainey says, but he has to shout because the kids are, well, screaming and Moxie answers with a wail.

Goodbyes are hollered. The front door slams. Engines fade down the road.

Sam finds an envelope of cash crammed in the back of a drawer with 'for emergencies' scribbled over it. He picks up. Puts it back. How can he take it when their dad was *just saying* they had no money for groceries? He's obviously saving this for worst-case scenarios.

But Sam is a thief. This is what he does, isn't it?

He stuffs the wad of notes into his pocket, guilt wrapped around his throat.

He pokes his head out the door.

The house is suddenly quiet.

Sam slips across the hall and peeks through the stairwell. A De Lainey-flavoured explosion has hit. Someone's pyjamas have been threaded through the railings and a bowl of half-eaten cereal sits on the second step. A sea of blocks covers the floors and the TV flashes a muted kiddie show.

Then Moxie storms into view, looking like a goddess of vengeance and war. Jam handprints stain her neck like blood and her eyes are fire. She wears Wonder Woman pyjama pants and a once-white singlet and she drags a struggling preschooler towards the bathroom.

'Quit it, Toby,' she orders. 'You're having a bath. *Another bath*. Because that's what happens when you put cornflakes down your shirt!'

The bathroom door squeaks. Water turns on. Toby howls like he's being murdered. The baby toddles after them, cradling a pot of jam.

Sam's getaway path is clear.

Except he doesn't want to get away.

His heart knots and his limbs ache, not from the flu any more, but with this dull feeling like he's making a mistake. But he *can't stay*.

He takes the stairs silent and fast, but he presses his fingers to the front door for one moment while his heart crumbles and the stolen money in his pocket burns.

He leaves.

He has to run to catch the bus, backpack jangling wildly like he's carrying half of Christmas. He uses stolen cash to get downtown, feeling sick about turning up at the mechanic's after beating up that apprentice. And also because Avery might be gone.

Where else can Sam go?

Back to the De—

Yeah, OK, hold that thought and put it in a deep box and don't touch it again.

He gets a few odd looks on the bus and then remembers the bruise on his cheekbone and his dishevelled hair and tired eyes.

He looks like trouble.

He finds a cafe for a lunch, an iced coffee and two tomato and pepper sandwiches. The De Lainey cash just slips through his fingers. This is his life. Steal and spend and stay alive. One good day – OK, the best day – with nice people doesn't change his reality.

His reality is stealing until he and Avery can afford their own house. If Avery hasn't run away or got hurt or freaked out or been arrested—

Don't think like that.

Sam walks into the mechanic's, bypassing stacks of tyres and oily toolboxes and a truck unloading crates of spare parts. It's not a big shop and the brick walls are painted swimming pool blue. Sam usually comes in the back, but not today. Not in case bloodstains still cling to the rough cement steps.

He jams his hands in his pockets and strolls in like it's no big deal. But his eyes skim the workshop for the apprentice he beat up. Which is why, distracted, he walks straight into the boss.

The boss wears grease-stained overalls and his hair is salt and pepper. 'Sammy Lou.' He has a voice like old engines. 'For the fiftieth time, your brother doesn't get visitors in work hours.'

Sam's heart leaps. He's still here.

'Sorry,' Sam says. 'I'll wait till his break.'

'Break?' The boss gives a rattling laugh that's the opposite of amused. 'You know what's breaking around here? My *mind* on why I kept that kid on. He's incredible at fixing engines, sure, but hell to everything else about him.'

Sam hangs his head so hair flops in his eyes and his shoulders bunch pitifully. He's practised this look for maximum patheticness. 'I'm really sorry for distracting him. He's been eaten up with worry about what he did, sir. He just needs—'

'Oh, save it.' The boss jabs a thumb over his shoulder. 'Just don't distract him. I'm two days behind on work thanks to your brother wrecking one of my cars and the fact my other boy got jumped. If he gets behind schedule, I'll take it out of his paycheck and your ass. I am *this close* to firing him, I swear.'

Sam ducks under the boss's arm and hurries

towards the back of the shop. So Avery got his second chance. And no one's figured it was Sam who jumped the other apprentice. They're good. Great, even. He sees Avery leaning over a Toyota with its hood popped, his coveralls slung around his waist and a black tank tight around his chest. His bare arms are stick thin and smeared with grease.

Sam thumps against the car and peers in like he knows about engines. He doesn't.

Avery looks up, eyes brightening for a second – but then his lips cut into a frown.

Is that about their fight?

'You stayed,' Sam says.

'What?' Avery pauses, arms half lost in the engine. 'What are you talking about?'

'The other night? You said you were steal— um, *getting* a car and then driving away. With or without me.' Sam meant to say it offhandedly but it comes out twisted.

Avery's eyes narrow. 'That was just *talk*. Does my boss know you're here? He's super angry at me, so ... so just get off the car.'

Sam shoves off. 'Sorry. Because of the paint?'

'No.' Avery's voice pinches around the edges. 'Because you're just like Dad and *I hate it*.'

It's a long thin knife straight into his heart. So Avery knows what Sam did. Oh, he definitely knows.

Avery drops his spanner in the toolbox and his hands flap, too hard, too fast. 'You hit him, you h-h-h-hit him—' He stumbles backwards, trying to stop himself cycling. 'My boss couldn't fire me because we're so behind, but-but-but you said you wouldn't *hit people any more*.'

'I'm sorry.' Sam smothers his panic because if Avery flips out here, the boss will toss them both. And this is all Avery's fault anyway, right? 'But hey, you were the one who screwed up and got drunk and drove that customer's car into a wall. You need this job.'

'That was an accident. I got – confused.' Avery's eyes flick everywhere but to Sam's face – not always an indicator that he's lying since Avery doesn't do eye contact anyway, but Sam can tell when he is. Especially when Avery jabs his fingers into Sam's chest – right on the bruise.

Distraction.

He's lying.

Sam bites back his pained whimper.

Avery's voice rises. 'You *meant* to break someone's hand. I don't want – I-I hate it when you're like that. I hate it. I hate it.' He stops flapping, thumb touching the corner of his mouth. His scar.

Agonising heat flushes Sam's cheeks. He's nothing like their dad and Avery's hitting low to say it. He wants to shove him back, but he can't. He'd never touch Avery to hurt him. Never.

'You need this job.' Sam's voice is low. 'So we can save up for the house.'

'There won't ever be a house!' Avery lets out a real cry then and Sam has to grab his flailing arm so he doesn't punch a toolbox and break his fingers.

'Avery, stop. *Please*. I'm sorry.' Sam tries to stroke his arm, but Avery snatches free.

He scowls.

But his breathing evens out.

'Even if we came up with the money,' Avery snaps, 'I'm only seventeen. I can't rent.'

'It could just be something small—'

'No, it's impossible. Shut up about it.' Avery's teeth clench. 'And stop ... stop being like *him*.'

'Then stop drinking,' Sam shoots back. 'I mean it. Don't ever do that again.'

Avery's lips pull back in a snarl. But he just flips Sam off and storms back to the car. He starts dropping and fumbling tools, a good way to get the boss coming over in a rage, and Avery is fresh out of second chances. It drives Sam mad, because Avery is good with engines. He can take apart anything and put it back together clean, oiled and working ten times better. You give him a problem with a mechanical solution and he'll find it.

But he has to stay calm. Not get overwhelmed. Not let anyone see him freak out.

People understand a cute seven-year-old boy screaming on the floor because he's autistic. They call the police when that screaming little boy becomes seventeen.

The police must not find the Lou brothers.

After what Sam did at school last year? He just, he ... he can't—

No, they can't be found.

Sam wants to shout: *Look, Avery! This is exactly why you can't be alone! Who'd calm you down if I wasn't here?* But he doubts Avery even realises what Sam does for him.

Forget it. They're brothers. This is what brothers do. Sam will hit *himself* before resenting Avery for needing help, OK?

He fiddles with a loose thread on his jeans. Moxie's jeans. He can't believe he forgot to change. He can't believe he's still clawing for the impossible wish of having his own home. But he needs a dream as big as the moon or else he's just an invisible boy with empty hands.

He sighs and tucks the leftover cash he stole from the De Laineys into Avery's back pocket. He'll add it to their savings.

'Can we not fight?' Sam whispers.

Avery braces his arms against the engine and lets his head hang down, shoulder blades sticking up like achingly sharp wings. 'S-stop hurting people. You'll hit the wrong person someday and get yourself killed.' He looks up, eyes like broken oceans.

'Then stop screwing up,' Sam says.

They let their impossible requests hang in the air, bitter as failure.

CHAPTER 9

Even though they look dishevelled, all grease stains and undone shoelaces and tired eyes, the Lou brothers can sit on the edge of a water fountain on the Esplanade, unnoticed. No one looks twice. Sam swings his legs, plastic milkshake cup clasped in sweaty hands.

They're here to work.

The sun is high and hot and the shops and restaurants and tourist traps along the beachfront are alive with the flurry of the lunch hour. Last night equalled cricked necks as they slept in the back of a stranger's car. Sam had to vanish before the boss arrived, although he stowed his backpack in a storeroom because Avery tried to unzip it and that's not happening. Then Avery, who's pulling double shifts while the other apprentice is off, was given an unexpectedly long lunch break because the boss had to go out of town. He clearly doesn't trust Avery alone in the workshop.

Fair.

Which ends up with the Lou brothers analysing tourist targets.

Their eyes are sharp and their list of needs specific: they want someone well dressed and distracted, hopefully sunburnt to proclaim tourist status. Someone happy or affectionate. Someone who'll care.

'I guess we'll do the hit-and-then-run-away routine,' Sam says at last.

Avery gives him a sour look. He still wears the grease-stained singlet from yesterday, but he has jeans on now and battered red Converse. He could use a bath.

There's a toilet block not far from the ocean where you can get a sixty-second lukewarm shower. It's supposed to be for sand-encrusted swimmers from the ocean, but it's downright helpful if you're homeless. It's downright unhelpful if you think of the De Laineys' warm shower and soap and comfortably softened clean clothes. Sam still has on the smiley-face shirt and Moxie's jeans. Does she wonder about him?

Why's he even thinking that? That's over.

Sam rubs the back of his sweaty neck. 'Well, we can't do the one where you fake-vomit. We're not set up for it.'

'OK, we can do the Hit 'N' Run job,' says Avery. 'I'm hitting, you're running.'

Sam gives him a flat look. Obviously that's how they divide the parts. He can't even fake hitting Avery. 'Stop calling them "jobs". What do think this is? A movie?'

'If this is a movie,' Avery tips his milkshake cup up for the last drops, 'then I want my money back.'

He hands his cup to Sam to throw out, because obviously that's what little brothers are for. Sam considers throwing it back at his face, but everything about him and Avery seems unbalanced at the moment. Like it's sliding. He wants to catch it before someone falls.

He puts it in the bin.

Avery stands, anticipation in his jittering arms. His eyes comb the crowd and he starts hopping up and down until Sam kicks his shoe to remind him to act inconspicuous.

Sam tugs at the collar of his shirt, too tired for this. His mind slips back to the butter-yellow house and the comfortable armchair in the sun and the way Moxie's hand brushed his—

Avery shoves him.

It comes so fast that Sam doesn't have time to brace himself. He takes a stumbling step backwards, falling against a passer-by in a tangle of limbs and hair flopping over his face.

'I'm sorry!' he gasps as the person shoves him off with a startled grunt.

Their handbag isn't quite zipped.

Sam's hand is in and out before he stands up.

Then Avery is in front of him, shoulders knotted, jabbing a finger into Sam's chest. Right on the bruise. Sam's wince is real.

'You want to run that by me again?' Avery shouts.

Sam slaps his hand away. 'Hey, take it easy.' He's not faking, though. Avery's a little too into it today.

'Shut the hell up!' Avery shoves him again. He puts in more force than usual, like he hasn't left their recent list of frazzled disagreements behind and it's playing out as his body uncoils frenzied tics. Not good. It'll be harder to gauge when he's about to—

Knuckles collide with Sam's jaw.

His neck snaps to the side.

His teeth sink into his tongue.

The boardwalk reaches up and Sam's face

    c
     o
   l
    l
      i
    d
  e
    s

with a dull thwack on the floorboard. His vision fractures.

Avery really *really* forgot to fake that punch.

Hands are already on Sam's arms, grabbing him, asking if he's OK as he's roughly propelled into a sitting position. Blood dribbles down his chin. Someone gives a heartfelt gasp.

A tall man in a Hawaiian shirt pushes Avery back and Avery starts jumping again, swearing viciously while his arms go like windmills. People back off and stare. Sometimes Sam feels guilty about this – using Avery like a sideshow distraction while he slips wallets. But they'll never get enough for a house just with Avery's mechanic job.

Voices flood over Sam.

'Are you all right?'

'Hey kid, can you stand?'

'Call the police.'

Sam snatches at an arm to steady himself. 'I'm fine.' The words slur without trying. He gets tangled up in someone's handbag as they haul him to his feet. His hand darts toward a back pocket.

Behind him, Avery's shoved Hawaiian Shirt, fingers moving in a lightning dance to steal a wallet.

Someone gives a grateful cry. 'Here comes a security guard!'

Sam's body tenses. He wipes knuckles across his lips, smearing blood, as he looks for the grey uniform of security. They need to run now. He'll have to drop the wallet he's just barely tucked under his shirt. He needs to get Avery—

And then his eyes catch on a girl with a knot of frizzy brown hair, wearing a loose tie-dye vest over a white shirt and cut-off jeans. She hangs over a stroller with an armful of serviettes for a baby with its face in an ice cream cone. But she's paused, wipes halfway to the baby's face.

Moxie stares at him.

Sam jerks away. Did she see his face? She didn't. She wouldn't have.

Please.

His breath tangles and he looks desperately at Avery, who now stares with saucer eyes up at an enormous security guard.

It's Sam's fault. He let himself get distracted.

They should be gone by now.

Sam doesn't think. He just reaches out to the closest Good Samaritan and yanks a wallet out of his pocket.

'What? Hey!' The person lunges at him.

Sam tips two fingers in salute and then—

runs.

The security guard grabs for Sam's shoulders, but Sam ducks under his arms just as Avery turns the opposite way and bolts. He vaults a flower garden with wild abandon, bark chips and purple petals spraying under his shoes. Then he's gone.

He never looks back to see if Sam made it.

That's fine. Sam takes care of himself.

Sam dives into the crowd at breakneck speed, leaving a trail of shouts after him. The security guard chases, shouting into his walkie-talkie. But Sam's already down the street, weaving around cars as they blast horns and hit brakes, and then he runs until he's thoroughly lost amongst tourist hats and buskers and restaurants serving vinegar crabs and hot salted chips. Noise runs over his back. Bodies shove him out the way.

He's hidden.

He's lost in a crowd.

He pulls up the hem of his T-shirt and wipes blood off his lips. Then he tugs the stolen wallet and iPhone out of his back pockets. The last wallet is still in his hand. Not a bad haul.

He walks and flips through them.

Tosses the first one out – just cards and silver coins.

The second is a fat tourist wallet. Fifties and twenties. He shies into an alcove as a group of kids on skateboards shove past. Then he drops that wallet in a flowerbed. The phone he'll give to Avery, whose friends can fix it for selling. If he can find Avery.

His fingers press gently at his jaw. Another bruise. It's not like that's usual for him, right?

But this is Avery. He hates hitting.

Sam shouldn't have got distracted, but it was *Moxie* and his eyes only caught hers for a second and he doesn't want her to recognise—

Stop. Stopstopstop. It doesn't matter. She's nobody to him.

Sam chews the inside of his aching cheek and wanders around the rows of shops, but there's no sign of Avery's oil-stained elbows. Great.

His eyes flick over crawling traffic to the boardwalk and ocean beyond. The sea is cut emeralds and the sparkle hurts his eyes. But he keeps looking. Searching.

Part of his thundering heart knows he's not really looking for Avery.

And he sees her again.

Moxie De Lainey.

She's across the road now, one hand pushing the stroller while the other gestures wildly at her dad, who's got a plastic kiddie trike over one shoulder. Sam wonders if she's talking about him.

Yeah sure, Sam. The entire world revolves around you. She probably (definitely) didn't recognise you.

She probably (definitely) didn't care.

A group of noisy shoppers passes and Sam melts behind a display of handmade hats and beaded anklets. His fingers move automatically to pocket something when a scream splits the air above the growl of the traffic.

'TOBY! *STOP.*'

Sam's fingers freeze. His head snaps up.

There's a break in the traffic and a small bundle of colour has tipped over the sidewalk and run for the road.

Sam doesn't even think.

He shoves away from the hatstands and flings himself over low buckets of flowers separating shoppers from the road. Cars stream forward. Sam's shoes hit the road. He left his beating heart back on the footpath, because right now he moves silently, airless, his fingers reaching out to snatch the hem of a small T-shirt and pull a kid into his arms. He twists so his back is to the oncoming car.

Moxie stumbles on to the road, her face stricken, legs stretching to cover the short distance.

'Moxie,' Sam says.

Just a whisper. Just a breath.

It's all happened so fast. No chance to think.

He throws Toby into her arms, which seems to take for ever and yet no time at all.

A horn blasts.

Undone shoelaces twist around Sam's ankles.

He takes a breath.

The car hits.

CHAPTER 10

He folds in on himself, a rag doll, all loose arms and stuffing spilling on to the road.

For a second the pain is bright and white hot, the road sheering the skin off his arms and the soft tenderness of his cheek. Then the world stammers to an abrupt halt. It doesn't hurt. He doesn't care.

He just needs to know if the little De Lainey boy is OK.

Car doors slam. Voices rise in panicked flurry. Blood, hot and thick and metallic, coats Sam's arms.

He pushes himself up.

'Wait, kid! Don't move. Let me call an ambulance—'

The driver is sobbing. Someone has a phone out, frantically dialling.

'No.' Sam tastes hot bitumen, salty blood. He scrambles to his feet. 'No, I'm fine.' His T-shirt sticks to his hip, his skin raw as skinned fish.

He looks for Moxie.

She sits in the gutter, Toby clutched to her chest, as her father pulls them both into his arms. Their backs are to Sam. Their father's shoulders shake.

But there's not a scratch on the little boy.

Sam clutches at the car hood for a second.

'Kid, just sit down.'

An adult reaches out to steady Sam, but he shrinks back. 'I'm fine.'

Moxie looks up over her father's shoulder. Her eyes are fierce and relieved as the aftermath of a storm.

Sam turns away.

He slips amongst the growing crowd and they move back – probably so he doesn't get blood on them. As soon as he's on the footpath again, he breaks into a run. He's fine, he's fine *fine fine*. His body screams so he just runs faster. Blood slicks down his arms. Hot tears crowd behind his eyes but he doesn't have time. Just get away. Move. Don't let people see. Don't let them notice.

He slips behind a row of shops and grabs at rough bricks to steady himself. The footpath ends here. No pedestrians. He sinks into the gutter, grabbing his stomach. The ground pulses and agony flashes in his guts.

He puts his head between his legs and vomits.

Tears spill next, hot and fat down his cheeks. His hand goes to his left side, where he took most of the hit. He peels it back gingerly to view red oozing road rash. His mind has completely stopped functioning so he just stares at it until the bile comes back up his throat and he pukes again.

A shadow falls over his head.

'Whoa,' Avery says. 'If that's a stomach bug, stay away from me.'

Sam closes his eyes, tasting blood and tar.

'I was looking for you but some idiot just got hit by a car up there and I got distracted and—' Avery stops. The shadow drops from Sam's head, and he winces because the brief respite from the sun was nice, and then Avery is kneeling next to him, grabbing his arm and twisting it to show raw skinned flesh. 'Sammy.' His voice is high and panicked.

'So,' Sam says, his voice thick, 'that idiot might've been me.'

Avery's fingers tighten on Sam's wrist and he fairly explodes. 'What the *hell*, Sammy? You could've died! Why would you even – you idiot. You c-c-could've died! We can't go to hospital or the c-cops will find—'

'I know!' Sam snatches his arm back. He wants to shove Avery and his panicked flapping hands away. Sam hurts he hurts *he hurts*. 'I don't need a hospital. Shut up, OK? I'm fine.' He presses fingers lightly to his left side again and his heart trips.

'You're lying! You're *lying*.'

Sam glances sideways at him. Avery's hands spin as he crouches by Sam. His eyes have a frantic edge to them and no, just no, Sam hasn't energy to tug him back from a meltdown right now.

'Avery,' he whispers, 'it was a little kid. I just … I had to.'

'You did *not*.' Avery says it so forcefully Sam sinks into himself a little further. 'You and your stupid Superman complex are going to get us killed. So just shut up.' Avery grabs Sam's shoulder. 'Now c'mon. We'll go to my friend's place.'

Oh, great. Avery's *friends*. Shifty assholes who screw Avery around and probably run drugs and worse. They're the reason Avery showed up to work so drunk he smashed a car.

'No,' Sam says, voice rough. 'I don't like them.'

'What? You want to try Aunt Karen's?' Avery's voice is high and sharp. 'She'll call the police on us. Now stop being a b-baby and—'

Sam pushes himself out of the gutter. His skin is flame and ice all at once, his pulse a suffocating fury behind his eyes. 'Screw you, Avery.' His voice bounces high and low, raw as his bloodied skin. 'You don't understand a single freaking thing. Those people you hang out with are bad—'

'We're not exactly good!'

'—and,' Sam's voice rises, 'I don't want to be around them and end up as messed up as you.'

Avery stiffens.

The terror in his eyes, the anxious knots, and the frantic clawing at Sam's shirt – it all stops. His eyes go blank, guttered out. He retreats. Sam watched this happen when bullies went at him at school. When teachers sent him out of class for his annoying tics. When Aunt Karen told him just what she thought of his attitude. When their dad hit him.

Avery just shuts down.

Sam has never made him do that before.

Avery rises and skitters back. 'Fine. You don't need me and I don't need you.'

'Avery, I didn't mean—'

But Avery's turned in a flurry of spinning hands. And he runs.

Great. He's probably going to freak out and Sam won't be there to catch him and –

Well, fine. *Fine*. Anger suddenly whitens behind Sam's eyes. Let him melt down somewhere alone and figure out what a stupid little jerk he's being.

Sam shoves to his feet and limps down the street. People stare, but he focuses ahead. He rounds a corner and has to lean against a wall, leaving a palmprint of blood against the bricks. He looks over his shoulder. Avery hasn't come back. Sam didn't realise, until that moment, that he desperately wanted Avery to come back.

Sam sinks into a crouch and puts his head on his knees. He cries.

Because it hurts.

That's the only reason.

CHAPTER 11

The boy from nowhere sits at a bus stop with empty hands and a bloodstained shirt. He flipped it inside out so at least the garish smiley face, now streaked with blood, doesn't make him look like an extra in one of Jack De Lainey's horror movies.

But if he doesn't move
if he doesn't breathe too deeply
he might be OK.

A bus arrives and he gets on behind a group of struggling shoppers who are tangled in bags of baguettes and tinned tuna. No one notices Sam. He leans his head against the window and closes his eyes. Obviously he should go steal another house. But he's not staked anything out. It could take for ever to find one. And he hurts.

He hurts too much to pick a lock.
He hurts too much to rob a family.
He hurts too much to breathe.

If he goes to hospital, they'll get his name, his details, call his aunt, call the police – he can't. If he goes back to the mechanic's, Avery's boss will ask questions. If he goes back to the De Laineys'—

What is he thinking? That's not an option. One stolen day doesn't equal him crawling on to their doorstop looking like he ran through a cheese grater. He doesn't even know them. They don't know him.

They wouldn't *want* to know him.

He puts a hand to his side and his skin feels hot and tight and ragged.

Yet somehow, probably because the pain is screwing with his common sense, he ends up back in front of the butter-yellow house.

He leans against their fence, hidden behind thorny rosebushes, and watches the occasional figure move behind the windows. A battered jeep sits in the driveway and the sound of the TV spills out of the open windows. Sam can't just sneak back in. He doesn't even have his backpack since it's still at the mechanic's. A small pang presses against his chest as he realises Avery might go through it without him around. Please no.

His backpack is proof he's just as screwed up as Avery. Worse. If you count how he hits things.

He wonders if Moxie is back. If she recognised him. If Toby is really all right.

He can't just go in. Unless …

Unless he says he's Moxie's friend.

Or Jeremy's.

Depends on who's asking.

Pain and desperation eat up his sense and he slips through the front gate. He finds a tap around the side of the house and splashes water on his face. Nothing to do about the gravel burn on his cheek, but at least the first thing they see won't be blood. He has to come up with a story. He ... fell? Good one, Sam. No one will see through that.

He shakes water out of his eyes and slowly walks up the front steps.

It's all in the body language, Sam realised a long time ago. You want to con someone? Be confident. Act like you're supposed to be there, like you know what you're doing, like your hand is supposed to be slipping down their bag, their pocket.

So Sam walks on to the De Lainey veranda like he belongs. Like they're expecting him. It hurts to stand straight, but he'll do it.

The front door is already open. He raps knuckles on the doorframe.

A hand shoots up from the sofa and waves vaguely. 'Come in,' says a tired voice. 'Unless you're an axe murderer. Then stay out or whatever.'

'Wow, Jeremy. That was convincing. No axe murderers will come in now.'

There's a muffled thump and yelp and a body falls off the sofa.

Sam steps in, muscles coiled. 'It's Sam.'

Jeremy's head pops up from behind the sofa. A soft grin spreads across his face. 'Hey, Sammy! Here for Moxie?'

Sam comes in a little further. One step. Two. He's committed now, isn't he?

'I just came to pick up my clothes.' It tumbles out of his mouth in a rush and it's a solid excuse.

'Oh, right.' Jeremy flops back down. Perfect. He can't see Sam at all now. 'I thought it was weird you forgot them.'

Please don't notice I'm still wearing your shirt.

'Moxie is out,' Jack says. He appears to be lying on the floor, eyes still on the TV. 'Dad's bribing her with gelato. Favouritism.'

'They'll be back soon, though,' Jeremy adds. 'Make yourself at home.' He nudges Jack's head with his foot and his whisper isn't so subtle. 'How did our little sister make a *friend*?'

'Weirder things have happened.'

'Like what?'

'Like your face.'

'Dude, you're literally insulting your own face right now.'

Another muffled thump and yowl.

Sam realises they don't know what happened to Toby. It's been an hour, maybe two, and Moxie hasn't returned. Maybe Toby is actually hurt? Maybe Sam thought he looked OK but what if there's a broken little De Lainey boy in a hospital somewhere and it's Sam's fault because he didn't move fast enough he didn't help he didn't he—

He closes his eyes so tight they burn.

He slips towards the staircase. He takes them two at a time and ducks behind a corner as Grady, headphones on, jerks a vacuum cleaner into a bedroom and kicks the door shut. The roar of the vacuum covers Sam snatching a nondescript black tee off the floor and then shutting himself in the bathroom. His heart rabbits so fast he can scarcely think. What the *hell* is he doing? He can't just ... he can't be doing this.

But he is.

The De Lainey bathroom is in that strange limbo land where someone obviously just vacuumed the floor but didn't actually *tidy*. Piles of dirty clothes spill out of a hamper and rows of shampoo bottles have been carefully cleaned around without disturbing them. Buckets of bath toys block the way to the sink. Sam has to stand half in a pirate ship while he peels off his shirt and sponges down his side. There's antiseptic under the sink and he splashes it liberally on the sponge.

He presses that to his side
and nearly passes out.

For a second he doesn't know if he'll hold in the scream. He shoves the clean T-shirt in his mouth and bites hard. When is he going to grow some freaking brains? He pulls away the antiseptic sponge and gazes blearily at the damage. He's scraped raw from the bottom of his rib cage down past his hip. His face has a palm-sized scrape over it and his arms are flayed from elbow to wrist where he twisted to hit the road. Like the glorious idiot he is.

In summary, half of Sammy Lou still clings to the bitumen downtown.

He keeps the shirt shoved in his mouth, and pours antiseptic on the rest of the wounds. He closes his eyes but tears still sheet down his cheeks.

The vacuum shuts off.

Sam slides the fresh shirt on over his feverishly shaking body. He stuffs the bloodied sponge in the bin and then waits with sick agony for his cover to be blown.

'Jack!' Grady shouts. 'You're growing bacteria with all those filthy plates in your room! Clean it up. *Now.*'

Jeremy's voice drifts from downstairs, sweet and innocent. 'Don't be insensitive, bro. Growing bacteria is all the social life he can hold on to.'

Something crashes followed by manic laughter.

'I am *so sick* of both of you,' Grady hollers.

Please go downstairs.

Footsteps stomp away, Grady shouting that they need to grow up.

Sam is out of the bathroom and skidding down the hall into the office before Grady hits the last step. He clicks the office door shut.

And he's alone.

Safe.

He rests his forehead against the wood and asks himself, for the hundredth time, what is he hoping to achieve? It'll end badly. And now his skin is red hot and feverish, like his wounds are full of crushed glass. If someone bursts in here, what would he do?

Sink to his knees and cry.

At least they seem to have forgotten they let him in.

The noise downstairs suddenly escalates and Sam's shoulders tighten. New voices clamber through the crack under the door – Moxie's higher tone of lemon and sharp corners and their father's deep rumble. A baby shrieks. And, above it all, Toby's shout of, 'AND THEY GAVE ME A B'OON.'

Tension floods out of Sam's bones so fast his spine turns to water.

Toby really is fine.

'—hit by a car,' Moxie is saying.

Voices mix and tumble.

'What?'

'Is he OK?'

'We went to the hospital to get him checked out—'

'I GOT A B'OON.'

'It's a mad epic balloon, Toby. Hit Jeremy with it.'

'—no, the baby's fine. He was strapped in the stroller the whole time—'

'—totally need to get him one of those kiddie leashes.'

'He's not a dog, Jack!'

'And then this kid just grabbed him out the way—'

Sam looks down at his hands. They're shaking. He cracks open the office door to hear better.

'Hey, quit hitting me with that balloon, you little terror.'

'Who grabbed him—'

'I don't know. I just ...' There's a slight lull in the stream of shouting, like everyone's waiting for Moxie to finish. 'I mean, I thought it was someone we knew, but it happened so fast and the kid just ran off at the end.'

'He got hit by a car and then *ran off*?'

'How hard did it hit him?'

'... bleeding everywhere.'

Voices jumble into indistinct coils again and Sam loses track.

So Moxie hasn't put it together yet – but she will, right? She'll piece together the boy she saw stealing wallets, with the boy who jumped in front of a car for her brother, with the boy who appeared out of nowhere to eat their Sunday lunch.

And then he'll have to run again.

He crawls on to the armchair and curls up, pain eating his heart.

BEFORE

Sammy is ten and he lost Avery.

This isn't happening. This *can't happen*.

He gets caught up with a teacher who asks if he started the fight in the playground today, so he's eleven minutes late to the gates. Avery isn't waiting.

Avery is supposed to wait.

Sammy rips apart the school grounds looking. Playground. Sports field. The overgrown bushes behind the toilets where he hides from bullies. Trees. Bleachers. Bus shelter.

nothing nothing nothing

Don't panic. Maybe he walked home alone?

Except they've lived with Aunt Karen for three years and Avery's never walked home alone. Sammy's not even sure he could without getting lost.

Sammy runs the whole way, tattered backpack punching his spine. He dumps it by their letterbox and runs inside. Aunt Karen's old station wagon is in the driveway so maybe she picked Avery up?

Aunt Karen's making chilli beef at the stove and the air's thick with peppers and oil – which flushes Sammy's face with anger because Avery won't be able to *eat that* – but there's no time.

'Where's Avery?' he gasps.

Aunt Karen flicks her cigarette in the sink. 'What are you talking about? Why isn't he with you?'

no no no no no

Sammy twists his fingers in his shirt. 'I don't know where he is! We have to go look. We have to—'

Aunt Karen whacks the wooden spoon against the pot to cut him off, and Sammy thinks he's going to catch it. But she just looks annoyed, greying hair stuck to her forehead. 'He's just avoiding chores, Sammy, and your dramatics are tiring. Go do your homework and—'

'No, we have to go find him *now*!' It bursts out of Sammy in a shout.

Aunt Karen's lips thin. 'That's enough attitude, young man. He's not a baby. He'll show up when he wants to.'

She doesn't understand.

They've lived here for three years and she doesn't understand Avery at all.

Sammy doesn't wait. He flies out the door like a starburst and he's on the streets, calling and calling for his brother. He goes to the park, full of prickles and rubbish. Nothing. He flies across footpaths. To the shops. Back to school. Home again. Back to the streets. Nothing.

It's dark.

The air chills and smells of car exhaust and loneliness.

He trips and skins both knees and running turns to agony.

He runs anyway.

Avery could be lost, or *taken* by strangers, or hurt or scared or freaking out and hitting his head and no one will be there to catch him.

Sammy trails, dejected and exhausted, back to his street. Blood and gravel stick to his knees, sweaty shirt glued to his chest. Someone leers at him across the street and he wants to cry and hold his brother.

Avery could be dead.

It's all Sammy's fault.

He's nearly at the house before he notices the police car in Aunt Karen's driveway. His heartbeat stutters and fear pricks his skin. A cop strolls to the front door and knocks while another, a man with the boots and belt and gun and *everything*, opens the cruiser's back door. There's a glimpse of white-blond hair.

Sammy runs.

He has energy after all.

He smacks into the car door, his hollowed-out lungs burning, and tongue so tangled the words barely come.

'I'm sorry,' Sammy says. 'I'm sorry, he's s-sorry, we're so so sorry. He didn't mean it. Pleaseplease please don't take him to jail.'

Avery's hunched in the back seat where they put the bad people. His school shirt is inside out because he hates itchy seams and he has a huge police jacket swallowing his thin shoulders. He's running his toy car up and down his face. A bruise blooms over his filthy cheek, but he's *all right*.

The policeman, crouched by the door now, catches Sammy before he falls. 'Hey, whoa there, little mate. This is your brother?'

'I'm Sammy Lou,' he says. 'He's Avery.'

'I know.' The policeman is young with slicked black hair and brown skin. He has a split lip, but he smiles anyway. 'See, our friend Avery here was a bit lost and scared and couldn't tell us who he was, but we figured out his school uniform and got hold of the principal.' His eyes take in Sammy's shredded knees and sweaty face. 'You were out looking for him?'

'I'm sorry,' Sammy says again. 'I'm *sorry*. Please let me have him back, I won't ever lose him again—'

'Hey, kiddo, calm down.' The cop smiles again. 'We're bringing your brother home. Not taking him away.'

Sammy thinks he might cry.

He will not cry.

He glances over his shoulder at the lady cop talking to his aunt now. There are folded arms and frowns.

Sammy tries to reach into the car, but Avery shies away.

'Come on, little mate,' says the cop. 'I'll help you.'

Sammy steps back as the cop gently pulls Avery

out – except suddenly Avery throws his arms around the cop's neck and wraps his legs around his waist. Digging in like a bite. Like a barnacle. Like desperation.

The cop staggers in surprise, and then laughs. Avery's small for twelve, but still too big to be carried, and yet the cop wraps his arms around Avery's back and heads to the house. Sammy hops after them, teeth chattering. Avery doesn't like adults, but right now his face is buried in the cop's shoulder.

They must've been so, so nice to him.

Aunt Karen's face is stony as they arrive. 'Will there be charges since he hit an officer?'

Sammy's heart plummets.

The cop's cut lip.

You *can't hit a cop.*

'No!' Sammy turns to the lady, so drunk on fear that he grabs her hand. 'Please please. He didn't mean to.'

The woman gives a small smile. 'Ah, you must be Sammy. We thought Avery was Sammy for a while because that's the only thing he'd say.'

Sammy feels sick. Avery needed him and he wasn't there.

'Please,' Sammy whispers. 'Don't take him to jail.'

'Of course not.' The lady cop turns back to his aunt. 'Look, usually we deal tough with violence against officers, even with kids. But I can tell your nephew has a disability and was terrified out of his mind being alone on the street like that. But what I don't get –' her voice hardens '– is why you didn't report him missing straight away.'

Aunt Karen matches the hardness, cut for cut. 'He wasn't gone for that long.'

'Five hours,' Sammy says.

His aunt shoots him a poisoned look.

The lady cop folds her arms. 'Look, ma'am, if your kid with special needs goes missing, you call it in immediately.'

'Can I put him inside?' says the other cop.

Aunt Karen nods tersely and tries to lead the way, but the lady cop blocks her with one arm and keeps going with her lecture. And Aunt Karen has to listen.

To all the ways

she's neglecting and forgetting and hurting

Avery.

Good.

Sammy follows the policeman to the lounge, where he tries to pry off Avery and absolutely fails. He gives another laugh and then rubs Avery's back for a while. 'Come on, kiddo, home now. Safe and sound.'

Finally Avery lets go.

Sammy fetches his favourite softest sweater so he'll give up the cop's jacket. Then Avery runs his toy car up and down his arms and looks at the floor.

Too old for cars. Too old to be carried. Too old not to know his way home.

'I'm sorry I couldn't find you.' Sammy hugs him and Avery leans in with a sigh, running his car over Sammy's cheek.

Sammy nearly smiles.

'I'm lost,' Avery whispers.

'Not any more.' Sammy casts damp eyes to the cop. 'Thanks.'

'I can tell you're a good brother,' the cop says, but then he sees Sammy's knuckles. 'You get into a fight?'

Sammy thinks of his dad, fists and belt buckles and shark eyes. In jail.

He tucks his hands behind his back. 'No.'

The cop raises an eyebrow. 'All right, Sammy, let's talk seriously for a moment. You know what happens to people who punch others?'

'They go to jail,' Sammy whispers.

The cop nods, the lightness gone from his smile. 'It's trouble. A lot of trouble. You sort yourself out, hey? Your brother needs you and I don't want to ever put you in the back of my car.'

Sammy nods, heart thundering.

It's a lie, the nod. The cop wouldn't understand. If kids hurt Avery, then what else can Sammy do? He has to hit them. Like today at lunch with those boys following Avery around the playground mimicking his tics and calling him horrible names and Sammy had to make them stop. He had to.

But he's not like his dad. He'd never never go too far.

Aunt Karen comes back inside and holds the door angrily open for the cop. He waves to Sammy and gives Avery a special smile and shakes Aunt Karen's hand.

'You need to put some measures in place to make sure this doesn't happen again,' he says quietly. 'He's small now, but hitting a cop ... when he gets older, it'll go badly.'

'I understand.' Aunt Karen's jaw is screws and hammers.

The police leave.

Aunt Karen locks the door and marches into the kitchen. She comes back out with the wooden spoon, the shout already on her lips. 'I've had enough of this, Avery. You know better. Get up. Right now.'

Avery whimpers and tucks his head into his arms.

Aunt Karen grabs him by the elbow, jerking him to his feet and swinging the spoon in a smacking arch on to the back of his thighs.

Avery sobs.

Sammy shoves between them, all fire flares and burning blood. 'No!'

'Well, *someone's* getting punished so this doesn't happen again.' Aunt Karen raises the spoon. 'You're embarrassing me and wasting everyone's time, you despicable, nasty little boys. You're going to end up just like your father.'

'Then hit me!' Sammy shouts while Avery crumples and rocks and clutches his stupid toy car.

Sammy matches Aunt Karen's eyes, flint for charcoal.

Her teeth clench. 'If you think he'll learn from it, you're wrong. That is a selfish little brat right there.' She spins Sammy around, one hand fisted in his collar.

The spoon slaps the soft backs of his thighs like fire.

Sammy seals his lips tight.

He looks at Avery.

Avery stares back, mouth open and face smeared in dried tears and snot. He flaps his hands harder at each *thwack snap thwack* of the spoon raising welts on Sammy's legs. But Avery doesn't scream for Aunt Karen to stop. He just looks confused and scared.

No one saves Sammy.

It's OK, right? He's used to it. So long as his brother is safe.

CHAPTER 12

Sam lies upside down on the worn armchair, a tattered book in his hands. His legs hang over the back of the chair, feet resting on the wall. He's tried at least fifty-two positions, but apparently the chair's eternal comfort wears off after living in this office for three days.

At least reading upside down keeps the hair out of his eyes.

He licks his thumb and flips the page.

He's not been in here the *entire* three days, obviously. He slunk out at night to steal painkillers from the chemist. Then he cased out a few houses. He just hasn't ... moved ... into ... them yet. And while the De Lainey house is rarely *completely* empty, there are moments when someone takes washing outside or hustles the babies to the playground or the entire family collapses under quilts and heavy eyelids and star-spun dreams at night – and then Sam wanders the house and eats blueberry jam sandwiches and steals a clean shirt.

There are actually a lot of benefits to living secretly in a house that's inhabited.

Leftovers, for instance.

Jeremy's Greek zucchini and halloumi falafel is incredible.

Jack's spaghetti sauce is like seventy per cent cheese, which seems wrong, but tastes great.

Moxie's reheated spring rolls are disgusting. Apparently it's possible to kill food not once, not even twice, but several dozen times using a spatula, chilli sauce and a microwave.

Sam's totally aware he's fallen into a pocket of unreliable paradise, but he doesn't even care. He can walk without limping now and his arms are scabbed and less raw. His backpack is still at the mechanic's and he just tries not to fret about it.

The only worry that gnaws at his chest is Avery. Always, *always* Avery. He hasn't seen him in three days.

But he'll be with his friends. Maybe if Sam ignores him for a while, Avery will start appreciating him.

Sam licks his thumb and flips another page.

He feels so guilty.

It's past ten in the morning and the house smells of peanut butter and banana toast, a painful reminder that he's hungry. Moxie has the babies and one of them has been crying since six.

There's a crash downstairs followed by a wail and then Moxie yelling, 'That's how I feel about today too, but do you see me crying about it?'

A stupid fantasy plays out in the back of Sam's

head, where he goes downstairs and holds the baby while Moxie catches her breath and then she smiles at Sam and her fingers interlock with his and they lean super close and—

Footsteps pound up the stairs.

'Toby, *no*. You're not using my box of industrial glitter.'

'I need it!'

'What? To bathe in? Put it down before I turn you into a pie and put you in the oven.'

'I'm not a pie!' Toby shrieks.

'TRY ME.'

A small smile tugs at Sam's lips. At least they're not all huddled over a hospital bed and a little boy of broken bones. He'd jump in front of a car a thousand times over if he never had to see that petrified horror fracturing Moxie's face again.

He's also figured why no one goes into the office – it was their mother's.

He's seen Mr De Lainey's handwriting on odd sticky notes, but a different hand has scrawled over stacks of ledgers, journals, phone books and the backs of photos. Dust lines the bookshelves. Her bookshelves? The walls are taped with curling pictures of a woman with thick chocolate hair. She holds babies and pushes gap-toothed twins on swings and pulls funny faces with a miniature Moxie. He wonders what happened to the De Laineys' mother. Did she walk out too?

Sam can't remember his mother's face. He

wonders where she went, that day when he was seven, and if she ever felt bad about skipping out on her kids. Leaving them with *him*. Their dad and his fists and his molasses eyes. She's just another reason to never, never trust adults.

He's about to change positions – *again* – because blood has rushed into his head and his skull hurts, when the office doorknob turns.

Sam drops the book.

He shoves himself off the armchair, eyes clawing desperately for his hiding place in the cupboard.

But he doesn't have time.

The office door swings open and there's a snatch of Moxie in a halter-neck shirt that looks like it's been refashioned from the living-room curtains, and she's looking over her shoulder at a tantrumming Toby.

'... because it's illegal for kids to use glitter, actually. You have to be, like, twenty-five and then you can apply for a glitter licence—'

A huge ice cream tub of glitter is tucked into the crook of her arm.

'I am twenty-five!' Toby shouts.

'Nice try,' Moxie says and turns.

Sam's on his feet, hands outstretched, not sure if he intends to slam the door in her face or plead for her to wait. Listen. Don't call the police yet.

I can explain.

Except he really really can't.

Their eyes meet.

Air escapes Sam's lungs like they've been punctured. He has no words, no thoughts, nothing to change the shock unfolding on Moxie's face.

Toby stands behind her wearing a Batman mask. 'Who's dat?'

Moxie screams.

She hurls the ice cream tub at Sam. The lid pops. The air fills with a soaring, shimmering rainbow arc.

Sam gives a muted cry—

and then two litres of glitter hits him straight in the face.

It explodes over him, light as dust, and sticks like a second skin. It's in his mouth, up his nose, plastered on his eyelashes.

Moxie keeps screaming.

Toby joins in.

Sam stands for just a heartbeat longer, glitter settling in pools around his feet – and then he runs.

He shoves past Moxie, vaults over Toby and flings himself down the stairs, shedding glitter in his wake. He jumps the veranda steps and his shoes hit cement.

Faster. *Faster.* Get out of here and don't ever look back.

He keeps going until his new scabs split and his aching bones remind him he got hit by a car three days ago. He staggers to a stop, clutching the stitch in his side. Asking himself why why why did he do this?

He didn't want it to end like this.

He tries to wipe glitter off his tongue, but ends up getting more stuck to his teeth. It rakes his throat.

Get away from here.

He listens for sirens. For someone to shout *stop that thief.* For a De Lainey brother to burst out of nowhere and lay into Sam until he's no more than a smear on the footpath.

But the streets stay still, except for a faintly clicking sprinkler and a yappy dog.

Walk, Sammy, just keep walking.

Where?

Anywhere but here.

Sam is all scraped elbows and cheeks stained with glitter as he walks into the seedy part of town where Avery's friends live. He doesn't want to be here. But considering he looks like a craft store threw up on him, he's low on options.

There are simple rules for surviving a lifestyle like his. Number one: don't get caught.

And he freaking blew that.

The apartments are all identical bricks, endless rows broken by rotting dumpsters and cars cranking out bad exhaust on mucky lanes. He smells pot and wet cardboard and there are smashed beer bottles everywhere.

It makes him angry, all over again.

Because this is exactly the sort of neighbourhood Sam and Avery grew up in, living stuffed in caravans or units or cars, forgotten between their parents' vodka bottles and mysterious bags to deliver. Aunt Karen's street wasn't much better. And Avery's just trotted right back in.

Because it's familiar.

Because it's home.

Yeah OK, the Lou brothers are still criminals. They steal. They lie. But Sam wildly, passionately *hates* the thought of this being their Forever. Ever since they were little, he's talked about living in their own house. A home. Endless conversations. Endless plans as they walked to and from school. Their own home would mean no adults with hard slaps, no one judging Avery's tics, no one walking out on them again. All they need is money, right? Every dollar from Sam's thieving and Avery's job is squirrelled and saved for this.

It's not impossible. No matter what Avery says, Sam refuses to believe it's impossible.

He stops outside a row of apartments. Paint peels. Windows are barred. Piles of junk sit in gutters. Is this even the right number? He's torn between hoping Avery is here, and wanting him to be at work. Just so long as whoever opens the door doesn't take one look and call the cops.

Does he know anyone who doesn't want him in jail? He needs new friends.

Or any friends.

A friend.

A non-judgemental dog maybe.

'What is my life?' he mutters and knocks.

A thump sounds on the other side, followed by, 'Go to hell.'

Sam pounds his fist on the door again. 'Is Avery Lou there? I'm his brother.'

Silence.

Sam kicks the door. A car crawls past and he glances at hard faces staring at his shimmering back. In this street of broken glass and rusted pipes, he is a prism of colour.

Footsteps thump and the door cracks open to show a sliver of Avery. His eyes are soft with sleep, hair mussed, and he's shirtless with every rib on his concave chest showing. Great. Sam can go right back to feeling guilty that he hasn't made sure Avery's been eating.

'Wow, it is you,' Avery says. 'I thought you hated this place.' He pauses. 'And me.'

Sam grits his teeth. 'You know that's not true. Now can I come in? I'm about to be arrested.'

Avery opens the door. 'I guess that's usual. But I—' He breaks off with a choke.

Sam shoves past, leaving glittering footprints. Honestly, it wouldn't be that hard to catch him. Screw the yellow brick road – just follow the sparkling glitter path to Sammy Lou. And he's pretty shy, but God help him, he is two minutes away from ripping off his clothes.

Avery opens his mouth. Closes it.

Sam rakes a hand through his hair and feels glitter stick to his scalp. 'I need a shower.'

'You need a pressure hose,' Avery says. 'What …
how?'

'I screwed up stealing a house, OK?' Sam folds
his arms. 'Just lend me some clothes and—'

Avery bursts out laughing.

It's his real laugh, all light and giddy, and it
shakes his whole body.

Usually Sam loves that laugh, but today he kind
of wants to murder someone. He *itches*. 'Super
mature, Avery.'

Avery clutches his stomach and slams the front
door. He sags against it, hand over his eyes while
he laughs and laughs and laughs.

Sam waits.

'I just can't even look at you.' Avery presses his
knuckles into his eyes. 'It's too much. It's too funny.'

'Would you shut up and listen?' Sam snaps.

Avery makes a show of holding his breath.
He nods.

Sam starts, 'So I was stealing a house—'

Avery cracks up again.

Sam is done. He's just done. He's ruined the one
good, one pure thing he had with the De Laineys.
He's got literally nothing on his back except for
stolen clothes and seven tonnes of glitter. And his
brother is a jerk.

'Screw you, Avery,' Sam says. 'I'm really
uncomfortable.'

'Is it on your teeth?' Avery swipes a hand over
the back of his eyes, his shoulders still shaking with

134

suppressed hysterics. He looks so much younger when he's laughing. 'Well, you're officially the prettiest Lou.' Avery sets himself off again.

Sam hopes he hacks up a lung.

He stalks past Avery, brushing himself off so someone will have a fun time cleaning up. Although from the looks of this place, no one's cleaned in a decade. Downstairs consists of a kitchen squashed in one corner and a few damaged sofas around an unreasonably expensive TV.

While the De Lainey chaos was all toys and clothes and sewing projects and buckets of seashells, this apartment is mouldy pizza boxes, empty bottles and broken boxes. The coffee table – which has three legs, the fourth being a pile of textbooks – is piled high with laptops, phones and a knot of chargers. Stolen, obviously. The carpet smells like cat piss. A curtain partitions off what probably was the dining room but is now more mattresses on the floor and clothes and spilled rubbish.

Sam rubs the bridge of his nose. 'Can I please just take a shower?'

'A shower is not going to fix this.'

Sam closes his eyes. That's a mistake. All he can see is Moxie's stupefied expression, her shock melting into terror, her first instinct to be self-defence. Against *him*. A criminal. A creep hiding in her house. Hot, anxious knives carve his stomach.

Avery finally registers the look on Sam's face and folds his smirk away. His fingers flap anxiously

135

and he goes to dig clothes out of a broken suitcase. 'Don't be mad at me.'

'I'm not mad.' He *is*, a little, but he'd rather lie and skip having to calm Avery down later because he's terrified of angry people.

'So what happened? Does this story involve you making out with a clown?' He grins suddenly.

'Hilarious,' Sam says. 'Why aren't you at work?'

Avery picks up a shirt and shakes it out. Crumbs fall out of the folds. He shrugs and flips it over his shoulder since Sam didn't specify *clean* clothes.

'What? Oh. Day off.' But he has too many lying tells. Like how he immediately hunches over, waiting for a blow. 'Shower's upstairs,' he says, fast. Distracting.

Sam sighs and follows him upstairs. The rail is broken in four places – how does that even *happen*?

'How many people live here?' he asks, while Avery slams a hip against the sticky bathroom hinges. There are other closed doors, muted voices behind them.

'Um, I don't know? They let me take the sofa and I don't have to put in for rent.'

'Um … and why would they do that for you?'

Avery gives him a cutting look. 'Because I have friends. Good friends. I'm helpful. Sometimes I drive for them at night when they're doing jobs.' The hinges unstick and Avery tumbles in. 'I don't even always have to sleep on the sofa.'

A sharp pang hits Sam's guts. What exactly is he

saying? 'But they're all way older than you.' *They're using you. They're bad news. Are you a getaway driver? Please, oh please, do not tell me you're sleeping with someone.* Sammy does *not* have the energy for that conversation.

Avery dumps the clothes on the sink and roughly clears a spot between bags of makeup and shaving kits and tins of hairspray. 'Red towel behind the door is mine.'

'We probably need to talk,' Sam says, trying to keep his voice level.

'OK. About what?' Avery's face is so open – *so naive.*

Sam scratches glitter behind his ear. Later. Just do it later.

'About why you're covered in glitter?' Avery says.

'Never mind,' says Sam. 'It won't happen again.'

It will never, never happen again.

CHAPTER 13

Hot water and soap can scrub out a multitude of evils.

Just not glitter.

Sam spends a good seventy per cent of his time in the bathroom swearing and the remaining thirty per cent raking fingernails over his scalp and always, *always* coming up with more glitter.

He gives up.

Why couldn't Moxie have just slapped him? Why did she have to go into the office at all? He needed that fragile paradise. He needed it so he could breathe again.

He hesitates over his glitter-covered clothes – De Lainey clothes. Then he stuffs them into a garbage bag.

Forget it, Sam. It's over.

Sam has to turn up the cuffs of Avery's jeans, but the shirt is uncomfortably tight. Meaning – it actually fits, instead of the loose ones he's been stealing off the older De Lainey boys. Sam likes clothes he can disappear into instead of tight ribbed cotton that shows his bones and sunken stomach.

He stomps downstairs, meaning to ask Avery for something else, but Avery sits on the sofa with his legs kicked up on a coffee table. And he's not alone.

A girl with blood-red hair, expensive clothes, and cool eyes sits beside him. She's at odds with the trashed house, the broken sofa they sit on, and Avery's bedhead and half-suppressed hand-flapping tic.

Avery's put on a shirt, but he still looks dishevelled beside this girl.

They're both drinking beer.

Avery won't look at Sam and Sam knows he has to fight this. He tugs the neck of his shirt and scuffs across the room to stand in front of them.

The girl looks him up and down coolly. 'I'm Vin.'

'You look slightly less like the glitter apocalypse,' Avery says. His fingers mess about with screws and a broken hinge to distract him from flapping. Once upon a time, it was little cars.

Sam tucks his hands into his jean pockets. 'Um, hi … Vin. Well, Avery and I can get out of your hair now.'

'Avery lives here.' Vin has a smooth voice, soft and rich, but Sam's stomach clenches. He's not sure if it's because this girl is taking Avery away from him or because her voice is so cold.

'And you too?' He can't imagine Miss Ironed Jeans living here.

Vin smiles and leans back, one arm covered in

gold bracelets slung lazily over the back of the sofa. 'Sometimes.'

'And how'd you meet?' Sam says, aware his voice is more accusatory than conversational. 'Over drinks? Because you know Avery's barely seventeen, right?'

'OK, OK.' Avery shoves himself off the sofa and sets the beer down. 'It doesn't matter.' He grabs Sam's arm, but the skin is still mostly scabs and bruises and Sam snatches away with a muted hiss. 'Oh,' Avery says, 'you still look like roadkill. How's your side?' Before Sam can grind out a reply, Avery snatches the corner of Sam's shirt and jerks it up. The skin around Sam's left side looks raw from the scalding shower. A few scabs have knocked loose and left pinpricks of blood.

Sam jerks his shirt back down. Avery's always woeful at personal space, but Sam's not in a patient mood today.

Vin, however, has a flicker of interest in her cold eyes. 'What happened?'

'He threw himself in front of a car,' Avery says. 'He thinks people will like him better if he saves them.'

Sam's fingers curl into fists. That's *not* why—

Is it?

'Avery,' Sam tries again, voice quiet, 'can we go? I need to get my backpack from the mechanic's.'

'Oh, right. Let's—'

'I'll take him over,' Vin says.

No way. 'Thanks,' Sam says, 'but we'll just—'

'OK.' Avery starts fiddling with the hinge again and casts an anxious look at Vin, one Sam doesn't like because it obviously has history and Sam's not used to missing pieces in the puzzle of Avery Lou. It freaks him out, what happens when he's not here.

It freaks him out when Vin scoops her hair over her shoulder and Avery gets this soppy look on his face. Like she could ask for the sun and he'd scramble to get it for her.

Sam didn't imagine it'd go this far.

And he's stupid stupid stupid, but he knows the thousand little pins in his stomach are jealousy. That Avery can be such a mess, but someone still likes *him*.

'Be nice,' Avery whispers.

Sam is nice.

Sam is nice while he gets into Vin's car – a partially refurbished sports car, half painted and missing hubcaps, with Avery's touch all over it. He's obviously fixing it up for Vin. Is that why she likes him? The car runs smooth as an oil spill and Vin goes twice as fast as the speed limit. Sam is nice even though he's seriously queasy before they pull up in front of the mechanic's. The place is open. An unfamiliar man talks with a customer over a car.

Sam's chest aches. Avery's replacement? He said he had the day off but ... he was lying, wasn't he?

Sam reaches for his seatbelt buckle but Vin

catches his sleeve. Sam is nice instead of punching Vin in the throat. He knows he's being unreasonable. All Vin's done is drive him here, which is decent, and befriend Avery, which makes Sam want her dead.

'I'll go in,' Vin says, 'since Avery told me you've got a history here.'

Decent. The girl is just being decent.

Sam slumps back in his seat and watches Vin glide into the mechanic's and have a few words with the new guy. No one seems angry. Vin flips her deep red curls over her shoulder and laughs, then she vanishes. Sam taps anxious fingers on the window and hopes Vin just picks up the backpack without looking inside. She might think the backpack is full of coins, right? Sam's a thief. Coins are logical.

Any thin threads of hope he has snap instantly as Vin strides out of the mechanic's with the backpack in one hand – and walks away from the car.

No.

Sam scrambles for his seatbelt. He flings himself after the fast disappearing Vin, his mind crumbling in confusion.

no no no no no no

He tears down an alley after her, but they're right by the wharves and Vin goes straight for the oil and muck-slick ramp lined with fishing boats and forklifts moving crates. She circuits them and pauses by the water edge.

'Hey!' Sam's voice echoes, too shrill. He springs forward. 'No! Wait—'

With a cool look of frosted steel in Sam's direction, Vin swings the backpack up and

over and

d

   o

     w

       n

into the sea.

The cry that escapes Sam's lips is hardly human.

He flings himself down the wharf, realising too late that he should've gone straight for fists and Vin's perfect face. Vin catches him from behind and pins his arms to his sides. She's strong and tall and knows how to lock her arms around a writhing body. She slams Sam against a cement pillar and for a horrible second Sam thinks this is the end. He's going to be thrown between fishing boats into the frothing, rank sea to drown and he'll never see Avery ever ever ever—

'Chill out, kid.' Vin's voice is calm as a finely tuned engine. 'Avery said you'd freak out, but I thought you'd just yell a bit. I'm letting you go now. Don't hurt yourself.'

Arms release Sam and he tips forward, hitting the rough cement on his knees and looking down, down, *down* to the water below. It's too far to swim, the water too filthy, climbing out again too impossible.

His cheeks are wet.

His backpack is gone.

Somewhere in the far back of his skull, the words *Avery said* tick over in a shower of betrayal.

'He told me about your crazy habit.'

He told. Of course he did ... when Avery starts talking, he'll tell anything to anyone. He doesn't even understand when he shouldn't. But how long has he known about the keys?

'You want to survive this life, you need to take a knife to that sensitive little heart of yours.' Vin folds her arms, stance easy and confident, and despite the sluggishly working dockyard, no one pays attention to them. She towers over Sam, a glacier of cold eyes and fancy heels. 'I'm working on that with Avery, so sure, I'll fix you up too. I need a kid like you. A good lock pick. You're so small ... and fast, right?'

Sam stares at the scabs on his palms.

'But you need to shed the baby face. Harden up. I mean look at you, kid. You're crying over a backpack. You're too soft.'

Even if Sam could explain the keys – explain how, if he fit them together, they were a map of the last year where he had nothing except stolen houses and fantasies of imaginary families – he wouldn't tell it to someone like Vin. He couldn't even explain it to Avery. The keys were promises.

They were all he had.

Vin hauls Sam to his feet by the back of his

T-shirt. He doesn't struggle. Dimly, he's aware he could hit Vin now – really hit her. But his arms hang loose at his sides.

Avery knew Vin was going to do this. He knew.

'You want a house, right?'

Finally, Sam looks up, his lashes thick with tears.

'Get your shit together, stop being sentimental, and work for me,' Vin says. 'You'll get money and then you can get what you want.'

Sam's mouth works, but it takes a moment for the words to come out. 'Doing what? Drugs?'

Vin gives a laugh and slides on aviator sunglasses. 'Sometimes. But I prefer to use my crew to gut houses, just like you do. Plus a few tools of persuasion to get bank details out of the occupants.'

Sam stares at her. 'Armed robbery?'

'Something like that.'

'But Avery works at the mechanic's.'

'He did. But yet, he's extremely good at taking apart doors.' Vin starts back towards the car. 'I know you're only a kid, so come on. I'll buy you some chips on the way back. We'll make a hardass out of you eventually.'

Sam wipes his face on his T-shirt and stares at the water. He could at least try to climb down there, swim, hopefully not get crushed between cement walls and boat hulls. Except he doesn't want to die. Except Avery let this happen, wanted it to happen, and Sam will do anything for his brother. If he doesn't go with Vin now, he'll be sleeping on the street.

We gut houses like you do.

They have no idea.

It's not about the stealing from houses. It's about stealing *the houses*. He puts his wishes into small metal keys and tucks them in his pocket to keep him breathing.

Right now, his lungs are rust.

He follows Vin.

CHAPTER 14

Avery drops down on the sofa where Sam's sprawled. The TV is on, sound muted, and Sam's flipping through channels with kaleidoscope swiftness. Avery pokes the back of his neck. Sam doesn't react.

'How long did you know about my keys?' Sam doesn't actually want the answer, but he's been lying around this house for two days and his voice is hollow from disuse.

'I looked at them when you slept. All the time. Hundreds of times.'

'Not creepy at all, Avery.'

'I liked them,' Avery says. 'But Vin says—'

Sam flips channels faster. 'Just leave me alone.'

Apparently Avery doesn't understand that phrase because he rubs a hand through Sam's hair and then shows Sam his palm. 'Still glittery.'

'Surprise,' Sam says, flat.

'Vin's just trying to help us.' Avery flicks his fingers by his ear and then stops suddenly, ramming his hands under his thighs.

Sam shoves hair out of his eyes and gives

Avery a long hard look. 'She's stopping you stimming?'

'Everyone says it's annoying.'

'That's not ... Look, Avery, you need to tic.' *Or you melt down later*, he doesn't add. Isn't it painfully obvious?

Avery chews his thumbnail, eyes on the TV. 'I can take care of myself.'

That's a hilarious joke.

'You didn't tell me how you got caught,' Avery says.

Sam doesn't want to, but somehow it tumbles out like colourful marbles – the butter-yellow house and where it is and why he liked it and then how he lost it. Avery looks worried and Sam's story trails off. It doesn't matter anyway. It happened. It's over.

There are things with sharper edges to unpack.

Sam sighs. 'Do you know how long you go to prison for *armed robbery*?'

Avery springs off the chair. 'I just said I can take care of myself.'

Sam's about to pursue this argument but the front door bangs open.

Vin glides in, folding sunglasses and tossing her perfectly groomed hair like the pretentious jerk she is. She wears white pants and stilettos today and carries a thick red wallet and a greasy bag of takeaway food. Sam's still isn't sure how old she is. Twenty-four? Twenty-five? She has a smile for everyone and is very hands-on and affectionate. And it always seems like a rehearsed act.

She dumps the greasy paper bag on the coffee table. Then she kisses Avery on the mouth. She kisses a lot of different people, Sam's noticed. He thinks Avery knows too, but Avery will just anxiously skim away from confrontation, and Sam has *no idea* how to talk about this with someone who doesn't understand unspoken rules. Avery deserves to be kissed by someone who wants him, not wants to use him. But talking about kissing and sex is too awkward, OK? It shouldn't be Sam's job. He's only fifteen.

Except it always is his job.

'Avery, your little brother just gets cuter by the day.' She drags off her heels and throws them amiably. 'I bought an extra kebab if he wants one.'

She empties the bag, tossing a tin foil wrap at Avery and then Sam. She flops in a sofa and unwraps hers.

Sam accepts the kebab even though every time he sees Vin, he kind of wants to break her kneecaps.

'He's not that cute.' Avery sets to work destroying the kebab but not eating it. It's soggy with oozing meat and sauces and a wild mixture of greens – exactly the opposite of what Avery will ever eat. Vin hasn't figured it out? Or is this another thing she's *fixing*? No tics. Eat your food mixed. Be normal.

Avery's eyes take on a panicked sheen while he tries not to flick his fingers.

Sam entirely hates Vin.

Why is Avery putting up with it though? Because he likes her? How can he adore her while his body betrays how scared he is?

Sam feels sick. He wishes he was sandwiched between Moxie and Jeremy on a sofa with sand in their hair and waffles in their stomachs. He wants to twine his fingers with Moxie's and explain himself. Apologise.

Vin licks juice off her thumb. 'How old are you anyway, Sammy? Thirteen? Fourteen?'

Sam frowns. 'Fifteen.'

'You're so *small*.' Vin stuffs more kebab in her mouth. 'Perfect size to fit through a window.'

Avery shoots her a frazzled look. 'No. He doesn't want to do stuff like that. Just leave him alone, Vin.'

'I said I'd toughen him up for you,' Vin says. 'I can make something out of the Lou boys.'

'Yeah, well, I can do that,' Avery says, like he's the big brother for once.

Vin's eyes narrow. 'Avery, help me out in the kitchen for a second.' She untwines from the chair.

Avery trails after her like an obedient puppy, which leaves Sam staring at his dripping kebab until he just abandons it on the already gross coffee table. He stares at the piles of laptops, the brand-new iPhones still in their boxes. He doesn't know how Vin isn't caught, but she's clearly good at this. She gets her teeth whitened to prove it.

A muscle twitches in Sam's jaw. He knows he's being a self-righteous ass, considering he's a thief too, but he hates this. All of it. He's taking Avery away after this and they can figure it out—

Something thumps in the kitchen. Someone.

Sam springs towards it, tripping over boxes of stacked junk.

Avery's up hard against the wall. Vin has a fistful of his shirt and is pressing against his collarbone. Her eyes are bottomless and frigid. She's got height on Avery, she's got steel he'll never have.

'—don't disagree with me,' Vin is saying. 'There's a place I want to crack and the best way around the security system is the window. That kid can fit.'

'I said n-no.' Avery's voice shakes.

Vin rams him against the wall again, harder this time and Avery's head snaps backwards and hits the plaster.

His voice takes on a desperate edge. 'Vin, please. I-I-I don't want him to get hurt—'

'After all I do for you.'

'Stop it!' Sam's muscles coil, tense, stretch. He springs into the kitchen and shoves Vin off.

Vin's breath escapes in a stunned gasp and she releases Avery and stumbles backwards into the sink. Cutlery slips and clatters to the floor. Her frost eyes snap to Sam, but Sam's moving, fast as running water.

He leaps and his fist shoots forward, knuckles slamming into the soft cartilage of Vin's nose.

She screams.

Blood sprays hot over Sam's fingers.

Avery gives a startled yell and grabs Sam's waist. 'Sammy, *don't*—'

But fire blazes in Sam's lungs. Intoxicating adrenaline sprawls up his throat and rushes into his muscles, that feeling he gets every time he loses it. Every time he explodes.

Vin snatches a tea towel and presses it to her face. Blood soaks her shirt. She roars something but Sam's ears are full of power and his fist is still clenched, and all he can think of is going at Vin again

and again

and

again—

Avery wraps his arms around Sam's chest and clings so tightly Sam can't catch a breath. 'Don't don't.' His voice cracks. 'D-don't hit people. You don't – c-can't … Sammy, *don't*.'

Vin throws the tea towel on the ground, but blood still streams from her nose and her look is black murder. Sam drops his curled fist to his side, his breath coming fast. He can't feel anything. He's spun out of invincible clouds.

'Let go of me, Avery, just – let go.' Sam's voice rises. '*Avery, stop it.*'

Avery drops to his knees on the floor, arms curled over his head, rocking and rocking.

Vin raises bloody fingers towards the door. 'Get out.'

Sam's anger is cooling, leaving his hands shaking. 'Fine.' His voice feels far away. 'Come on, Avery.' He wipes blood on to his jeans and reaches for his brother. Tries to grab his wrist.

Avery jerks back.

Vin's voice explodes. 'GET OUT.'

Avery unfolds from the floor and for a second Sam thinks they'll both run for the door and keep going until Vin is a faded, bitter memory. But instead Avery slips past Sam and bolts for the stairs, fingers flicking in front of his eyes and head tucked to avoid invisible blows. Sam tries to tell him to stop, come back, but the words stick.

A door slams upstairs.

Sam has to go after him, calm him down and make it better, say sorry for yelling at him – for scaring him. How could he *scare his brother*? But then Vin's suddenly got a fistful of Sam's shirt and drags him towards the front door. He trips on the threshold.

'The quiet ones are always the psychos,' Vin growls, her face and shirt a bloody waterfall. Then she hurls him out and slams the door. Locks click. Avery's crushed expression and broken eyes play again and again in Sam's memories.

Sam waits

just a minute
to see if Avery will come out.
He waits an hour.
Then he walks while slivers of hope fall out of
his pockets and splinter on the ground.

CHAPTER 15

The lock comes apart under Sam's thin, light fingers.

He uses paperclips and pretends he doesn't miss the real lock picks that Avery gave him a few years ago, wrapped in an old chip packet and tied with a bow while he hopped on the spot in giddy excitement. 'Happy birthday, Sammy, go steal me the moon.'

Now the only thing he wants to steal is Avery.

Except right now, Avery doesn't want to be around him. Sam scared his brother. He *scared his brother*. He has to stop doing this, losing it. Hitting people.

Sam breaks into a house and his footsteps echo on empty tiles. The *For Sale* sign was a pretty solid indicator that he'd have no trouble here. The thick coating of dust on the light switches says it's been vacant a while.

There's nothing to take except handfuls of cobwebs.

He wanders into a small bedroom and curls up in the corner.

Close your eyes and pretend this is a bed.

Pretend you don't smell stale air and mouse bait. Pretend those are waffles on the stove, covered in maple syrup.

Pretend Avery's in the garage, taking apart the engine on his first car. He never stops talking about how badass it'll be when he finishes.

Sam tries to fit Aunt Karen into a cosy armchair, but she has a cigarette between furious lips instead. Was she ever happy with them?

He puts in the De Lainey father.

And then a handful of De Lainey kids.

And somehow the house fills up with piles of Lego and yogurt tubs and Moxie putting caramel sauce in a coffee cup. Her eyes meet his, chocolate curls spilling across her cheeks.

His words come cracked as a broken plate. 'I'm sorry.'

The fantasy turns to puffs of dust and curls of ghosts and he's lying in an empty room, crying hot salty tears into the carpet.

CHAPTER 16

'Hi, Moxie. I'm sorry I was lurking like a sick creeper in your house. The truth is none of you actually know me and I just invited myself in because I'm pathetic.'

Sam holds a spool of yellow thread out to the hydrangea bush.

The bush waves encouragingly at him.

Sam clears his throat. 'This is an apology present. I didn't steal it. Well, I mean, I stole the money for it, so technically I guess I stole it. I don't know what your favourite colour is, but yellow reminds me of happiness, which reminds me of your house.'

The bush appears to have lost interest in his spiel, or else the wind died.

'So what I really want to say is ...' Sam rubs his cheek, picking off remnants of road rash scabs. 'I'm sorry?'

The bush does not accept his apology.

To be fair, it was a terrible explanation and an even worse apology and he doesn't think a bobbin is really going to fix this. But he has to try. He doesn't have anything to lose.

He doesn't have anything.

His shoulders ache for his backpack. He rubs a thumb over bruised knuckles on his right hand and wishes he'd done more to Vin.

No. You're not allowed to think about Vin. Or how you scared Avery so much he stayed.

Sam needs to get himself together, get Avery someplace safe – a home. They need their own home. How much longer can he dream about this before he suffocates?

Sweat soaks the neck of Sam's T-shirt and the sun raps an unfailing rhythm on his shoulders. His borrowed shirt is too tight and his undone shoelaces are still coated in glitter.

This can't go well.

He formulates a different apology to a lamppost that sounds like, 'Hey Moxie, I'm not a creep, I swear,' which is *exactly* what a creep would say.

He's so screwed.

He sits in the gutter in front of the De Lainey house, fiddling with the yellow thread. Behind him the house is awake with alternating peals of laughter and shrieks. Moxie shouts, 'EAT YOUR PEAS' and there's a wet *thwap* of, presumably, peas hitting the floor.

Has Moxie told her family about catching him in the office? It's been over a week and he's been in and out of a few stale houses. He didn't take a single key. He feels sick whenever he sees them now. He should hurry up and knock before the De

Lainey brothers get home and beat the holy hell out of him.

Get up, you spineless coward.

He picks himself out of the gutter, dirt and gravel sticking to his jeans, and forces himself to the front door. His fingers curl to knock and then hesitate. From behind the door come strains of the TV and then the whir of the sewing machine.

He knocks.

His heart stutters.

The sewing machine shuts off and there's a muffled growl of, 'If those girls are fake-knocking again, I'm going to turn Dash into an Elven mop—'

Then the door rips open and she's right there, all long tanned legs and wrists full of hair ties, in a patchwork shirt of rusty orange.

Sam awkwardly holds out the thread. It's so *tiny*. He's such an idiot.

Confusion fades from her face and fury washes down. Betrayal stings in her eyes and her lips part, but she hesitates like she doesn't know what to scream at this boy who hid in her house.

'I'm sorry,' Sam says.

Moxie slams the door in his face.

OK.

Well, that's fair. He deserves that.

He hesitates a second, rocks on his heels, and then leaves the spool of thread on the welcome mat. His feet march him away on autopilot, which is good because his anxiously hoarded courage is gone. He feels weak and sick and like the most filthy, pathetic worm to ever crawl the earth.

He's reached the gate just as the jeep pulls into the driveway. Boys covered in concrete dust vault out. Doors slam.

'Hey, is that Sammy?'

He can't do this. He doesn't want to be hit.

Sam rips around the front gate, his shirt catching and tearing on the latch.

'Sam, wait!' One of the twins strides around the rosebushes.

Sam runs.

He's fast fast fast and when he glances over his shoulder, Jeremy stands in front of his house, one hand shading his eyes as he stares after Sam's flying legs.

Sam's stupid to come back.

It doesn't occur to him until he's three streets away, that Jeremy's face was puzzled, not angry. That his fists weren't raised. That maybe he wanted to talk, not to hit.

CHAPTER 17

He can't go back to Avery. Or the De Laineys'. And the last empty house he broke into made him feel like the air has been crushed out of his lungs.

He's tired. He's so, so tired.

He ends up outside Aunt Karen's crumbling little house, made of whitewashed bricks and a leaky roof, pea-green curtains hiding sparse furniture. He scuffs the toe of his shoes against the letterbox again and again while he waits for her car to pull into the driveway. It's nearly five. She knocks off from the petrol station around now.

She used to.

He hasn't been back in over a year.

A blue station wagon rattles into the driveway and Aunt Karen gets out. She's fighting with the name badge pinned to her shirt and doesn't see him. Instead she rips out the pin and circles the boot of the car, jerking at the sticky lock until it pops. She's dyed her hair lighter, but her throat still sports loud jewellery and the frown lines are the same.

Her fingers close around shopping bags before she sees him.

For a second they just stare at each other, her eyes narrowing and his widening. Like maybe he can make himself look younger, innocent, *sorry*.

What should he say? *I'm so out of options and I'm so tired of screwing up, that I came back?*

He forces his feet forward. 'Hey, Aunt Karen.'

She gives her head a little shake, like she can't believe what she's seeing. The hems of her black slacks are frayed and her grocery bags are pitifully light. Tuna, it looks like, powdered milk and rye crackers.

'Are you in more trouble?' Her voice is as sharp as the tins rattling in her grocery bags. 'Are the police chasing you?'

Well, obviously. They haven't caught up with him from last year at school when he … he can't think about it.

'I'm not being followed,' Sam says, 'if that's what you mean.'

He thinks of doorknobs, unscrewed like puzzle pieces on the tiles, and Avery's brightly proud smile over what he's done.

He thinks of sprawling over the scratchy carpet with homework drenched in red crosses.

He thinks of curling up at the foot of Avery's bed because he'd wet his and he was too old for that and neither of them wanted to wake up Aunt Karen and ask for help and get punished.

'Where's Avery?' Aunt Karen says.

'Living with some people ...' Sam leans forward and takes a shopping bag from her. She lets him. 'He's OK.' No, he's not. 'He, um, works a real job. With a mechanic.' A lie now.

'I never threw him out, you know.' Aunt Karen folds her skinny arms. 'Just you.'

Sam looks down. His shoelaces are undone. Perpetually.

'If he needs to come back, I'll do something about him.'

He's not sure what that even *means*, but Avery will never come back without Sam.

'And you? What have you been doing?' The words come tight, forced – like she doesn't really want to ask.

'Nothing.' Sam's mouth is full of cotton. 'I don't have anywhere to live.'

'Oh, so you're crawling back for help, are you?' Veins flex purple in her neck. 'After all you've done, you ... you despicable little boy.'

Sam's chest caves in on itself.

'I'm not taking you back,' Aunt Karen says. 'You go inside my house and I'm calling the police. They can figure you out.'

'I just ... I'm sorry—'

She snatches the shopping bag off him. 'Really? I can see your hands, Sammy. Still fighting? Still hitting people? Do you know what you deserve? To be locked up. No second chances. No sly apologies.'

Sam opens his mouth, but the lump welling in his throat will only release the dam holding back panic and tears. She won't budge for that either. She'll say *crocodile tears* and *I know what game you're playing*.

He wouldn't be here unless his world had crumpled to nothing.

'Sorry is not enough,' Aunt Karen says, vicious.

'But can I just have one night? Please? I'll go in the morning—'

'I told you what will happen if you come inside.'

Sam's voice cracks. 'It was an accident—'

'Oh, don't start.' She storms towards her front door, swinging the bags so hard they hit her legs.

Sam looks desperately at her back, needing her to understand. He'd do anything to have one person stop and listen to him. See him. Truly stop and *see* him.

He runs after her, heart falling through his chest. 'You always gave Avery another chance—'

She spins and drops one of her bags so it spills across the grass. Her hand shoots up and cracks across his face.

It takes a moment for the sting to catch up.

Sam stares, his mouth open, red fingerprints across his cheekbone.

'Unlike you,' Aunt Karen's eyes are pinpricks of venom, 'Avery never had blood on his hands.' She catches his wrist then, flipping it over to his scabbed knuckles.

'I was protecting him,' Sam whispers.

'Bullshit.' Aunt Karen drops his wrist, like she can't bear to touch him any more than necessary. 'You like the power you get from hurting people. You're just like your father.'

Sam can't speak. He can't. He'll cry. That's not him. That's never him.

'I thought Avery would be the death of me, with those insufferable tantrums and flapping.'

Sam digs his fingers into his shirt, trying to anchor himself. Trying to keep himself here. 'Don't talk about Avery like that,' he whispers.

It's like she doesn't hear him. 'But no. It was the little one with his bloodlust who ended up being the devil.'

Sam's face burns from her slap.

Aunt Karen says, voice suddenly crisp. 'Are you coming inside? You can sit down while I call you in. You know you deserve it, Sammy Lou.'

A cute name.

Not Samuel. Just Sammy Lou.

The wrong name for a boy who's all fists and split skin.

Does he deserve it?

you do you do you do you do

He turns.

He walks away.

'I thought so,' Aunt Karen calls.

He gets to the end of the street before he stops and looks back. She's picking tins of tuna off the grass and tucking them back into the plastic bag. Her shoulders stay stiff. Her face sets. She never cried over a Lou boy before, why would she start now?

BEFORE

Sammy is thirteen and this is definitely going to end in tears.

Or broken bones.

But he has to pull Avery out of his shutdown slump.

Sammy pushes the old trampoline with the frayed mat – gifted by the neighbours who were going to dump it before they moved – close to the house and he kicks off his shoes and shouts for Avery to come over. It's dusk and the world is full of fireflies and sweet-smelling grass and endless possibilities.

'I'm going to fly,' Sammy says as Avery slumps over, lost in a gigantic hoodie because he's having a rough day.

He's having a rough life.

High school sucks.

He's aware of how different he is now. He cares. He tries to fit with the kids in their class, but he speaks at the wrong time and flicks his fingers by his ears and they call him crude names and pretend to be nice until they trip him in the halls

167

and laugh. It's stupid, wanting friends. But Sammy understands. He wouldn't mind a friend. He also wouldn't mind not having to spend hours making up rules for Avery.

Like, (1) people don't mean what they say, and (2) don't stand so close, and (3) don't *touch* anyone ever, and (4) never never never take your toy car out of your pocket. You're fifteen and they'll rip you to pieces if they find that out.

Sammy's worried school will kill Avery.

But he can fix this, right? He fixes everything.

Avery watches from slitted lids as Sammy bolts forward like his heels are on fire and leaps on to the drainpipe. He scales it like Spiderman. Hand over hand, propelled by momentum and sheer will. He snatches at the gutter and then hauls himself up, ripping his shirt on a rusty hook and scraping his ribs. But he's up. His arms go out for balance, and he stands on the roof, just him and the horizon and the moon already fat against the deepening indigo sky.

Then he backs up – and runs – and leaps – and for a moment he's

f

  l   g

    y   n

      i

And as he falls, he cups his hands in the sky and catches the moon for just a heartbeat before his feet hit the trampoline and the rusty springs groan.

It throws him back up so high his stomach spins out and he windmills his arms with a shout.

A happy shout.

He slows the bounces and twirls to make a ridiculous bow.

Avery pulls his hood off. 'You're going to kill yourself.'

'At least I caught the moon first.'

'You can't catch the moon,' Avery says, bitter. He shoves his hands deep in his pockets, probably thumbing his toy car. His secret.

'I can do whatever I want.' Sammy trots back to the house. 'I'll catch the moon and steal it. Are you coming?'

Avery is coming.

Sammy thinks he'll have to boost him up, but Avery's surprisingly agile at scaling the drainpipe and then balancing on the tin roof. Note to self: stop babying him already. Avery runs and Sammy's heart skips into his mouth and crashes against his teeth, because he thinks Avery's overshot.

But it's fine.

Avery lets out a whoop and his hair fans out in a corn silk halo. His eyes light up and he flaps wildly as he bounces – forgetting that he's supposed to *be acting normal now*.

He's just happy.

Sammy can breathe again.

Sammy turns his next jump into a backflip and nearly hits the trampoline on his face. But his world is a rush of air and power, static in his hair, and grass stains on his knees. And it's good. Everything is good. He jumps again and again. He backflips. He shouts. He throws his arms around the moon before his heels hit the mat and in those moments the world belongs to Sammy Lou.

And he can take what he wants.

Then Aunt Karen's battered blue station wagon rolls into the driveway. Both brothers are on the roof this time, sweaty and bright-eyed and drunk on night air and when she starts shouting, they just laugh.

'What the *hell* do you think you're doing?' Aunt Karen grips her thin handbag and raises a bony finger. 'Get down right now. Right now! Sammy!'

Get down and get your ears slapped, she means.

Not tonight.

Sammy nudges Avery with his elbow. 'Together?'

'You,' Avery whispers, 'and me. We.'

They burst across the roof in a howling run and spring off the edge, their mouths full of the moon and eyes full of stars.

Aunt Karen hollers at them.

They hit the trampoline and bounce high and the poor abused mat gives a wailing *r-iiiiii-p*

and they go straight through and hit the grass.

Idiots.

They smack together as they tumble through the split. Lightning shots of agony jolt up Sammy's legs and he rolls, grabbing Avery's head before it slams into the ground. They tangle for a second in the uncut lawn. Chests heave. The trampoline waves torn threads in apology.

'Anything broken?' Sammy says. 'Because we kind of have to run right now.'

Avery moans and touches his cheek where he collided with Sammy's head. 'Your stupid skull broke me.'

'But worth it?'

Avery's lips are a fractured smile.

Aunt Karen storms over, shouting about *inappropriate behaviour* and *ruining her house*. Sammy rolls out from under the broken trampoline, making sure Avery is on his heels, and then they bolt into the street and leave Aunt Karen raging behind them. She'll lock them out. But so what?

His fingers tease lock picks out of his pockets, relieved they're not broken.

'Where are we going?' Avery's panting, but his face is flushed with the thrill.

Sammy slows and they limp, out of breath and bruised, on the footpath. He throws his arm over Avery's shoulder. They're height for height right now. 'We're stealing a house, because you know what we need?'

Avery shakes his head.

'We are the kings of nowhere,' Sammy says. 'We only need us.'

He's a very good liar.

CHAPTER 18

The wallet is hot and heavy in Sam's sweat-slick hands.

Sickness twirls fists in his stomach as he digs out fives and twenties and shoves them in his pocket. He can practically hear Aunt Karen clicking tongue against teeth and saying, *You despicable little boy*.

He tosses the wallet in a nearby bin, not even checking to see who's watching, and leaves the crowded shopfronts to go wander the Esplanade. Alone.

It's the hottest kind of summer day, where everyone smells of coconut sunscreen and carries cups of pink and green gelato. Sam has a headache. From sun beating on his bare head? From sleeping on the ground? From replaying every horrible encounter he's had this week with every person he knows?

He massages the knot in his neck and scuffs down the boardwalk. Gulls shriek and tourists jostle past in floppy hats with fat wallets he could be taking. Except he doesn't want to. He just doesn't care any more.

Ahead there's an old woman sitting on a tarp, handmade wares spread before her for the tourists. Seaglass necklaces and hand-painted bowls and boxes of postcards. Sam slinks past but then sees fat squares of fabric sitting in a box.

He thinks of Moxie and her sewing needles and thimbles and her lemony frown.

He stops and picks through while the woman haggles with other shoppers over sunglasses and handwoven hats. His fingers brush soft cloth patterned with superheroes and sunflowers and peacock feathers.

'That's ten for two, boy,' the old woman says.

Sam picks rolls out and shoves them in his jean pockets. He drops the notes he just stole into the woman's lap. Three times what she asked for. But they're making him sick.

'This OK?' he says.

She smiles.

The first person to smile at him in days.

CHAPTER 19

Because Sam is stupid, he ends up in front of the De Lainey house again.

His heart gallops double time and his throat is full of thorns. When is he going to understand that it's *over*? She slammed the door in his face. Does he need someone to pound the message home with fists? What's it going to take for him to stop? The police to show up? They'll nail him for theft, house burglary, stalking, trespassing, assault—

The sun bakes these pleasant thoughts into his skull, burning his fair skin beetroot red.

It's been a few days since he left the spool of thread. He should turn a *few days* into *for ever days*. Do everyone a favour.

Come on, cut the self-loathing. If he's going to be here, he might as well knock.

The scrolls of material fit nicely in two hands. Pity he's soaking them with sweat.

He takes the steps like an old man in need of leg surgery. How can he dread this front door and yet long for it so much? He needs to get himself together. He's an embarrassment.

His knuckles tremble at the door,
fingers made of glass
ready to shatter when he meets her furious gaze.
He knocks.
Feet patter inside.
The doorhandles twist and then pauses. She knows it's him, doesn't she? Finally it cracks open and there's a sliver of Moxie – one brown eye and white shorts and a top of indigo lace.

'Oh my God.' Her voice is flat. 'You are actually a stalker.'

Sam swallows, trying to dredge up the apology he rehearsed which has suddenly packed bags and fled. His dry lips part and then he raises the fabric rolls.

'Because you, um, s-sew,' he says.

'What is your *problem*?' Moxie doesn't open the door further and definitely doesn't accept the gift. 'Were you actually living upstairs like a creepy psycho? Like … *why*? Who are you?'

She's talking to him, so that's progress, right?

I had nowhere to go, he wants to say. I'm the boy of nothing and nowhere. I'm invisible and forgotten, a thief of dust and cobwebs and house keys.

'I'm nobody,' is what he says and he knows it's all wrong.

'I checked with all my brothers.' Moxie's eyes narrows. 'None of them knows you. And look, I appreciate that you saved Toby's life, which is why I didn't tell my dad you broke into our house. But that's it. Repaid. Now take your creeper self somewhere else.'

He doesn't argue, doesn't tremble. He takes a step backwards and lays the cloth on the doormat again. 'I really am sorry.'

Her glare is broken bricks and betrayal. She slams the door.

Sam leaves without another word. He gets past the rosebushes and across the street before he dares glance over his shoulder.

The front door is open again. She stands on the veranda, arms folded, watching him and glaring as the light summer breeze plays with the corner of her top.

She doesn't call out after him.

But he notices the material is tucked under her arm.

CHAPTER 20

'For your girlfriend?' The florist has tiny rosebuds painted on each fingernail, the pink the exact same shade as her hair. Sam concentrates on her hands as they find the price tag on the tiny pot of geraniums and hopes she doesn't notice his panic.

A wild antelope with tigers on its tail probably looks more chill than Sam in a florist's shop.

'Um, not exactly … um, not my girlfriend.' Sam rakes fingers across his sunburned scalp.

'Oh, boyfriend?' the florist says.

'I mean, she's not *my* girlfriend. I screwed up and I'm trying to say sorry.' Shut up, please, Sammy, just close your mouth.

The florist looks at him. He picked up the plastic flowerpot, no bigger than his hand, in the 'on sale now' section. Five bucks. He's scraping together twenty-cent pieces until he lifts another wallet. Except that Moxie would burn these flowers to ash if she knew he'd stolen money for them.

Well, she'll most likely do that anyway.

Why is he doing this?

She made her opinion of him very clear before—

But it's wrong. This is all *wrong*. He didn't mean – he isn't that person – he just wants—

'Hmm, I think you need help.'

Sam's eyes snap away from the florist's hands to her face. The sympathetic look in her eyes startles him.

'How mad are we talking?' the florist says. 'Because flowers send a message, you know. And an orange geranium is more like "Hey, I think you're cute" instead of "I screwed up royally and I'm sorry".'

Sam knows this.

He should've lifted another wallet. But it's excruciatingly hard without Avery working in tandem, as a lookout or distraction.

He went to see Avery yesterday, waited until Vin's car wasn't there and then broke in to find Avery pulling apart a CD player. Destroying more than fixing. Avery was deep in *shutdown mode*, which always comes after he spins out. So Sam got three jumbled sentences and a keening wail when he suggested they leave together.

Sam left alone.

It's not like he has anywhere better to force Avery to come. Although a stupid pulse in his heart wishes Avery would ask Sam if *he* was all right. Just once.

Yeah, OK, stop. It's not Avery's fault he can't look at a face and read the lonely pain.

'Well.' Sam shakes the hair out of his eyes.

'She um … slammed the door in my face.'

'Ohhh,' says the florist.

'She said I have problems.' Sam scuffs the toe of his shoe against a bucket of paradise lilies. 'She maybe called me a creep.'

The florist makes a sympathetic *tsking* sound.

'Which I'm not,' Sam adds, quickly, looking up. 'I'm not a creeper. It's a huge misunderstanding and she won't give me time to say sorry and—' He stops, a rope knotting around his throat.

'Ouch.' The florist taps her manicured fingernails on the countertop. 'I do hate to say this, because it's not exactly good for my business, but it sounds like flowers are not your fix. I'll give you a solid piece of advice.' She leans elbows on the register. 'When a girl says "no", what she actually means is *no*.'

Sam's shoulders sag. 'I just want to say sorry. I don't …' He swallows. 'I'm not asking for a second chance.'

The florist sighs and for a second Sam thinks it's the typical *I'm so done with you* sigh he's used to. He's ready to flee, but the florist scoots out from behind her counter and strides over to a bucket of roses. She folds her arms, surveying them.

Sam trails after her. 'I don't have … much money.'

'I believe in good apologies.' The florist clasps hands together. 'Chivalry is not dead! And you're kind of adorable. So if you put on a button-down shirt and get a haircut and –' she glances down at

Sam's ragged shoes and dirty jeans '– hmm, yeah, do something about everything else too – then you have a chance. But we need to abandon the flowers.'

'Um,' says Sam, 'you're a florist?'

'I keep a store of options.' She crooks a finger at him. 'Follow.'

He does.

She walks him to the back of the store, where huge flower arrangements give way to a rustic shelf made of vintage ladders that trail vines and fake butterflies. Boxes with bows of purple and gold and cinnamon sit in pyramid piles.

Chocolates.

'I only have five dollars,' Sam says.

The florist smiles. 'I can work with that for a good cause.'

Sam peeks up at her through tangles of blond hair. 'Do you have caramel?'

CHAPTER 21

His knuckles are practically healed now as he knocks at the De Laineys'. He tried to take the florist's advice. He *really* tried. He found an old comb in the free bathrooms by the sea and probably gave himself lice. But at least his tangles have been tamed? And ... a lot of glitter resurfaced.

He also washed his shirt and spent all day drying it on the rails where the surfers hang out. Consequently he has the worst sunburn over his pale shoulders.

But he did an OK job, right?

So long as he doesn't vomit in the De Lainey rosebushes between now and when someone answers the door.

That will not help.

There's the *click-clack-click-clack* sound of a small De Lainey on a trike, likely doing laps around the kitchen table. Deep in the house, a baby wails.

Maybe she didn't hear?

He waits and waits, hands slick around the chocolate box that's probably melting into a caramel puddle. Maybe if he leaves it here and—

181

The door shoots open, a full swing, which is more than the five centimetres he got last time.

Moxie stands there, tear-stained baby on her hip, wearing a yellow and white henley T-shirt covered in apple sauce and snot and green felt pen scribbles.

Her frown intensifies.

'You,' she says.

Sam holds the box of chocolates half in front of his face. Possibly proof his intentions are honourable. Possibly a shield. 'Hi.'

'Are you seriously not going to quit, you creeper?'

He reminds himself to speak. Don't vomit. Stand up straight. Look her in the eye. Don't lose it.

'I just want to say sorry,' he says. 'And explain. And th-then I'll go and I swear you'll never see me again.' He rushes the words so they slur together like he's some nervous boy a heartbeat from tears.

Which is exactly what he is.

Toby appears behind Moxie's legs and rams his trike into the wall. He falls off with a shriek of laughter.

'There is no explanation,' Moxie says, voice flat, 'in this big wide world, that will make why you were *living in my house* make sense.'

'I broke in,' Sam says, voice high and breathy. She's here. She hasn't slammed the door. She's listening. He's maybe got five seconds. 'When you were away. And I – I just needed somewhere to sleep and then you all came back and I tried to leave b-but your brothers …' He stops, no air in his lungs. 'You all thought I was someone else's friend. So I stayed. Accidentally. I *swear* it was an accident.'

Moxie's scowl remains.

'And your family was so awesome …' Sam looks at his undone shoelaces.

'You lost me there.' Moxie gestures to her shirt. 'This little monster,' she jiggles her hip and the baby's lip sticks out, 'just threw his *whole* breakfast at me and Toby's been using me as an art board. I haven't slept in two days because the baby's teething and apparently I'm the only one he wants. And I'm like *this close* to screaming and losing my mind because they expect me to be their mother and *I'm not* and—' Her voice catches, jagged and breathy. Then she narrows her eyes like she's been caught, vulnerable and bare, and it's his fault.

Gingerly, Sam offers the box of chocolates.

Moxie's gaze snaps from the golden bow up to Sam's pleading eyes.

She takes the box. 'There's glitter in your hair.' She shoves past him, posture like a queen. 'And you're not forgiven.'

But she took the chocolates.

Sam's heart dares to beat again.

Moxie plops herself down on the veranda steps, settling the baby beside her and then turning full attention to the box. She undoes the bow and the shadow of a smile passes her lips. 'How'd you know to get caramel?'

'That day I spent with you?' Sam says. 'You practically married the caramel sauce.'

Moxie raises an eyebrow at him, but it's not caustic. She looks curious.

She plucks a chocolate and bites. For a moment, she's forgotten Sam because her guard drops and she just looks like a frazzled girl who's melting into the bliss of sweets.

Toby hurtles out the door, apparently sensing chocolate, and Moxie reluctantly hands him one to stop the incessant stream of 'Please please please—'

'Do yourself a favour,' Moxie says to Sam, 'and don't collect brothers.'

'I only have one.' Sam shifts awkwardly, not sure if this is his cue to sit or leave. 'Older.'

'Older is nearly as bad, but at least toilet trained.' She glares at Toby, who has chocolate all over his face. Then she looks up at Sam, the guarded look of queens and conquerors falling back over her eyes. 'Time to start your working penance.' She points to an upside-down kiddie pool on the lawn. 'Fill it for the brats and then we'll talk.'

Then we'll talk.

Sam realises, with a pang, that he'd probably do anything she asked in this moment.

It takes longer than he anticipated to wrangle the pool into submission. The hose isn't attached and Moxie gives no helpful advice, so he has to battle through that alone. Then flush out the pool. Then fill it. By that point, Toby wants to help and ends up untwisting the nozzle while Sam adjusts the tap pressure.

The hose is pointing at Sam.

Sam gets a faceful of water.

He gives a garbled shout and falls on his butt in a rapidly flooding puddle. When he finally gets the hose off Toby, fills the wading pool, turns the water off, and limps back to Moxie – he's dripping and she's laughing.

Laughing is good, right?

Sam plops on the step next to her and wrings out his shirt.

Moxie sticks the chocolate-smeared baby in the pool while Toby throws handfuls of grass in to totally destroy Sam's attempts of fixing up a *clean* pool.

'Oh, you should see your face,' Moxie says, shoulders still shaking with quiet laughter.

'I just got that pool all nice ...' Sam trails off as Toby runs over with a bucket of dirt and jumps in. 'Never mind.'

'Now you see why I look like this.' Moxie drops back on to the steps beside Sam and helps herself to another chocolate.

He makes a mental note: when you've pissed someone off, bring chocolate first not last.

They sit in silence for a while as the babies destroy the pool and Moxie makes short work of the chocolate box. She holds it out to Sam and he hesitates, then takes one. He's not sure that's how apology chocolate works but he'll do whatever he can to prolong this moment. Because it seems she's accepted the apology.

Which means he really has no excuse to come back after this.

'So you're homeless,' Moxie says. Not like a question.

Sam's caramel gets suddenly stuck in his throat. 'Yeah.'

'What about your parents?'

He doesn't want to talk about this. Especially not with her, not with someone who's actually seeing him. Once you start talking about fathers who beat the crap out of your brother and aunts who hate you and older brothers who still drop in screaming meltdowns – you start sounding like the kind of wind that whines through all the cracks of a house. The kind you wish would shut up and never come back.

'Not around,' he says. 'It's fine. I just – I make do.'

'In my house, clearly. How long were you even there?'

'A ... a few days.'

Moxie gapes. 'Days? We had no idea for *days*?'

'You don't go into that office much,' Sam says.

'No.' Moxie looks away again. 'It was ... it was my mum's space. She did all the books for my dad's building business and it was like her "no kid" zone. So she could catch a break.'

Sam picks at the hem of his T-shirt. 'Yeah, my mum walked out too.'

There's no answer, so Sam keeps picking at threads, until he realises Moxie is staring at him. Hard. He flinches. He's said the wrong thing.

'No, my mum died.' Moxie's voice is strangely emotionless. 'Cancer. She ... she had it after Dash was born too. That's why there's like seven years between Dash and Toby. Then it was gone and Toby was a surprise, so I guess she and Dad decided he'd need a playmate.'

The playmate in question tries to eat one of Toby's proffered dirt pies. Moxie doesn't seem fazed.

'Then the cancer came back and she chose keeping the baby over chemo,' Moxie says. 'I mean, she was trying everything else to fight it but ... she died a year ago, two months after the baby was born.'

The weight of the story sticks in Sam's throat. He knows you're supposed to say something comforting when people talk about tragedy. But he doesn't *have* conversational skills. When it comes to people, he screws up and runs away. The end.

So all he says is, 'I'm sorry she was stolen from you,' because thieving is what he knows and this is most definitely a theft as cruel and sharp as knives.

The curious look is back, flitting in the corner of Moxie's eyes. 'Thanks. That's … that's exactly what it feels like. And I'm the oldest girl so everyone thinks I'll just fit the space she left, but …' She seems to shake herself a little and then yanks a hair tie off her wrist and scoops her frizzy mane into a ponytail. 'Wow. I totally did not mean to blurt that at someone I just met.'

'We met that Sunday,' Sam says.

'Met properly,' Moxie concedes. 'So now you know I'm a motherless snark who bites and you're a homeless creep who sneaks into people's houses and steals their lunches.'

So maybe he hasn't made any progress.

'But you also saved Toby.'

He scrapes hands through his hair again and ruins his pathetic attempt at combing.

Moxie looks pointedly at his arms. 'I'm not forgetting that.'

He drops them to hide the healing scrapes.

'But you were stealing wallets on the Esplanade that day, right?' Her voice levels back to brisk sharpness. 'I didn't tell anyone that either. Currently my family knows you appeared out of nowhere to spend Sunday with us and then vanished.'

'Why didn't you tell them I'm a thief?' Sam says, soft.

'Because you saved Toby and I didn't want you to get in trouble. Ugh.' She groans and tosses the empty chocolate box on the veranda. 'I have to tell my dad the truth. All of it.'

Sam squeezes his eyes shut and for a moment the world is summer sun and grass clippings and children shrieking over splashing water and hot roses and a girl who smells of caramels.

'I'll go.' He knows this is the end. 'I wanted to explain and I wanted to apologise and ... I did ... both.' He stands, awkwardly dusting grass off his jeans. He's still damp, but a few hours walking will solve that.

Walking to nowhere.

'Wait.' Moxie stands too. 'My dad could help you. I mean ... where will you go?'

Sam shoves his hands into his pockets. 'I'm not ... I'm not excusing myself, but I steal to live. If your dad finds out about me, the only thing he can do is hand me over to the police. And there's other stuff. There's ...' His voice trembles, too high, and he makes an effort to even it out. 'I can't go to prison. I just can't. I have to look after my brother ...' Avery would die if Sam got caught. He'd never cope.

Moxie chews her lip, her face strangely vulnerable. 'OK. I get it.'

There's silence. Sam's toes tip over the edge of the world and he's dizzy and hopeless. This is the part where he goes away and her life goes back to normal.

'I can't cook,' Moxie says, very suddenly. 'I burn everything. It's a literal nightmare.'

Sam remembers scrubbing the blackened pot.

She meets his gaze and he realises her eyes are the same golden brown as her caramels.

'Do you know how to make pancakes?' she says.

CHAPTER 22

Sam cracks eggs into a bowl and scoots the butter away from Toby's curious poking fingers. He also pretends he's not watching Moxie. But his face turns hot as he collects ingredients – without Moxie's direction. Because yes, Sammy Lou knows his way around the De Lainey kitchen quite fine.

Awkward.

Moxie takes this in with thin lips. She hoists herself up on the bench and bounces the fussing baby.

'You don't seem like an axe murderer,' she says finally.

Sam carefully pours perfect circles of batter into the frying pan. He searches for a response but his words are lost, perpetually lost, stuck in hollows where people have scowled or flicked his ears for not answering fast enough.

'You have flour on your nose,' Moxie goes on, 'a clear "not-an-axe-murderer" sign. And you were OK-ish that Sunday.'

'OK-ish?' Sam repeats.

Moxie shrugs.

Sam's heart flutters ridiculously and he clutches

the egg flipper to stop his fingers shaking.

Toby finally gets his hands in the butter and pulls it on to the floor. 'Oops.' He turns huge brown eyes up at Sam.

Moxie has a very satisfied look on her face. 'Oh, how fun it is to serve penance.'

Sam cleans it. He flips pancakes. He even holds the baby for a terrifying nine seconds while Moxie finds some teething rusks in the pantry. The house is noisy with fans working overtime, butter crackling in the pan, and Toby staging a brief tantrum about wanting butter and jam on the same pancake but not *on the same pancake*.

They sit on the table, an impromptu midday picnic, and eat as many pancakes as they can hold. And Sam makes a fine pancake. They're crisp around the edges and perfectly cooked inside. He's been making them for ever, especially when he was nine and it was all Avery would eat without panicking.

Moxie tears a pancake in half. 'So if you have an older brother ... why doesn't he take care of you?'

Sam feels a little sick. 'Avery needs someone to take care of him.'

'Ah.' Moxie reaches over and wipes the baby's mouth with the edge of her T-shirt. 'And where do you sleep when you're not creeping in my house?'

'Anywhere. Other houses. They're usually ... empty.'

'Where are you going tonight?'

It's a trick question. He cycles through a million lies and half-truths and tries to block out the picture of the warm armchair in the office.

'Probably the park,' he says, and then quickly adds, 'it's a warm night so it'll be nice.'

Moxie snorts. 'Nice? Liar.' She slides off the table, tugging a sticky baby after her. 'I know you excel at dishes, so have at it. I'm putting the boys down for a nap.'

Toby looks up from where he's fingerpainting in jam. 'No!'

Moxie eyeballs him. 'Oh yes, sir. And another bath.'

She hauls a kicking Toby and an overtired flailing baby upstairs and Sam tackles the dishes. He does feel bad for her. He obviously has the easier job here.

He wraps the remaining pancakes in plastic and hides them under the steps outside. For an easy grab and run.

Pitiful. Absolutely pitiful, Sam.

He doesn't mind the dishes, with warm soapsuds up to his elbows, but he's scared of finishing. Scared of leaving. He wipes every dish dry, just to prolong it, and finally Moxie comes downstairs. She's changed shirts and brushed her hair and looks a little self-conscious about it. But she still walks with her back straight, chin jutted out, and leaps over the back of the sofa. She folds legs underneath her in perfect triangles and then glares and crooks her finger at Sam to follow.

He does.

'They usually sleep for two hours,' she says, 'which is the time I love them the most. Sit.'

It's a small war to find space around the huge load of washing that covers most of the sofa, but Sam sits. His leg bounces. He's so close to Moxie and she smells of marmalade. Her clean shirt is a patchwork of pinwheels, all hues of deep purple and mint.

'You made this?' he says.

Moxie stretches her shirt out a little to admire it. 'Yes. I'm making enough pieces for a portfolio so I can get into an amazing art school. I was going to work on it all summer, but obviously no one in this freaking house cares about my future.' She makes a low growling sound and picks up the remote, snapping the TV on. 'Want to watch a movie?'

Of course he wants to watch a movie with her.

He never wants to go.

'Not horror.' She peers sideways at him through dark curling lashes.

Sam's smile is sheepish.

She puts on a superhero movie, all car chases and impossible powers and the occasional bomb detonating. He can't focus. All he can think of is how Moxie sits beside him. *Sits beside him.* And she knows who and what he is.

'There's still flour on your face.'

He scrubs at his cheek hurriedly.

'No, you missed it. More to the – oh, here.' She reaches across the infinite black chasm of theft and lies and hungry hearts and brushes flour off his forehead.

Something explodes on the TV screen but Sam stares at his hands, fingers tangled in nervous disarray on his lap, and Moxie is still watching him.

'You're kind of like Goldilocks,' Moxie says suddenly as the superhero and heroine swoon into each other's arms on screen amidst an exploding building. 'But with pancakes instead of porridge.'

'Goldilocks wasn't sorry.'

'But you are.' It's not a question.

Moxie's body relaxes and her shoulder leans against his. The pressure is warm and soft and everything. And he falls into it. Just a little. He won't let himself get too comfortable – he's not *that* stupid. But for the barest moment between patchwork frowns, he's wanted.

He falls asleep.

How *could he?*

Sam snaps awake so fast that he swallows his heart. His limbs flood with terror, *real* terror, because he can't be caught sleeping right out in the open in the De Lainey house again. Moxie is gone. The sun has dipped and the room is full of shadows. He's been nestled into the laundry, his head cushioned amongst tea towels and dozens of soft shirts.

And the house is anything but quiet.

Car doors slam outside and boots tramp across the wooden floors accompanied by the clash of voices.

'Dad said we'd knock off at *three*. Does it look like three to you?'

'Dude, we were waiting on that timber shipment. It's not Dad's fault.'

'I need a sandwich.'

'Shotgun the shower.'

'You can't shotgun the freaking shower—'

'Whoa, Moxie did the dishes?'

'Holy hell, she's finally been possessed by aliens.'

Mr De Lainey's voice booms from outside. 'Jack. LANGUAGE.'

Sam is suffocating. It's like last time, when he woke in the office to a flood of De Laineys and the knowledge that he was about to feel fists in his stomach. But this time he has nowhere to hide.

He's sitting in the L-shaped sofa in a mound of washing and Moxie is gone.

'The one who stinks to high heaven,' says Grady, 'gets the shower first.'

'But that's not fair.' Jeremy hops in a circle, unlacing his boots. 'Jack perpetually smells like a sewer. I was cutting timber with Dad. I have more sawdust than hair.'

'That's because you're bald.'

'It's called a crew cut and it was for a good cause.'

'Shotgun the shower!'

'I'll kill you, Jack.'

Jack glides past with a very self-satisfied smile and tosses a backpack on the sofa.

Directly on to Sam.

Sam catches it with his face.

'Oh,' says Jack, backtracking to stare. '*Oh*.'

Sam scrambles to his feet, clutching the backpack to his chest. He has to run. He has to run *right now*.

And then the back door bangs open and Moxie marches in, the babies tumbling after her. Her arms are covered in glitterised stickers and there's grass in her hair.

'My friend Sam is staying for dinner,' she announces. 'And isn't it Jack's night to cook? He better get his stinky ass in the shower.'

Mr De Lainey appears at the front door then, leaning on it to take off his boots. He narrows his eyes at Moxie. 'Language.'

'Sorry.' Moxie raises her hands innocently.

'I'm overworked and underpaid,' Jack says.

Moxie waves vaguely at the room. 'Show of hands who cares.'

Grady has his head in the fridge and Jeremy just smirks.

'I hate you all,' Jack says and then cuts another look at Sam. 'Wait, he's your friend? I thought you said you didn't know—'

Jeremy throws his boot at Jack's stomach and he lets out an *omph*. Jeremy flees for the back door and Jack chases with a roar, question forgotten.

Sam abandons the backpack shield since he's apparently *invited* and slips over to Moxie's side. 'Do they … are you going to tell them?' His throat is dry.

'They still don't know you were the creepy intruder,' Moxie says. 'But I'll claim you as my friend and they'll forget I said you weren't. They're boys. Their brains are the collective size of a pea.' She looks at him. 'Hmm, oops.'

Considering his recent decisions, she's not wrong. 'What will you tell your dad?'

Moxie sweeps her dishevelled hair out of her face. 'Let's worry about that later. Right now we get to play a fun game called "dinner time chore avoidance". Oh, and I hope you had a nice nap.'

'You shouldn't have let me sleep.' His voice is distressed, even though he tries to hide it.

'You look tired, Sam. Now shut up and come and see my latest project.' Her voice lowers to a mutter. 'Because if I'm going to adopt you, then you might as well be a captive admirer.'

He is a captive admirer.

But not on the topic she has in mind.

He follows her dutifully to the corner of the room where her sewing machine is set up. They have to squeeze behind a bookshelf of toys and a play kitchen and then they've entered Moxie's domain.

A tall shelf overflows with boxes of pins and patterns, material and lace. There are a dozen half-done projects scattered on her table and piles of scribbled designs in blue and red ink. A dress dummy displays a pinned outfit of emerald green. When he looks closer, he can see the pockets have been embroidered with tiny yellow daisies.

'Is that the thread I gave you?' He rubs a finger along them.

Moxie's smile is wry. 'Maybe.'

'I am a solid admirer.'

'You're a solid weirdo,' Moxie says, but he can tell she's pleased.

Dinner is loud and messy and intoxicatingly alive.

Sam sits squashed between Moxie and Jeremy and he feels safe. Probably because he's far enough away from the two smallest De Laineys, who still believe food is more fun to paddle in than eat.

Also because he's far away from Mr De Lainey.

Sam just … he can't with adults. They frown, they shout, they hit. Mr De Lainey seems like the opposite of that, but Sam's tattooed the caution to his bones. Just in case.

It's spaghetti, which seems to be the complete range of Jack's cooking skills. Jeremy made garlic bread and now they're arguing whether that counts as 'helping' and whether Jack is now required by household law to aid on Jeremy's cooking night. The baby faceplants in a bowl of sauce. Grady eats and reads and doesn't get a single drop on his paperback, which is probably a sign of dark magic. Dash has a sword bound with twine and twigs on the table and at least four people rotate in telling her to get rid of it.

Mr De Lainey leans over Sam and Moxie's heads to get at the cheese and manages to give Moxie a half hug and then rest a hand on Sam's shoulder for just a second.

Sam flinches.

But all the De Lainey father says is, 'Sam, it's great to see you again.' He smiles warmly, squeezes Sam's shoulder and then moves away.

Moxie pokes Sam's leg under the table. 'He's the softest squish you'll ever meet. He's buff because he's a builder, but trust me, he's the kind of guy who saves spiders.'

Jeremy leans over, mouth full of spaghetti. 'What are we whispering about?'

Moxie stabs at him with her fork. 'None of your business.'

'Less conspiracies, more eating.' Jeremy deposits two soft rolls of garlic bread on to Sam's plate. 'I'm still concerned Sammy's going to turn sideways and we'll lose him for ever.'

'We wouldn't want that,' Moxie says.

Sam shovels in food to hide the smile. His knee knocks against Moxie's – an accident, obviously – and she gently taps him back.

'So, Moxie.' Mr De Lainey clears his throat. 'I could only organise the concrete truck for this weekend, which means I need—'

'Wait, wait.' Moxie sets her fork down with

a crack. 'You're taking my weekend now?'

Her father sighs. 'Moxie …'

'Oh, it's fine.' Moxie's teeth clench. 'Obviously I'm just a home-grown babysitting service.'

Sam casts an anxious glance at her, suddenly seeing fissures and fractures through the walls of the De Lainey life.

Moxie snatches her fork and stabs a meatball. 'I am *not* their mother.'

'Mama!' says the baby, a handful of tomato sauce squishing through its fat fingers.

'No,' Moxie snaps. 'No and *no*.'

The baby's lip juts out.

'Seriously, Moxie?' Jack says. 'Can we just eat without one of your self-pity sessions?'

'You can't talk!' Moxie whips to face him. 'You *never* have to look after them. I'm only fifteen. I'm a kid too. And they're exhausting and … and frustrating!'

The baby pops open a wide pink mouth – and *howls*.

Sam winces.

'All right, let's calm down,' Mr De Lainey says.

No one listens.

Jack rolls his eyes at the dagger look Moxie gives him. 'It's not like you're the only one working.'

'Jack, maybe shut up?' Jeremy says.

'I never get to stop,' Moxie shoots back. 'Who got up for the baby last night? Me.'

'I'm sorry—' Mr De Lainey tries again, but

Moxie is already half out of her chair, bunched fists on the table.

'Who's been up since five with Toby? Me.'

Sam slowly eats another piece of garlic bread, feeling guilty for even seeing this. But in that moment, his heart tugs for Moxie.

He gets it.

A life tangled with siblings who can't look after themselves? Sam gets it.

'Who gets called "mama" like eighteen times a day, which is like a stab in the guts every single time?' Moxie's face is red. 'ME.'

The baby's howl escalates so Toby joins in at a clashing pitch and Mr De Lainey scrabbles to try and soothe them both.

'We all miss Mum,' Jack says. 'You're not special.'

'Shut up!' Moxie shoves away from the table, nearly tipping the bench, and Sam grabs it as it wobbles wildly. 'Shut the hell up, Jack!'

'Moxie, *language*.' Mr De Lainey is barely heard over the chaos.

Grady snaps his book shut, snatches car keys, and walks outside.

'Grady,' Mr De Lainey calls, sounding a little desperate. 'Hey, just wait a—'

The front door bangs.

Mr De Lainey puts his head in his hands.

Moxie flips around in a whirl of purple and mint shirt and storms towards the stairs.

Jack snaps garlic bread in half. 'Oh, so now

she's going to get out of the dishes? It's like Moxie is the only one "suffering" around here.'

'Just stop, son,' Mr De Lainey says quietly.

Moxie gets to the bottom step, fingers clenching the rail, and then she twists back to Sam. 'Come on.' It's a command.

Sam jumps out of his chair, stuffs a last piece of bread in his mouth, and ducks after her. They sweep upstairs and leave the clatter of crying below. Over the top, Jeremy's saying, 'Wow, way to go, Jack,' while Jack snaps, 'I miss Mum too, OK?' and Dash yells for someone to shut up the kids. And then a wail cuts above them all from the three-year-old:

'*I want Mama!*'

Moxie pulls Sam into her bedroom and slams the door.

For a second he just stands awkwardly on the duct tape divider that separates elven catastrophe from a sewing cyclone. One step and he'll end up in a button jar or a box of tin foil play-coins.

Moxie flops on to her bed and buries her face in her knees. 'You can officially take back your comment about my family being "awesome".' She lets out a bitter laugh.

Sam gingerly tiptoes across the room, hesitates, and then climbs on to the bed next to her. Half his nerves knot and shred, like she'll scream at him *how dare you come this close, you creeper and stalker and thief?* But she doesn't.

They sit shoulder to shoulder, listening to the dimmed chaos downstairs.

'I've seen worse,' Sam says.

Moxie tips her head sideways, cheek still resting on her knees. 'Do tell.'

He bites his thumbnail and then forces himself to stop. *Don't tell. Don't be miserable and needy or she won't want you around. Don't don't don't—*

'My dad used to beat the hell out of my brother and me.' Sam's biting his nail again, not realising. 'But ... we were little and my brother's autistic so he just caught it more ...' His thumb's bleeding.

She stares.

God. He should *not* have said anything.

'It's fine now.' He tries to pin a smile on his face. 'Long time ago.'

'OK, wow. I am such a jerk.'

'No ...' Sam's heart thuds. 'No, please. It's – you're allowed to hurt. It's not a contest.'

Moxie sighs and digs fingers into her scalp. She swivels on to her stomach and reaches under the bed to drag out a small box. A packet of marshmallow chocolate biscuits is snatched and shared and they both chew in silence.

'I really miss my mum,' Moxie says. 'I'm being a complete jerk to Dad, but ... I'm tired and I hate trying to be her and—' She bites savagely at a biscuit.

Sam looks out the window at the darkening sky. They're quiet. Alone. Comfortable.

'I should go.' Sam doesn't move. 'Thanks. For ... today.'

'Are you sure talking to my dad would ...'

'End with me in prison.'

'Because of the stealing?'

Sam's heart speeds up. 'Yeah,' he says, the lie soft as butter on his tongue. He thinks of the school. The blood. *Running away*. 'I'm sorry ... I'm ... I'm really, really sorry.'

Moxie stretches out her legs, and it's probably definitely an accident, but she leans harder against him, her hair tickling his ear.

He'd give anything to stay like this.

'Just sleep in the office again,' she says finally.

'But you nearly murdered me for—'

'Throwing a bucket of glitter at you is not murder, you drama queen.'

'You try getting it all off.'

'You didn't.' She reaches out to brush behind his ear. She presents fingers of glitter in proof. 'The difference is now I'm inviting you.'

'But your family—'

'I'll figure it out tomorrow.' She offers him the biscuit packet. 'It's just one night.'

BEFORE

Sammy is a breath and a whisper away from fourteen and he just wants time to stop.

Life has grown complicated, his wishes and wants screwed like broken marbles in his lap. He can't do this. He doesn't know how.

He stuffs another wad of toilet paper up his bloody nose and tips his head backwards against the brick school wall. Shouts and voices have dimmed as kids load into buses. Now there's just the pound of a basketball on the court where stragglers play – where Sammy sits forgotten in the corner. Bloody. Tired.

Shoes slap on the court and kids shout in annoyance as Avery suddenly hurtles through the middle. His shirt is inside out, collar popped, tags fluttering.

He looks happy.

Sammy's worried.

Avery arrives out of breath and drops to his knees in front of Sammy, fingers fluttering. 'I kissed someone.' His eyes are the darkest seaglass, shimmering with anticipation.

Sammy stares at him.

'I kissed Elle,' Avery says. 'But she said "no way" to being my actual girlfriend and to ask someone else so I asked if it has to be a girl or can it be a boy and she laughed and said whatever I want –' he speaks faster and faster '– and did you know you can pick whoever you want, which is good because sometimes boys are as pretty as girls and she said she'll still kiss me sometimes because I'm cute and dumb and then her brother West is fixing up his uncle's Hyundai and said I can hang out and watch if I want and—'

'OK, whoa. Stop.' Sammy pulls the paper out of his nose. 'You're talking way too fast.'

Not just talking. He's going way too fast for Sammy to keep up. In everything. Being a year above Sam in high school means Avery isn't around him all the time and is instead watching fifteen- and sixteen-year-olds – watching and copying and *wanting*.

He's going too fast.

He's not like them.

He's going to get hurt.

Sammy claws for words, but they sift through his mouth like sand. 'You can't go around kissing. Not yet.'

'Why not?' Avery rips at the dandelion weeds in the cement cracks.

Sammy tries to steady himself. He aches. The cut under his eye where a backpack buckle clipped him is swelling and he's trying not to use his left hand until he figures out if his fingers are just bruised or – worse.

He's not ready for *this* kind of conversation with Avery.

'Because,' he says, closing his eyes, 'they're messing with you. To *hurt you.*'

Avery frowns. 'Or maybe they like me.'

Sammy's about to say 'as if' but catches himself. He knows this school is full of rejects and cruel smiles and barred windows, but does it matter if Avery can't see that? Isn't that nice for him? 'Are you sure these kids want to be your "friends"?'

'Yes.'

Sammy cuts him a hard look. 'Do you even care about them or just the fact you can see a car being fixed?'

Avery opens his mouth. Closes it. His bottom lip juts out and he looks wounded. 'I want to go to their house and maybe learning to fix cars can help me get an after-school job at a mechanic's somewhere.' His voice brightens. 'I could earn money, right? Money for our house.'

This is Sammy's wish, the dream he holds like a broken box, careful so the edges don't cave in. He talks about it when they lie in bed, Avery crushed against his side because he sleeps better when he's back to back with his brother, matching their breaths.

Sammy has the dull feeling that he's being manipulated.

'Did you say you're going with them *now*?' Sammy says.

'Yup.' Avery points to the front gate where a group of teens is messing about, waiting.

Not the kind of people Sammy wants Avery around. All crass jokes and cold smirks.

Does Sammy want Avery around anyone? OK, fine. No. He'd keep him in his pocket if he could, safe and warm, with hands over his ears when kids start shouting sick slurs at him because of his tics. There are a few kids at school who are nice enough, like August and her boyfriend, but Avery can't tell the difference between someone laughing with him and *at* him. He picks friends badly.

'You're not going to anyone's house,' Sammy says. 'We're going back to Aunt Karen's.'

Avery's eyes narrow. 'You don't want me to have friends.'

'That's not—'

'You don't think I deserve anything good to happen to me.' He starts rocking on his heels, eyes damp.

How's Sam supposed to explain? How's he supposed to be fiercely proud Avery's growing up and fiercely protective at the same time?

He doesn't know how to let go of Avery. Doesn't think it's the right time.

'Look,' he says, soft and calming so Avery stops the wild rocking. 'Look, there are rules for this sort of thing, OK?'

'OK.'

Sammy clutches for handholds in this slippery surface. 'The rules ... well, you can't kiss people and hang out at their houses if ...' He sees Avery's fingers slipping into his pocket. Ah, perfect. 'If you still have toy cars.' Sammy tries to keep the triumph out of his voice. 'You can't have both. It's like being a kid versus growing up. You either have the toy or you have kissing.'

No way is Avery going to give up that car.

A reason amongst *millions* that he's not ready for this.

Avery pulls the toy car out of his pocket. It's silver now, paint worn off and wheels gone and edges smooth from six years being comfortingly thumbed in Avery's pocket. He flips it over with long thin fingers, staring.

Sammy tests his nose. Still bloody? He wads up more paper and knows he won and they can go home. Sam will make sandwiches and Avery will trawl the newspaper for houses they can dream could be theirs and—

'OK.' Avery puts the toy car in Sammy's hand.

Sammy's heart gives a thin, thudding leap and then just—

stops.

Avery bounces to his feet. 'I'll be back at six or something.' His eyes flick to the teens by the gate. One waves him over.

Sammy's fingers close over the toy car. 'W-wait.

What exactly are you – wait, Avery, we need to talk about—' He snatches a corner of Avery's shirt. 'Please, just *listen*. Don't do … don't …' He wants to rip out his hair. 'No kissing and don't let anyone touch you.'

Avery looks down quizzically at Sammy currently touching his shirt.

'I mean,' Sammy says, teeth grating, 'under your clothes. If clothes cover it, you can't touch it. It's the rule, OK? Till you're … eighteen.'

He holds his breath, desperate for Avery to accept this.

Avery frowns. 'OK. It's the rule.'

'You know West is a jerk, right?' Sammy's voice is too high.

Avery frowns and pulls out of Sammy's grasp and then he seems to take in, for the first time, Sammy's swollen cheek and bloody, crusted nose. 'You hit people. That's worse than anything West does. It's bad, Sammy. It's so so bad.'

Sammy's teeth clench. 'I didn't hit anyone. I promised I'd stop, didn't I? They jumped me.'

Avery flicks his fingers by his ear. 'I have to go.'

'Avery, please …'

Let him go, Sammy. He doesn't belong to just you.

'Just please,' Sammy whispers, 'don't let them hurt you.'

But Avery doesn't hear because he's already crossed the basketball court and vaulted over the broken-down fence to trot up to his new friends.

His smile is puppy-dog wide. Innocent and anxiously excited. West drapes an arm over his shoulder. Laughs at him.

Or with him?

These kids are older and they'll push him into things he's not ready for.

Sammy looks down at the toy car in his hand. A tear hits it, hot and wet.

He's crying?

He's stupid to be crying.

When he looks up again, the group has gone and he's alone in a near empty school – just overgrown grass and a forgotten basketball and crinkling food wrappers.

Alone.

His knuckles tighten around the toy and then he gives a tiny, melted cry and throws it. Hard. Fast. Gone.

He drops back against the wall of the school, head curling against his legs as the universe spirals out from under his fingertips.

CHAPTER 23

Their routine becomes pleasantly seamless after a week.

Sam lurks in the office until the house clears out and then he emerges and tucks himself into Moxie's day. This generally involves tricking the little boys into eating breakfast and wrestling them into clothes while Moxie snatches a few minutes at her sewing machine. Then the babies promptly ditch their clothes in favour of the wading pool. Sam and Moxie oversee while eating salted caramel popcorn and lying on their backs under a frangipani tree.

They talk.

Sam turns out his pockets and discovers there are words in the bottom. They come out faster the more he's around Moxie. And she doesn't glare when he stammers or roll her eyes at his opinions.

Wow, he actually has opinions.

'I'm actually not descending into madness with you around,' she says later, scrolling through her phone and eating popcorn. 'Or thinking too much about my mum.'

He checks her eyes quickly, waiting for the sad cloud and the stiffness that always follows mentioning her mother. But today her smile is sad and small and then she just shrugs.

'Maybe I'm a *tiny* bit glad you sneaked into my house.'

'Has your dad noticed that, um …'

'That you never leave? He commented that you're always around, *but*,' she flips a kernel into her mouth, 'he still thinks you go home at night.'

'Are you going to tell him?'

'Obviously. Soon. Someday.' Moxie twirls her phone to show him a photo of a model with wind-scrubbed hair and a wild rainbow shirt. 'See this? This could be you.'

Sam looks up, alarmed.

'If you modelled for me, which would do wonders for my portfolio. You'd need to cut your hair though. I'll bribe you with chocolate truffle cupcakes.'

'But if you bake them, isn't that more of a threat?'

'Careful, sir,' she says. 'There is a time-out corner and I will use it on you.'

Sam self-consciously tucks his hair behind his ears. 'I don't have money for a haircut.'

'Right.' Moxie chews her lip. 'But do you actually like it long? Because you could just get it tidied. You look like a haystack.'

'It gets in my eyes,' Sam says. 'But I can't—'

Moxie sits up suddenly, screwing up the picnic blanket they're sprawled over. The baby and Toby are licking watermelon ice blocks and slapping them on Sam's arms intermittently. He's a sticky mess.

'I'll cut it.' There's a dangerous spark in her eyes.

Sam is decidedly nervous.

'I'm good with scissors.' Moxie makes a snipping motion with her fingers. 'How hard can it be?'

They decide to do the responsible thing and watch YouTube clips first. Moxie fetches her sewing scissors and Sam sits on the bottom veranda step.

'Take your shirt off,' she says, 'so I don't get hair on it.'

His heart should not speed up as much as it does right then.

He shrugs out of it obediently and balls it into a knot. He decides to not look at Moxie's face at all considering he still has remnants of road rash and smudged yellow bruises. No girl's heart is going to stammer at seeing him half undressed, that's for sure. And he doesn't want to see disgust in her eyes.

His shoulders hunch over slightly and she sits behind him on the steps.

She ruffles fingers through his hair. 'It should be just like cutting out a dress.'

'Please don't cut out a dress in my hair.'

'Ye of little faith.'

Grady's jeep clunks into the driveway at that moment and three sawdust-covered boys tumble out. They're arguing loudly about how much caffeinated energy drink you could consume before giving yourself a stroke and they don't notice Sam and Moxie until the little boys run to the fence and shriek for attention.

'Hey, babies.' Jeremy swoops in, folding himself in half over the gate to kiss their watermelon-sticky noses. 'And what cities have you felled today? How have they—' He looks up and then nearly falls face first over the gate.

Jack is there in an instant, a devilish grin spreading over his face. 'Whaaaaat did we interrupt here?'

Moxie snaps her scissors at them. 'Haircutting. You're next, Jack. I might take off a few ears while I'm at it.'

Jack's grin fades. 'Over my dead body, pipsqueak.'

'That can also be arranged.'

Grady stomps over and surveys everyone with a tired sense of indifference behind his glasses. He sneezes once, mumbles, 'Hay fever,' and then shoves through the gate and into the house.

'He's going to get the shower first,' Jack says.

Jeremy clambers through the gate. 'Sneak.'

The twins charge indoors, and Jack manages to give Sam's shoulder a rough playful shove on his way up while Jeremy yells, 'Relationship goals!'

That's not ... what Sam and Moxie are. They're friends ... right?

Moxie snorts and waits till they're gone before scooting closer. Her knees press against Sam's shoulder blades and she runs her fingers through his hair again. Spiderwebs of sensations dart across his skull.

'Don't move.' Moxie snaps the scissors experimentally, which instils zero confidence in Sam.

The scissors snip.

Wisps of corn silk strands drop on to Sam's shoulders.

'So I may have been planning this for a while,' Moxie says. 'I'm making this waistcoat, see,' she goes on, unaware of the explosions happening under her fingertips every time she touches him. 'It would look so good on you. And as a budding designer, I really should have bodies behind my clothes occasionally.'

Sam's brain struggles to catch up. 'Me? But I'm ...'

'Remarkably pretty. Don't let it go to your head.'

Cool metal touches his neck. She fluffs hair out from behind his ears. Can she feel them burning hot?

'Plus you kind of owe me, because after all I'm giving you a great hair—'

The scissors snap shut.

Moxie jerks back. He misses the sensation of her touch for half a second and then she says exactly what he doesn't want to hear.

'Oh no.'

Sam's shoulders straighten. 'What do you mean "oh no"?'

'Um.'

Panic hits. '*Moxie.*'

'OK, OK, don't stress. I just …' There's a tense pause. 'Crap.'

His hands fly to his head, but she smacks them away before he can feel the damage. Moxie twists, scissors swivelling so Sam has to duck to avoid losing an eye.

'JEREMY,' she hollers. 'JEREMY, I NEED YOU.'

There's a thud inside the house and then Jeremy appears with a sandwich in one hand.

'Words I always want to hear,' he says, 'especially from my annoying little sis— Oh wow, Moxie. That's not good.'

'*What?*' Sam says, his voice four notches too high. 'What's going on? How bad? Moxie? *Moxie.*'

'I don't understand,' Moxie says. 'I watched three tutorials.'

'That is confusing,' Jeremy says. 'Surely three tutorials are enough to become an expert.'

Moxie turns on him, a lethal grip on those scissors. Sam drops his face in his hands.

'Either help,' Moxie snaps, 'or feel my wrath.'

Jeremy rolls his eyes and hops down the steps. He holds his sandwich out and Moxie trades him the scissors. Then he takes her spot behind Sam and rumples a hand through Sam's hair. It's considerably less exhilarating.

'Shorter at the sides and longer at the top. You'll look great.' Jeremy snips much faster than Moxie was going.

Sam's going to be bald.

'You have a buzz cut,' Sam says, voice thin. 'What do you know about haircuts?'

'I used to have extremely long hair, my friend,' Jeremy says cheerfully.

Moxie takes a bite of his sandwich.

'Hey,' he says.

'Focus.' Moxie snaps her fingers at him and then nudges Sam with her toe. 'He donated it to cancer kids. How long did it get, Jeremy? Halfway down your back?'

'It was a mane of beauty.' Jeremy sounds wistful. And totally unfocused.

Sam resists covering his ears in hopes of protecting them.

'You were majestic,' Moxie says. 'Like Rapunzel.'

'Oh, the glory days.'

More hair falls on Sam's shoulders. A *lot* of hair.

'Aaaand ... done!' Jeremy snaps the scissors shut and lays them on the steps. He brushes off

Sam's shoulders and then pats him on the head. 'Go find a mirror.'

'I don't want to,' Sam says.

Jeremy shoves him off the steps and yanks his phone out of his pocket. He flips it on to camera and then spins it so Sam *has* to look.

OK.

It's not too bad.

His head feels strangely naked and he can actually *see*. Jeremy's raked it back from Sam's face and without the weight of the length, it's naturally mussy.

'Also,' Jeremy says, holding up a hand that sparkles in the afternoon sun, 'I believe you've got glitter in your hair. Unexpected, I admit, but I'm a fan.'

Moxie chokes on the sandwich and hurriedly hands it back to Jeremy. 'Well, wow, Jeremy! I think you should quit the building industry and take up hairdressing.'

'All those faces I could gently caress.' Jeremy grins at Sam and then the mischievous light in his eyes dims.

'Thanks.' Sam rubs the back of his bare neck, suddenly worried he didn't say thank you fast enough.

Then he notices Jeremy's looking at his ribs. Oh, right. He snatches his shirt, even though his back is itchy with rogue strands.

'Are you all right, Sam?' Jeremy's voice is soft

and he's obviously looking at the still healing road rash.

'It's nothing.' Sam looks away.

Moxie picks up the scissors and taps them against her palm. 'The ribs, however.'

'Unacceptable,' says Jeremy. 'He's staying for dinner right, Moxie? I'm cooking. We'll stick some potatoes to this skinny lamb.' He pockets his phone but his tone goes serious for a moment. 'But really, Sam. If you're not getting enough to eat, you come here, OK? Any time.' Sunshine crackles back into his eyes. 'I'm making brownies.' He ducks back into the house.

'Make it caramel!' Moxie yells at his back. 'And thanks for saving us!'

'Welcome.'

Moxie twirls on Sam and folds her arms, tilting to the side to survey him. 'That was fun.'

Sam itches his neck. 'Not really, no.'

'And you have a whole face. Fancy that.'

She hops down the steps so they're level on the grass, so close that if he stretched out his arms he'd have to hug her.

She musses his hair again, frowning as she arranges it. 'And you even have eyes.'

She can probably hear his heartbeat as he rockets out of his chest. She's so close, her hands all through his hair.

'I like your eyes,' she says. 'They look like infinite blue skies of possibilities.'

Is she ... would she ... kiss him?

'That really wasn't so traumatic now, was it?' Moxie steps back, half a smile perched on her lips, but no longer touching him.

She has no idea, does she? What she does to his heart.

CHAPTER 24

'Ow,' he says, dispassionately since Moxie doesn't seem to care where she stabs her pins. Sympathy is not her strong point.

She mumbles something around a mouthful of pins that sounds like 'Baby' and then jabs another one into his shoulder.

He sits on the kitchen table while she turns him into a living porcupine. It's the weekend and he's been Moxie's shadow for fifteen days. The guilt of soaking in this sweet, simple summer and not fighting with Avery for so long weighs on his chest. He'll check on him tomorrow. Make sure he's eating. Make sure he's not on the edge of a meltdown.

The house is strangely devoid of the constant flow of Jeremy and Jack's friends. They're having a morose game of Monopoly at the other end of the table with Dash who, as Sam has been forcibly told, is ten and three quarters, and is currently draining the life out of her older brothers.

'Mayfair,' she crows. 'And I have hotels.'

Jack drops his head on the table with a loud thunk.

'Hey, don't do that,' Jeremy says, petting him tenderly. 'You'll knock out your brain cells and you don't have enough to spare.'

Jack swears at him.

Mr De Lainey, of course, enters the room at that second. He has an eerie gift for appearing whenever his children are doing something disagreeable. He strolls over to the table and holds out his palm to Jack. 'Phone.'

Jack looks helplessly at Jeremy. 'He started—'

His father snaps his fingers.

Jack mutters something darkly unintelligible and slaps his phone in his father's hand.

'And bed for you, miss,' Mr De Lainey adds to Dash.

'But I'm winning!'

'And it's past ten.'

'It's *holidays*.'

'Dash.'

She slides off her chair and stomps towards the stairs. 'Don't forget, I whopped your pathetic butts.'

Jeremy rubs his remaining two-dollar bills together. 'Good game, Dashie.'

She beams and bounces up the stairs with Mr De Lainey in her wake.

'Don't make it late, kids.' He pauses halfway up the stairs. 'Is someone picking you up, Sam?'

Sam opens his mouth dumbly, and Moxie chooses that moment to stab him with a pin. He yelps.

'Soon,' Moxie says fiercely. ''Night, Dad.'

They wait till he's gone before Moxie and Sam exchange glances. Sam can't quite read Moxie's expression, but he thinks it's a mixture of relief – and guilt. His chest tugs. Two weeks is a lot of lying.

'OK, take it off,' Moxie says.

Sam shrugs out of the half-pinned material, jabbing himself several times in the process. She spreads it over the table and then goes to her sewing corner for extra supplies.

Jeremy sets up the Monopoly board again and Jack is on Jeremy's phone, texting rapidly.

'You don't need to warn everyone you've lost your phone,' Jeremy says. 'Half the time they just text me anyway. It's like, expected.'

'Dad picks on me,' Jack says.

Moxie reappears with an armful of garments. 'Your voice carries the furthest because you're a foghorn.' She tosses the clothes in Sam's lap and then hands him a small, lethal-looking weapon.

'Who do I kill with this?' Sam says.

'That's an unpicker, you goat. And these are second-hand clothes. This is where the "upcycle" comes into my stunning design work. We rip these old clothes to pieces and I remake them into something new.'

'Dead people's clothes.' Jeremy pops houses on the board.

Jack makes an exasperated sound.

Sam swivels the small torture instrument. It feels

like a lock pick. His body coils with a strange feeling – has he ever gone this long without stealing something?

'Someone needs to be helpful around here.' Moxie stares pointedly at her brothers. 'Since they're all completely useless.'

'Excuse me,' Jeremy says. 'I did reconstructive surgery on Sammy's hair and Jack cleaned the bathroom once. Last year, I think.'

'I rest my case,' Moxie mutters.

Grady appears, rubbing his eyes until his glasses are askew. 'What'd I miss?'

'Everything,' Moxie says. 'Here comes another useless De Lainey.'

Grady peers over Moxie and Sam's shoulders, where they're attacking seams in efficient unison. 'Why don't you just buy clothes? Save time.'

Moxie slams her scissors down, nostrils flaring. She stalks over to the huge whiteboard hanging by the fridge and wipes a corner free from the hubbub of family notes. She snaps the pen lid off with vicious intent and writes, in hard and tall letters: RANKINGS OF USEFULNESS.

'Oh, here we go,' Jeremy says.

She starts with Grady and gives him a four out of ten.

Grady slides on to the bench across from Sam. 'Ouch.'

Moxie writes her own name and a big fat ten next to it.

'This seems unfair,' Jeremy comments. 'You can't even cook.'

Moxie's frown is lemon. 'Excuse you? I can heat up lasagne. I look after the kids *all* the time now. And yesterday I reminded Dad that we're nearly out of chocolate. I'm keeping this family together.' She writes Jeremy's name as she says this and gives him a seven.

Then she writes *Jack* and gives him a one.

Jack throws his Monopoly money. 'Give me that pen, you little freak.'

Moxie blows hair out of her face and writes Sam's name next.

He rips seams nervously, the unpicker stuck between his teeth and his hair filled with cotton fluff.

The pen hesitates. Then Moxie gives him an eight.

'All right, this is rigged.' Jeremy frowns. 'I should be worth more than Sam. I cook! I specifically made you a salted caramel latte last night.'

'But I don't have one *right now*,' Moxie says. 'So it doesn't register on this scale.'

Jeremy shoves back his chair and heads for the kitchen. 'Blackmail.'

Moxie doodles a butterfly on the whiteboard, humming softly to herself. Monopoly forgotten, Jack looms behind her, all folded arms speckled with house paint.

His glare levels mountains. 'Why are you rating Sam so high? Do you have a *crush*?'

Sam's unpicker slips and he nearly stabs his own hand.

Moxie's lemon frown is back. 'The real question to ask, Jack, is why are you so annoying?'

'I still love you despite your faults, dearest,' Jeremy calls from the kitchen, popping the lid off the cocoa powder.

'Shut up, Jeremy.' Jack's mouth tips down at the corners and he looks surprisingly like Moxie. 'This scale is complete bull—'

Their father's voice thunders from upstairs. '*Jack.*'

Jack slams his hand against the wall. 'THIS HOUSE IS BUGGED.'

Upstairs, the baby wakes up with a howl followed by flying footsteps. Mr De Lainey, wearing pyjama pants and huge reading glasses, materialises at the top of the stairs like a force of power. He's all muscles and sinew and Sam decides he's still terrified of him.

'Jack,' the De Lainey father snaps. 'My room. Now.'

'I get in trouble for *everything*.' Jack storms towards the stairs. 'You lot could murder someone and stuff their guts in the freezer and get away with it.'

'There go my weekend plans,' Jeremy says.

Jack angles his body so his father can't see and shoots his siblings a rude gesture. Then he stomps upstairs.

Jeremy reappears with a tray full of mugs, steam

228

curling over the rims and marshmallows bobbing. He grins like a delighted Cheshire Cat. 'Soooo ... who has a crush?'

'Shut up.' Moxie takes a mug and sits next to Sam.

Jeremy and Grady exchange smirks.

'Sam is a lovely shade of red,' Grady says.

'Is your brain the size of a pea?' Moxie stabs material. 'He's sunburnt.'

She cuts a sideways glance at Sam. He wants to whisper, *do you have a crush*? But his tongue is stuck, his breathing shallow. It'd be so much worse if she did.

Boys like him don't get the girl. They go to jail.

CHAPTER 25

Sam sits on the floor, tangled in patterns and pins, with a measuring tape around his neck like a scarf and a bowl of cereal perched precariously atop several bolts of fabric. It's seven thirty in the morning. He wears Moxie's jeans and one of Jeremy's shirts and Moxie specifically wrote honeyed oat granola on the shopping list because it's his favourite.

He's so caught up in wrestling a pattern piece on to the right fold that he doesn't notice someone's stumbled down the stairs until a bone-rattling sneeze startles Sam into looking up.

Mr De Lainey has sunk to the bottom step, one hand on the banister and another clutching a tissue to streaming eyes. He's a mountain of a man, but flus don't discriminate. Sam's usual response to seeing Mr De Lainey is to quietly vanish, but this time he has a twinge of sympathy.

Mr De Lainey catches his eye and croaks, 'You're here early.'

I never left.

Sam is saved from fumbling an excuse as Moxie

stomps downstairs with the baby on her hip and a brittle frown.

'Dad,' she says, 'we're totally out of food. We're on the verge of starvation and – wow, you look awful.'

Mr De Lainey proves her point by sneezing. 'Sorry, sweetie. I meant to go ... go ...' He's lost to the rapidly disintegrating tissue and another sneezing fit.

'That,' Moxie says, hand on hip while the baby chews her necklace, 'is because you don't take care of yourself. Lemon tea and bed.'

'Moxie, I'll be fine—'

'Seriously, am I the only voice of reason around here?'

Sam collects his empty cereal bowl and makes for the kitchen. He hesitates, caution towards adults battering against wanting to do something nice for a man who's only ever been kind, and then he stuffs his nervousness in his back pocket and puts the kettle on. He fetches teabags, lemon and ginger, and Mr De Lainey's favourite mug. Moxie smiles at him, surprised and entirely pleased.

She should've realised, by now, that he'll do anything for a De Lainey.

'I'll go shopping.' Moxie tries to put the baby down but it squawks at her, so she sighs and shouts up the stairs, 'JEREMY! Drive me to the shops!'

Silence.

Moxie mutters something about lowering

his usefulness rating until Jack appears, hair like a cyclone and wearing a black shirt with a skull on it.

'Jeremy cannot return your calls right now,' he says.

Moxie narrows her eyes. 'Did he come home last night? Tell me he's not trying to get back with his ex-boyfriend again.'

Jack makes a wild cutting motion at his throat, but Mr De Lainey – flu or not – has an all-seeing eye.

'Right, he's grounded.' He sneezes. Moxie hands him the whole tissue box. 'Where's Grady?'

Jack bounces downstairs. 'He left super early to, and I quote, "prevent inevitable murder if I have to stay in this house one minute longer". I guess he's with his girlfriend.'

'If Grady wants to murder you,' Moxie says, 'he should totally live that dream.'

'Shut up.'

Sam brings over the tea and Mr De Lainey accepts gratefully. 'You're brilliant, son, thank you.'

Sam looks away quickly to hide the flush of pleasure.

'Then Jack can go shopping,' Moxie says.

Panic lights Jack's eyes. 'What? No way.'

'There's literally no food.'

'There's not actually a lot of money for groceries,' Mr De Lainey says, sipping tea. 'I just ... as soon as the house we're building sells, we'll be fine. But I've sunk a lot into it. Too much.' He rubs his reddened eyes. 'Jack, can you grab the emergency cash in the office? Top drawer.'

Sam's heart skips a beat and then

s t o p s.

'I'll sell a few pieces of furniture,' Mr De Lainey adds. 'Just to tide us over.'

Jack folds his arms. 'Great. We're going to end up on the streets, starving and destitute.'

Sam's looking anywhere but at Moxie. His pulse flutters, fireflies and knives, and Moxie frowns curiously at him.

Mr De Lainey sighs. 'It's not that d ... dram ... a – TIC.' It ends in a sneeze and he sloshes tea on the stairs.

Moxie snaps her fingers at Jack. 'Get the money. And keys. Also your brain, if you can find it.'

'I'm not going anywhere with you—'

'We need food!' She practically stamps her foot. 'Dad needs a twelve-year nap. Stop being so selfish, Jack.'

Mr De Lainey tries to say something like 'I'm not that bad' but he looks exactly that bad.

Jack storms off to search the office, muttering darkly, while Moxie pulls on boots and stuffs her frizz into a ponytail. The baby clings to her leg and sniffles.

Jack returns, car keys jingling. A pang slides down Sam's arms and he stuffs his fingers in his pocket, because he *wants*—

No, he doesn't. He's fine. He's over keys.

'I couldn't find any money in the office,' Jack says. 'And whoever put those blankets in there needs to clean it up. But I got your wallet and we can totally live off a hundred bucks.'

Mr De Lainey frowns. 'Did I use that emergency money already?'

Sam quickly takes Mr De Lainey's half-empty mug. 'Want me to refill this?'

Mr De Lainey blinks for a bleary second. 'Oh? That'd be great, Sam. I think I'm about to keep you.' He smiles.

Sam is a war of guilt and pleasure at Mr De Lainey's words. It wouldn't be like this if he knew what Sam was.

'We have to take the baby,' Moxie says, 'because I give up trying to put it down and suffering the screaming.'

'And take Sam,' Mr De Lainey says, voice thick, 'so you don't murder your brother.'

'Of course I'm taking Sam.' Moxie sniffs disdainfully. 'I wouldn't just leave him.'

It turns out that Moxie grocery shopping is a terrifying thing. She is a burst of violent fire and speed as she storms aisles with a list and clicking pen.

Jack shoves the trolley in her wake and looks bored and offended by everything. 'We're going to live off gruel.'

Moxie's voice turns dangerous. 'Listen here, Jack. We're in a tight spot and Dad's doing the best he can and if you can't possibly be a decent person, at least pretend, or I will wipe you off the usefulness rating board completely.'

'You are simply the worst creature,' Jack says.

Moxie's smile is sweet poison. 'At least I was planned while you were an unhappy accident.'

'That is *so* not true—'

'Mum only planned for Jeremy,' Moxie says. 'And she'd have so many regrets if she knew how—'

Sam taps her shoulder. 'Aren't we shopping?'

'The puppy has an excellent point,' Jack growls. 'And Moxie, you're not the only one who has a shitty time without Mum, OK?'

They eyeball each other, angry and raw, and Sam flinches. It's not like he expects the De Laineys to be perfect – he's not an idiot. But he hates when their wounds show, because he wants to fix it like he would try for Avery, and he *can't*. He wishes they'd realise, though, that you can't fill the hole of a missing mother by carving each other to pieces.

Surprisingly it's Moxie who caves and strides off, muttering about potatoes and stupid boys.

Jack follows, shoving the trolley with the fussing baby strapped in, and Sam trails behind like a sorry impostor. Usually he fits with Moxie. But the weight of stealing their money burns hollows in his chest.

The baby whines pitifully for Moxie, so Jack

plucks it out of the trolley and shoves it at Sam.

'Whoa,' Sam says, 'this is your brother.'

'It likes you.'

Probably because Sam spends his days pushing it on the swing and lying on his stomach in the grass while the baby uses him as a jumping castle.

He bobs up and down awkwardly.

Jack eyes him and then snorts. 'You look ridiculous. Get in.'

'The trolley?'

'Yes.' Jack shoves peanut butter and bread out of the way. 'Quick. I keep trying to get Jeremy to do this but he won't.'

That seems like a good indication that it's a bad idea, but Sam has a terrible weakness called: Do Whatever a De Lainey Wants.

He climbs in, knees at his chin, and squishes the baby to his chest. It stops crying and looks interested.

Jack has a devilish spark in his eyes. While Moxie is all sharp edges and paper cuts and Jeremy is buttery sweet and warm – Jack is spiky daring and recklessness.

'Have you ever been thrown out of a grocery store?' Sam says.

'Bring it.' Jack drags the trolley to his chest and then shoves forward, running like lightning down the aisle before jumping up and hooking his legs around the edges so it shoots forward.

It turns out their combined weight makes the

trolley go spectacularly fast. They soar the full length of the store, narrowly missing taking out a Vegemite display. People jump clear with gasps.

They flash past Moxie holding packets of spaghetti and she gives them a sour look.

Jack whoops.

The baby shrieks in delight.

Then Jack attempts to slow them down—
and fails.

They hit the ice cream freezers with a clatter and Sam covers the baby with his arms as peanut butter smacks him in the face.

'That – was – *awesome*.' Jack is still on the floor, his smile delirious.

'Ow,' Sam says with a broken face.

The baby pats his cheek. 'Ow-ow, Sammy.'

Moxie storms over. 'You are both *so* embarrassing.' She snatches the baby off Sam and throws a packet of spaghetti at his head.

He raises his arms in self-defence. 'Jack's idea.'

Moxie whirls on Jack. 'You're a terrible influence on him. I'm trying to raise him nice and sensibly and you're turning him into a De Lainey.'

Jack picks himself up, holds out a fist to Sam, and they hit knuckles right as the store manager strides down the aisle.

'You are both so stupid.' Moxie snaps her fingers in Sam's face. 'Why are you still smiling? Stop smiling. You are never going to be allowed back in this store.'

Sam tumbles out of the trolley. Usually the sight of angry managers is a clear indicator he should run – before they call security and nab him for shoplifting. But his pockets are empty. And Moxie said he was *turning into a De Lainey*.

It's the first time Sam's thrown out of a grocery store smiling.

BEFORE

Sammy is fourteen and there are knives in his belly.

He's so hungry.

He should be mad right now, since Avery unscrewed most of the door hinges, took apart every lock, and started dismantling the ceiling fans before Aunt Karen came home from work and screamed at him. Sammy should've stopped him, should've been there – but he was out practising with his lock picks on an empty house. He's fast now.

Fast at locks.

Slow to notice his brother cracking around the edges.

They're banished to their room without dinner, even though Sammy didn't *do anything*. He's so freaking hungry and the gallon of cold water he drank just gave him a stomach ache.

It's dark and too warm and he lies on his face in mussed sheets, picking at threads with fingernails gnawed bloody.

The bunk bed creaks. A small thump. Then Sammy feels the familiar weight of shivering, spidery limbs pressed against his back. The night's too warm for this and Sammy's hungry and tired and annoyed. But Avery rests his head against Sammy's spine and Sammy lets him. Counting breaths. Calming down.

'You want to tell me what's going on yet?' Sammy says.

Silence.

'I know you're freaking out about something. How am I going to fix it if I don't know what it is?'

Avery's whole body shudders.

Sammy closes his eyes, thinking of trying the bakery before school tomorrow since they often give away those pink-iced sugar buns if they're stale. He could eat nine right now. Twenty-nine.

'Is my brain broken?'

Sammy stiffens. His blood runs hot and he wants to rip out of bed and and and ... *smash something*.

He stays very still. 'Who said that?'

Avery presses his ear harder to Sammy's back. 'Everyone.'

'West? Elle?'

Silence.

'I don't really like them any more.' Avery's voice is small. 'They and the others ... they copy me. Like when I tic and—' He stops. 'They think I don't get that they're laughing at me. But I do.'

'There's nothing wrong with you.'

Silence.

Sammy rolls over and pulls the blankets away from Avery's head. 'Did they do something to you?

You have to tell me, OK? If they hit you or-or-or screwed around with you or—'

A sliver of light from the open window touches Avery's brow, knit with pain and something like fear. 'If I tell you then you'll hit them and you can't keep hitting people.'

Isn't Sammy supposed to be the reasonable one here? He groans and knuckles his eyes. 'I won't hit anyone. Just tell me.'

'No.'

'Avery.'

Avery rolls to face the wall. 'Every single person in this world is full of bullshit.'

Sammy's heart aches. 'Yeah, I know.'

Avery's fingers trace the cracks in the wall plaster. 'Can I ... can I have my car back?'

Sammy wants to hit himself, really really hard. His throat is dry when he says, 'I don't ... have it any more,' and he's never hated himself as much as now.

A shudder runs across Avery's thin shoulders.

'Avery?' Sammy whispers. 'Please talk to me.'

Avery starts to cry.

CHAPTER 26

It's quiet that Thursday and impossible not to feel drowsy while sprawled out on the De Lainey sofa buried under button tins. Moxie and Sam scour second-hand stores on the weekends when they're not babysitting. They come back with treasure. Peculiar costumes to rip apart. Strange tins of buttons. Odd hats to remake.

Moxie always looks so pleased when she's hauling a strange vintage curtain out of a box and whisper-shouting, 'Just imagine this as a *dress*!'

Their latest find was a four-litre bucket of buttons. He and Moxie planned to eat popcorn and sort them, except Moxie's best friend, still spending the summer overseas, wanted to video call, so Moxie barricaded herself in her room for 'extremely needed girl time'. The three older teens are out and Dash is showing her homemade Thirteen Elven Warrior Whatever footage to her dad. The house still smells of Mr De Lainey's moussaka – garlic and spices and béchamel sauce. He sold the desk from the office. He hasn't mentioned the missing money again.

Sam sifts through buttons. He loves how they feel, cold and knobbly, every one a different pattern and shape and colour. Avery would love doing this. Sam is consumed with sorting and nothing else.

Because this he can do.

This is safe.

He checks the clock and decides Moxie is due back soon. Time to put on popcorn. It's proof of how long he's been in the house that he knows where the electric popcorn maker is and how to outwit the sticky buttons.

He's rummaging for kernels when his eyes fall on the fruit bowl.

Mr De Lainey has left a tumble of house keys and wallet sitting there. The keys stare at him with rows of metallic teeth. The wallet is old, seams popping.

Sam stops.

Don't. Just ... *don't*.

But his hands are in the fruit bowl, popcorn forgotten, before his brain catches up.

Razors of guilt hook into his ribs until it feels like he's being pulled apart. He sees Mr De Lainey's disappointed eyes. Avery's understanding slice of a smile. Sam's backpack full of glittering keys sinking beneath the grimy sea. He owed everything to those keys. They kept him alive, kept him weighted to the earth when everything else threatened to cut him loose and send him spinning to die amongst the endless dark.

Fingers shaking, he unhooks the house key.

He puts it in his pocket.

He doesn't touch the wallet.

Cars pull into the driveway followed by a smattering of boys' shouts and revved engines, and then the door crashes open and Jeremy and Jack sweep in. Sam's heart catapults in his chest and he runs across the room, dives back on the sofa and covers himself in buckets of buttons. The pocketed key digs into his thigh.

whywhywhywhy what if they saw—

Sam takes a breath. No one saw. The twins will do the usual: raid the kitchen, argue about the injustice of being seventeen without their own car, and insult each other as they go upstairs. Moxie will come down soon.

Nothing happened.

Instead, two shadows fall over his head and – perfectly synchronised – they vault over the back of the sofa and land on either side of Sam.

He snatches at the tub as buttons fly into his face.

'Saaaaammy,' Jack says.

'Sam.' Jeremy pats Sam's knee.

Sam does the logical thing – he panics.

They know.

They'll see what a miserable pathetic creep he is. Who steals house keys? *Who does that?* They'll hit him and throw him out and—

'We need to have a little chat.' Jeremy fakes a demure smile.

Mischief lights Jack's eyes. 'About your intentions with our purest of little sisters.'

The air gushes out of Sam's lungs.

Oh.

Then he stiffens right back up.

Wait.

'Since you're here so much,' Jeremy says.

'Without supervision.' Jack throws an arm around Sam's shoulders and effectively pins him there.

This is worse than being caught with the key. 'I haven't ...' Sam says.

'Hush, hush.' Jeremy leans slightly into his grip on Sam's knee, proof that Sam is going nowhere ever again. 'Let the big brothers talk.'

'See,' Jack says, 'Moxie hasn't had a boyfriend before.'

Jeremy flicks Jack's head. 'Dude, she has so. Remember that kid with the glasses last year? I think she dumped him after he said girls don't like superhero movies.'

'Fine, a *serious* boyfriend,' Jack says. 'Sam is practically a live-in.'

They have no idea.

'We're not like that ... I mean, it's not ...' Sam says weakly.

'Shut up.' Jeremy is calmly pleasant. 'It is. You're just both babies and too shy to smooch.'

Jack's fingers dig into Sam's shoulder. 'And this is the part where we remind you Moxie has three strapping older brothers.'

Sam swallows. 'And you'll kill me if I hurt her? That's cliché, guys.'

'Moxie can pound you herself,' Jeremy says.

'And then when she's done,' Jack's eyes are evilly bright, 'we'd remove your entrails via your nose and use them to truss you up like a Christmas turkey and then toss you to the sharks while you wear nothing but your boxers.'

Jeremy gives Jack a tired look. 'Why so complicated? Just say we'll kill him.'

'We'll kill you,' says Jack. 'Bloodily.'

'Well, I'm *not* doing anything.' Sam clutches buttons. 'I mean – we haven't even … kissed or anything.'

'Oh.' Jeremy's face falls slightly. There's a pause. 'Do you need advice?'

Jack smacks his twin on the head. 'That's the opposite of what we're doing here.'

'Aw, come on,' Jeremy says. 'Sometimes the babies need helpful hints. But just small tips to match Sammy's small height.'

'Yeah, are you sure you're not, like, twelve, Sammy?' Jack says.

Sam glares.

There's a thump on the stairs and then Moxie appears. The goodness of catching up with her friend shines in her red cheeks – until she sees her brothers. Her brows tighten in that trademark lemon scowl.

'What,' she growls, 'is going on here?'

Jack rumples Sam's hair. 'We're just giving him the safe sex talk.'

Sam chokes.

Jeremy whacks him helpfully on the back.

Moxie folds her arms. 'Oh, so this is a display of dominating male chauvinism, as if you have ownership of me and feel it's your duty to "protect" me because I somehow "belong" to you.'

Jeremy spreads his hands out in innocence. 'We're just making sure Sammy has honourable intentions.'

'Do it again,' Moxie says, 'and you'll find itching powder all over your soap.'

'You don't even own ...' Jeremy starts.

Moxie is pure darkness. 'Would you like to bet?'

'We'd tell Dad,' Jack says. 'And you'd be in deep trouble.'

Moxie points towards the stairs. 'Don't even think of playing a blackmail game with me, because I have so much on you.'

Jack snorts.

Moxie tilts her head, tapping her fingers against her chin in mock consideration. 'I suppose I'll just randomly mention to Dad that your little *"summer begins, let's have fun!"* camping trip involved alcohol.'

Jeremy and Jack glance at each other over the top of Sam's head.

'You guys aren't allowed to drink?' Sam says.

'Our mother was Greek and Catholic,' Jeremy

explains, 'and Dad isn't but he's raising us like she'd want, you know? Safe and strict. So no drinking. Or swearing.'

'Or sex,' Jack adds.

Moxie smiles sweetly. 'There's one you'll never get to struggle with.'

Jack growls and starts to get up but Jeremy grabs the back of his shirt. 'We'll find you a nice human with low standards someday.'

'Don't Catholics drink wine?' Sam says. 'Or the blood of Jesus or something?'

'I'll beat you for your ignorance later,' Moxie says. 'It's just our dad has a zero tolerance policy on alcohol. So keep that in mind, *you two* –' she aims this at the twins '– and remember that Dad will literally lecture you for nine hours if he knows you've been drinking. Remember that time he grounded you for like three months and you had to always be in his sight?'

Jeremy sounds reflective. 'Ah. How could I forget? All our friends thought we'd died.'

Jack looks like murder. 'I hate you, Moxie.'

She batters her eyelashes. 'Love you too, sweet cakes.'

Jeremy pops to his feet and smiles brightly. 'Well! I have stuff to do! 'Night all!'

Jack extricates himself from crushing Sam, glowers at Moxie, and then follows Jeremy. They argue their way up the stairs about whether they can put Moxie in a box and sell her online.

Moxie plops down beside Sam. She picks through the button box for a quiet second and then casts a wary glance at Sam. 'What did they actually say?'

'Something about me needing to have honourable intentions.'

'Absurd. Especially considering I found you living dishonourably in our house.'

The stolen key burns hot in his pocket. He resists the urge to close his fingers around it. Protect it.

He shouldn't want the stupid key as badly as he does. What's *wrong* with him?

Sam's voice is soft. 'I guess you'll have to tell them soon. About ... me.'

'Holidays are nearly over.' It's neither agreement nor disagreement and Moxie doesn't look at him.

Suddenly she snatches the button box away and dumps it on the floor. He starts to protest, but she presses four fingers to his chest and his heart stops beating.

'Lie down,' she says.

He does.

His world grows crushingly tight. He doesn't know what to do. What he's allowed to feel. He doesn't know what she wants from him, if she even *really* likes him or just feels sorry for him or—

His head hits the perpetual pile of laundry and then Moxie lies down beside him. They stretch their legs out, squished tight together so Moxie doesn't fall off the edge of the sofa.

She puts a hand on his chest. Spreads her fingers out.

'Your heart is beating very fast.' There's a soft laugh in her voice.

Slowly, Sam slides his arm around her back – to help her not to fall.

Honourable intentions.

Moxie's head is on his shoulder, her hair soft against his chin.

He's holding Moxie.

He will never move again.

'We should probably talk,' Moxie says.

Sam closes his eyes. The house is so quiet, just the hum of the fridge and the click of cicadas outside.

'School starts soon.' Moxie gently draws a circle on Sam's chest. 'And I've lied to my dad all summer, which … I mean, I feel bad.'

A lump sticks in Sam's throat. 'I'm sorry. I shouldn't—'

'No. I wouldn't change a single day. It's been … it's been perfect. After my—' Her voice wobbles slightly and she takes a deep breath. 'After my mum died, I just wanted to cut holes in everything. Literally. I'd just started sewing, but I ended up wrecking everything I made. It sucked, OK? She left this tiny baby and all these kids and Toby calls me "Mama" by accident so the baby calls me it *all the time*. And I want to scream. I want to just be a kid and make art and not take care of everyone.'

Sam is quiet. He so deeply, so desperately doesn't want her to say he's been just a distraction.

He wants to be—

something.

Someone to her.

'And then Kirby went on that stupidly long holiday and I thought I'd spend the whole summer alone and, well, miserable. Then I found you. Stealing my family.'

'I was actually trying to steal your house.'

'All of it?' She draws an invisible smiley face on his T-shirt. 'Goldilocks.'

'I don't want …' Sam's voice cracks around the edges. What does he say? He doesn't want it to end? He doesn't want to leave? To lose her? He wants to hook his fingers into the last cracks of summer and hold on?

'I don't want it to end either.' She pushes herself up on an elbow and looks down at him. 'You snuck up on me, Sam. I felt bad for you and then you reminded me to care about things again. You fit so perfectly with me and I just … I like it. I like you. Obviously.'

Something floods through Sam's chest, something intense but sweet, like summer and starbursts and wild hopeless longing.

'I like you quite a lot too,' he whispers.

A smile curves half her lips. 'Can I ki—'

There's a thump like someone just ran bodily into a wall and then a throat clearing. 'AHEM.'

Moxie shrieks and falls backwards off the sofa.

Sam shoots upright, guilt plastered thickly on his face.

Jeremy stands on the bottom step, wearing comic pyjama pants and holding a toothbrush. He slides towards them cautiously and peers over the sofa at Moxie, now flat on her back on the floor, glowering.

'Sorry to break up ... whatever *that* was,' Jeremy says in a tone that doesn't sound sorry at all. 'But Dad said Sam can spend the night. So long as he calls his parents.' He pauses. 'He stays on the *sofa*. While Moxie stays in her *room*. Just to clear that up.'

Moxie looks at Sam and they both burst out laughing. Like he hasn't been staying here for weeks.

Jeremy looks confused. 'OK. Wow, you weirdos.' He turns to go and then backtracks. 'I guess you don't need advice, Sammy.' He winks.

Sam pulls a pillow over his face.

Moxie shoots a suspicious look from one to the other. 'Excuse me?'

'Nothing.' Jeremy cheerfully flees.

Moxie's eyes narrow but then she climbs back on beside Sam and he'll be lying if he doesn't admit he desperately hoped she would. They fit together more comfortably this time, his arm not so awkwardly around her and her face nestled against his chest.

'It's like I live here or something,' he says.

'It's like you live here or something,' she agrees. 'And since you live here and are therefore beholden to me for ever—'

'I'm worried.'

'—then you can't say no when I tell you about this party at the beach we always go to before summer ends. Basically our whole school shows up.'

Sam's breath hitches at the word *school*.

'It's a Catholic school,' Moxie goes on, 'so it's pretty calm. But we dress up fancy and dance and tell everyone they've grown over the summer, etcetera etcetera. Someone always smuggles alcohol and we light a bonfire. It's like the last holiday hurrah.'

'I ... can't. If someone knows me—'

'No one's going to know you. Unless you went to St John's, which seems unlikely.'

She's right, isn't she? No one will recognise him. His old school was across the town and full of kids who don't host *beach parties*. They'd smoke in battered parks and pay homeless guys to buy them vodka.

'So ... I could sit in the car,' he starts, only half joking.

She smacks his chest. 'Never. Will you wear the waistcoat we're making?'

It's a crazy waistcoat. Because, for starters, it's a *waistcoat*.

'Obviously,' he says.

She tips her head up and he looks down and her smile is so full of undiluted delight that he realises no one's ever taken her outfit-designing seriously before.

'I'll finish my dress,' she says. 'This will be my debut display.'

'And then ...' Sam reaches up to twist a finger around one of her curls. 'And then you go back to school.'

And he goes back to nowhere.

To being
utterly
invisible.

A shutter tips over her eyes. 'Can we talk about it later? We'll work it out. I'm not going to say goodbye.' Her voice is fierce. 'I promise.'

She's so close to his face now that his world is just caramel eyes and lips and the fierce fire that burns through this girl for ever and always. He wants to tell her everything.

That he steals keys because he's desperate to belong.

That he ran away because he had to, because of what he did at his old school.

That he wants to catch her a bouquet of stars and kiss her under the moon.

Her forehead presses against his for a moment and his thoughts melt and Moxie's world wraps threads around his chest till he can barely breathe.

She kisses him.

He tips his head up to catch it.

She's soft and warm, summer nights and sugar. His brain shuts off. His hands circle her back.

Then she pulls away – quickly – and the catastrophe of stars exploding in Sam's chest cuts off. He did something wrong. Of course he did. He screwed it—

'I'm sorry,' he's saying, breathless and panicked. 'I haven't ever kissed—'

She puts a hand over his mouth. 'Well, that I can tell. But wait.' She adjusts herself, scooting up higher on the sofa. 'There's something in your pocket digging into my hip.'

The key.

Sam's hands start to shake.

Moxie doesn't notice as she rearranges herself beside him and then rolls so she's lying half on his chest. She tilts his chin up. 'You have a lot of practice to do. It's OK to move your face, you know. And your mouth.' She punctuates this by kissing the very corner of his lips. 'I'm very, very happy to teach.'

His heart threatens to explode and his lips part to tell her so.

'Perfect,' she says. Then kisses him again.

And he thinks there is nothing in the world so beautiful as kissing Moxie and please let this never end, this one good and sweet thing—

until

a fist pounds at the front door of the butter-
yellow house,

and a voice shouts, 'Sammy Lou? You need to
come get your psycho brother.'

Sam's perfect world turns to rust.

CHAPTER 27

Sam and Moxie trip over each other as they scramble for the door. Tight fear spirals down Sam's spine, cuts through skin and bites bone. Pleasepleaseplease don't let—

He rips open the door while Moxie says, 'Wait, don't open it! Who the—'

Vin stands in the thin light whispering out of the De Lainey house. Vin, in a tight black lace dress, with a red leather jacket falling off her shoulders. It matches her hair. Blood and fire.

Her lips curl with disapproval.

'Who—' Moxie starts again, but Sam jumps in front of her, not sure if he wants to protect her. Or hide her.

It tumbles out in anguish. 'Where's Avery?'

'Currently embarrassing the hell out of me,' Vin says.

Shit.

Shit.

'It's not like I can call the cops,' Vin says, her tone acidic. 'But I figure you know how to stop an overgrown tantrum?'

It's not a tantrum. It's never a tantrum.

Moxie's fingers curl over Sam's arm. 'Who is she? What-what's going on?'

Vin's already turned on excruciatingly high heels, stabbing back down the path to her white sports car. Engine still running. Lights blazing.

She's going to wake up the whole house.

'I have to go.' Sam turns to Moxie, desperate now. 'Please, just ...' Just what, Sam? Just what the hell will you tell her? He can't fit his world with Avery into a single sentence and Avery needs him. Now.

So his fingers just slip through hers and he bolts after Vin.

'Tell me what's going on!' Moxie cries from the doorway.

He gets into Vin's car. She rips into gear and on to the road in a howl of mufflers and rage before he's even shut his door.

The soft kisses, the key, the warmth, *his stolen family* – is crammed out of mind. All he has is a desperate need for Avery.

'Tell me what happened.' Sam's voice is too high. 'Where is he? At your place? H-how did you even know where I was?'

'Avery never shuts up about you. If you tell him something,' she rolls her eyes, 'then I hear it fifty times a day. I could say your bloody house address in my sleep by now.'

He feels sick that someone like Vin knows where the De Laineys are.

Why would she even bother to fetch Sam to help after he hit her? Probably because Avery being taken by cops would put her shady businesses at risk. *Since he can't shut up.* Vin's only kindness is truly selfishness.

The car spins downtown. 'We were at a club and—'

'The *hell*?' Sam wrenches to face her. 'Do you even know him?'

'I thought he was getting over his pedantic sensitive stuff.'

He wants to hit.

He lays his fingers, flat and sweaty, on his jeans and forces them still. Breathe.

'He's autistic.' Sam grinds each word like crushed glass. 'If he was deaf, you wouldn't expect him *to get over it*.'

'Whatever. I'm not here for lectures—'

'You know what's too much for him? Lights, noise, tons of people, trying to figure out what you want all the time – goddamn *alcohol*. And you threw it all at him? Do you know what happened when he was nine and went into a club?' She starts to answer, but he cuts her off, almost shouting, 'He nearly died, OK?'

She gives an unfunny breath of a laugh. 'Kid, if you're about to flip out, I'll just dump you on the side of the road. I can only take one Lou tantrum per night.'

He knots his fists. 'Drive faster.'

They speed until they pull into the car park of a club, lights and pounding bass shuddering out the brick walls. It's like being hit in the stomach. It's like eight years ago and being strapped inside the car while his father thrashed pieces off his brother's fragile, fluttering soul. Sam rips out of his seat before they even stop. Cars pack the small space so tight it's hard to move, to see.

But there's a small cluster of people by a slick wall. Talking. Looking.

A scream, a *wail*, like someone's dying, pierces the night air.

Sam runs.

He doesn't hear Vin follow.

Don't don't don't let him be too late—

Sam slams through the thin wall of elbows and silk jackets and perfumed skin – and sees his brother.

Avery's tucked tight to the brick wall, black button-down shirt ripped open at the collar and long scratch marks cutting from throat down his chest. His own work. His fingers scrabble in loose gravel, open and close, open and close, like he's trying to hold on, before he flings his hands up to hit his head, his ears. His world is spinning out from under him.

He screams and screams.

They've pushed him too much.

The world has always been a hot coal on Avery's skin. He is made of raw nerves that touch and feel and see everything too hard and too fast, and if you burn him too much – you get this. Overload. Catastrophe. *Drowning.*

Sam shoves people back, yelling even though he doesn't mean to. 'He's fine! He's fine! Just go away.'

'Is it some kind of fit?'

'Get the cops.'

'I can call an ambulance—'

'No!' It's nearly a scream now. Sam wants to slam the phone out of the do-gooder's hand. 'No, just leave him alone. I've got him. I've got him.' He drops to his knees, reaching slowly for Avery. *'I've got you.'*

He should never have let it get this far.

Sam's selfish fault.

Then Avery slams his body against the wall, head cracking with a sick wet *thwump* against the bricks. His screams pitch higher. Sam explodes forward, snatching Avery's head before he can bang it again. He wraps his arms around Avery, hard and fast and suffocating, and as Avery swings out with fists and teeth – Sam holds tighter. Tighter.

Tighter.

Pressure.

Calm him down with pressure.

Avery's fist connects with Sam's stomach.

Again.

again

Sam takes it all with the smallest grunt. He crushes Avery's head to his chest and rocks, just keeps rocking, until Avery's thrashing arms suddenly go limp and he slumps into Sam.

'Sammy?' He looks up with frantic, damp eyes and blood pours from his lips.

Sam turns Avery's head so it fits against his T-shirt, blocks out the world. The lights. The people. Everyone's drifted away, muttering about *fits* and *crazy kids on drugs*. Sam doesn't care. He's just glad they're alone and Avery has space to breathe between cars and walls and the black star-bitten sky.

'I'm here.' Sam puts his cheek on the top of Avery's head. 'You're OK.'

'I c-c-c-can't—'

'You don't have to,' Sam whispers. 'I got you. I'll fix it.' He keeps rocking as Avery's bunched muscles uncoil, terror draining from his brother's trembling limbs. 'I'll get you someplace safe.'

He looks up, trying to find Vin so they can get Avery out of there. But all he sees are the taillights of a white sports car as it peels away and roars into the street. Without them.

... *embarrassing me*, she'd said.

Sam closes his eyes tight for a second, shoving back the haze of red and fear and panic. How's he going to move Avery? They have nowhere to go.

Life is always so sickeningly cruel.

He blinks fast and then looks down at the

exhausted, bloody boy in his arms, torn to pieces and sick with sobs.

Sam holds him tighter.

He knows where to go.

CHAPTER 28

Sam slips the key out of his pocket while crazed panic burns through his skull. He can't be doing this. He'll ruin everything.

He's doing this.

He unlocks the door quietly, props it open with a knee, and then grabs a fistful of Avery's shirt to pull him inside the warm butter-yellow house.

Getting him this far, with midnight buses and begging, no *forcing*, him to walk, nearly didn't happen. Sam is the monster right now, the monster who knows the world has cut his brother to splinters but forces him to walk through the pain. He hates being this cruel.

Avery's soul is bleeding out. He's on the slim edge between catatonic stillness and falling back into screams.

But they made it.

Sam knows tomorrow will be the end of his stolen home, the beginning of retribution. But right now all that matters is that his brother is safe.

Sam locks them inside and whisks across the room to be sure everyone's upstairs and asleep.

Part of him longs to slip to Moxie's room, for her to be awake so he can fall into her arms and explain. She'll be furious he ran out like that.

Their kiss, so sweet before, feels like memories of ash.

Instead, he drags Avery to the sofa and pushes him down, stripping off his tight, expensive-looking button-down and snatching a T-shirt that smells of soft eucalyptus soap from the eternal washing pile. He slides it over Avery's shivering shoulders, doing all the work because Avery just *can't* right now. The shirt is probably Jeremy's. Sam has so much stealing to apologise for.

Later.

Sam tugs off Avery's shoes and clears space so he can lie down.

Avery's chest moves in ragged lunges and his hands flap in front of his face. 'I c-c-c-can't ...' He stops. A sob tears free. Too loud.

Sam snatches a quilt and covers him and then, carefully – like when they were kids – he climbs on top of his brother. A blanket. A barrier. Pressure to calm him.

They lie there for a minute, still in the soft honeyed darkness. Avery's breathing slows as Sam holds him tight. A sandwich of Lou boys in a stolen house.

'We have to be quiet,' Sam whispers. 'But tomorrow I ... I'm going to fix it. Explain everything to the De Laineys.'

They'll cut him to his knees and beat him to death.
No.

No, the De Laineys are not like that.

'I think they can help us.' Sam scoots a little, checking that he's not crushing Avery too much. He used to research ways to help Avery at the school computers, reading about why some things destroy him and how weighted blankets help meltdowns. Failing owning one, Sam decided to be one. 'I'm ... I'm sorry I wasn't there. I should've been there.'

Avery rubs a palm up and down his cheek – where he used to drive a small toy car – and says nothing. Silence is usual for him after he's fallen on the world's barbed edges.

Then he goes completely still.

A small sigh escapes.

Sam closes his eyes for a second in relief and then carefully peels off. Avery's asleep in a flood of silver moonlight, his hair nearly white and his cheeks lit with spiderwebs of tear stains.

Sam would save him a million times. He'd *never* hesitate.

But you can't hide Avery.

Sam's perfect summer is a hot slap against his cheek.

He wakes to a toe in his ribs.

Sam snaps his head up with half a snort, backhanding drool off his cheek. He fell asleep

266

with his head tipped backwards against the sofa, arms crooked awkwardly, and butt numb from sitting on the hard ground all night. He blinks up at Moxie, who wears a breezy navy swing top and embroidered shorts, her arms folded, her scowl a line of demands.

Oh no.

Avery.

Sam jerks toward the sofa but it's empty.

'I need explanations,' she says. 'Many of them. And the fact that you slept through the screamfest that is our breakfast is disturbing.' She taps fingers against her folded arms and then her voice drops. 'What the *hell*, Sam?'

He kneads his eyes.

The front door bangs and Jeremy strolls out with one baby on each hip, belting out a Disney song at the top of his lungs. The crash is a momentary distraction for Sam to collect thoughts.

Explanations.

But his words have fallen out of moth-eaten holes in his pockets again.

He pushes his aching body to his feet, feeling the bruises now where Avery panicked and hit him last night. 'My … my brother needed help.' Where is he? Please please don't let him be lost—

'Did you bring your brother *here*?' Moxie hisses. 'Look, I haven't asked for every detail because I can see it hurts. But I have to ask now, Sam. I really, really have to ask what's going on?' She catches the corner of his T-shirt, like she thinks he might run, and her voice softens. 'Is this your autistic brother? Is he safe right now?'

'I don't know,' Sam whispers.

Their eyes meet, hers chips of steel and his crumbling seas.

'We need to tell my dad,' she says.

He opens his mouth to – what? Plead? Argue? Maybe just agree? But Jeremy sticks his head back through the open door and hollers, 'Sammy? Do you have an extremely cute and slightly taller doppelgänger? Because one is currently abusing our poor gate. Also, I think he's wearing my shirt?'

Sam springs for the door, Moxie hot on his heels.

He fairly falls down the veranda and crosses the grass, bypassing Jeremy who's pushing the babies around on their trikes. Sam left his heartbeat inside.

But Avery's OK.

He grips the worn gate, knuckles white, foot hammering the rhythm of his frustration. There's a fence between them, but it feels like a gulf.

'Where'd you go?' Sam says softly. 'Come back inside. I know this is … I know it's a mess, but I'm going to ask them for help. We … we have to.'

Avery looks away, hair falling over his cheek to cover the mottled bruise where he smashed his head last night. His eyes are smudged with exhaustion, his lips bitten bloody.

'If you tell, they'll s-send you to jail,' he says. 'All … this? You c-can't keep this.'

He probably doesn't have a word for 'this'. Friends. Sunday night waffles. Falling asleep with his head on Moxie's lap during a movie. Lying on the grass with mango pips. Hiding behind freshly washed sheets on the line outside to tell silly secrets.

Avery couldn't possibly comprehend what it is to have a home.

Sam leans across the gate. 'I'll risk it for you. I'll come clean and they'll help you and you won't have to go back to Vin.'

'I fit with Vin.' Avery's voice strains. 'Stealing stuff. Running away. I rebuilt her car.' His split lips tip downwards. 'I'm not … I'm not your pet, Sammy.'

A lump forms in Sam's throat. He glances over his shoulder where Jeremy is pretending not to stare and Moxie is openly listening, arms folded, eyes shrewd.

'Don't be like that.' Sam's voice stays low. 'I'm just taking care of—'

'I can take care of myself,' Avery snaps.

'You really can't.' Heat flares in Sam's chest. 'You just fall apart. You just screw up and have a meltdown and then I have to pick you—' Suddenly he hates that he said any of that. 'I didn't mean it.'

'Screw you, Sammy.'

'Just please stop … leaving.'

Avery presses knuckles to his eyes and for a second Sam thinks he might lose it again and hit himself. But instead he tugs his phone out of his back pocket and taps it against Sam's arm until he takes it. 'Fix all your problems.' He tries to smile but it falls apart before it begins. He looks wretched, tired and hollowed out.

Sam's throat closes.

'I like your hands better this way,' Avery says.

Sam looks down in confusion. His knuckles are smooth. No bruises. No cuts. Instead there are callouses from sewing and streaks of glitter pen from where Toby drew on him.

'If you tell them what you did at school ...' Avery licks the corner of his lips, tongue on the scar from their dad's fists. 'They'll turn you in and hate you and they'll ... break your heart.' His fingers dance on the gate. 'Vin says you're soft. You'll get hurt.'

'I'm already hurt.'

'OK, so come with me.'

Sam would rather bleed. He twists his fingers in his shirt and then forces himself to stop.

'You don't belong in a house,' Avery says. 'We're the kings of nowhere, remember? You. And me. We.' He tips his head, like Sam's a puzzle he can't figure out.

No one can solve the puzzle that is Sammy Lou.

They shouldn't even try.

Avery kicks the gate one more time and then pulls free, fingers fluttering like they hold invisible puppet strings. 'You can call Vin if you need me. But I'm leaving now.'

If *he* needs Avery? More like when Avery needs him.

But he thinks Avery means it. He thinks Avery's trying to be a big brother.

Sam could laugh. Or maybe just cry.

He's still trying to find an answer when Avery's shoes skim the street and he vanishes back to his world of shiny things to pocket between here and nowhere.

Sam holds on to the fence for a long, long time.

Finally Moxie crosses the grass, still damp with early-morning dew, and rests her chin on Sam's shoulder. He wants so desperately to scoop her into his arms and just hold her. But he doesn't.

'Can I tell you everything later?' His voice is made of weary bones.

'After the beach party,' Moxie says. 'Then we're officially talking to my dad. About *everything*.'

He just nods.

'Is he going to be OK?' Moxie looks down the street, but Avery's gone.

No, he's not. Avery's just going to crack again and again if he keeps this up. Sammy's lived with him for fifteen years and he *knows* Avery better than anyone.

Sam looks down at his fingers wrapped around Avery's phone. 'I'll catch him if he falls.'

'Who catches you?' Moxie says.

Sam stitches on a pretend smile. 'It doesn't matter.'

CHAPTER 29

Sam fits his hands into his pockets and walks self-consciously downstairs. He hates plenty of things: seeing Avery hurt, a lock outwitting him, his skin stinging from a beating, the thought of losing Moxie. But having dozens of eyes look at him?

He loathes that.

This is why he fits so well in the invisible boy's bones.

But when going to a party with the De Laineys, there's no escape from the volunteered honest appraisal.

Mr De Lainey is in the kitchen making gingerbread men with Toby, and Jack sits on the bench, legs swinging, on his phone. He tends to be glued to it when he actually has it. Six pairs of eyes immediately lock on Sam.

'Whoa,' Jack says, 'the eighteenth-century circus just arrived.'

Mr De Lainey wipes his floury hands on a towel. 'Sam! You look incredible. Moxie and you made this?'

Sam nods and looks down at himself to avoid their eyes.

The waistcoat is marvellous. It's burgundy and rust and charcoal and gold. Hundreds of thin strips of material are sewn so the colours merge in a rich ombre. It folds over his chest, six mismatched buttons on either side. And it's slim fitting. Sam didn't even argue about the tightness, mostly because he isn't painfully thin with protruding bones any more.

But the secret of his outfit is a key strung around his neck and tucked deep behind his shirt. No one will know. He needs it. More than ever, with the image of Avery walking away replaying every time he closes his eyes.

'You look like a particularly fine gentleman,' Mr De Lainey says.

No one has ever called Sam a gentleman before.

He wonders if Avery would laugh at that and then he feels sick – knowing that after tonight he tells Moxie everything and this summer ends. Aching, because he could face it if Avery was beside him. And there's that constant whisper deep in his bones that says maybe Sam and his hitting and unattainable dreams is the reason Avery is always leaving.

He can't think about it right now.

Moxie flies down the stairs in a rain of hair ties and buttons and an explosion of hair. Her eyes are wild and there's a comb clamped between her teeth. She frantically dumps herself on the bottom of the staircase and skewers bobby pins covered in white flowers into her braid.

'We're going to be late.' She rips open another packet of bobby pins and they scatter over the stairs.

Jack doesn't look up from his phone. 'The sun's not fully down yet. Chill, sis.'

Sam hides his smile and folds himself behind Moxie on the stairs. The first time they sat like this, positions were reversed and Sam was about to be scalped. Now they're always somewhat sandwiched together, her tucked against him while she whispers a joke, or him resting his chin on her shoulder while she tells him her wishes and fears.

He will never get tired of leaning on her while she leans on him.

Jeremy catapults down the stairs and vaults Sam and Moxie at the bottom. He skids into the kitchen wearing boxers and a collared shirt patterned with pineapples.

'Does it look OK?' His eyes are possibly more wild than Moxie's.

'No,' says Jack.

'What have you been doing all this time?' Moxie says. 'You don't even have hair to fuss over.'

Jeremy is too flustered to react. He fixes a few buttons and looks anxiously at his father.

Mr De Lainey pops raisins in his mouth. 'Well.' He pauses. 'Well ... you need pants.'

Jeremy looks down. 'Oh, yeah.'

'And a different shirt,' Jack adds, stealing gingerbread. 'Because we're identical and I'm not letting my face walk around a pivotal social event with that shirt on.'

Jeremy casts a desperate look at Moxie.

'Don't you also have that really nice salmon shirt?' Moxie stabs bobby pins in her hair.

Jeremy nods several times and bolts back upstairs. 'OK. Salmon. I need to wear a salmon. OK.'

Moxie glances at Jack. 'Does he have a new crush? Is that why he's flapping?'

Jack shrugs. 'Why are you asking me about his f— um, *frick fracking* crushes?'

'Did you just say *frick fracking*?' Mr De Lainey says.

'No.' Jack puts his phone behind his back. 'I'm not speaking again unless I'm talking about the Lord Jesus Christ, can I get an amen?'

'Amen,' says Moxie.

Their father sighs and looks very old.

Sam nudges Moxie with his knee. 'Are you going to show them?'

A proud spark flashes behind Moxie's eyes and she pops off the steps. 'Dad? Watching?'

She stalks to the centre of the room and raises her arms above her head. Her dress is yellow cotton, the bodice embroidered with half a million flowers. It looks like any other nice dress – knee length with a flared skirt and tulle peeking below the hem to give it 'body' as Moxie informed him. Whatever that means.

But the dress has a secret.

Moxie glances at Sam and he knows his smile is stupidly happy, but he can't help it.

She spins.

The skirt flares out to a perfect circle. The soft yellow panels peel open to reveal an explosion of colours. Rainbow stripes spin around her, each of the hidden folds laced with sequins and buttons to catch the light.

She is the sun and her eyes burn stars.

She stops spinning and her skirts twist and still around her, yellow cloth falling back to hide the hidden rainbow panels. Her smile is glory and pride and infectious delight.

Mr De Lainey looks like he's about to cry. 'Moxie, darling, you're *beautiful*. I'm taking a picture. Everyone on the stairs! And someone get Dash and the babies so I can have a family photo for once.'

Sam slips quietly out of the way.

The De Lainey kids assemble with fake groans – all chocolate-brown hair and summer-kissed skin and cheeks flushed with golden smiles. They shuffle and poke each other. Jeremy leans on Grady. Dash picks up Toby. A stray curl falls over Moxie's eyes.

Mr De Lainey has a phone in hand for the photo

but then pauses, looks over his shoulder and finds Sam. They share a smile.

And in that moment Sam's heart is so full it hurts.

It really, really hurts.

He can't lose this.

CHAPTER 30

The beach is a fairyland of lights like broken stars.

As Grady's jeep curves down the road along the bluffs, everyone's eyes fill with twilight and bonfires and rows of fairy lights. Cars are parked on the sand and an entire universe of people mills around. They're on the edge of town to hide the fact bonfires on the beach aren't strictly legal.

'It's mostly kids from school,' Grady says. 'And their friends and friends of friends. The rich ones started it. Rich kids get away with a lot.'

Sam won't argue.

They pull into an overcrowded car park and strike out for the sand together. Sam ignores his tightening lungs. He normally only enters crowds to lift wallets, and after weeks sprawled in the butter-yellow house, he's not used to the crush.

As they move into the mess of people, the sound hits – the roar and crackle of the bonfire, yells and shrieked laughs, people scraping coolers full of ice and drinks across the sand, a revving engine, music booming from one of the cars with speakers set up in the back.

Everything clashes together. Loud. Fast. Overwhelmingly excited.

Don't freak out. Just don't.

No one knows you. There is no way anyone here will recognise you.

Jack and Jeremy head for the cars, talking very seriously about drinking versus how much they like life.

'If we have one beer now,' Jack says, 'and then drink fifty buckets of water, Dad won't know.'

'He'll look into our eyes and *know*,' Jeremy says. 'Anyway, why are you saying "we"? I'm not your sheep.'

'Like you don't do everything I do.' Jack slings an arm around Jeremy's neck. 'Loser.'

The crowd swallows them.

Grady lays a hand on Sam and Moxie's shoulders. 'Time to be the boring older brother for a second.'

Moxie rolls her eyes. 'You're too old to be here anyway.'

Grady gives her a playful shove. 'I'm nineteen, not ninety. And all my old school friends still come. Also Isla's here.' He clears his throat. He's wearing contacts and he's not holding a book, which seems wild for him. 'So no drinking.'

'Obviously.' Moxie folds her arms.

'Don't wander off someplace dark.' Grady shudders. 'Because I'm not explaining that to Dad.'

'Now you're just being embarrassing.'

'And probably hold Sam's hand because I think he's about to faint.'

Moxie whips around to Sam who manages a thin and unamused smile. 'Ha,' he says.

Moxie slips her hand into his. 'This rule I can do. But seriously, are you OK, Sam? You do look peaky.'

Oh, totally fine. He's just avoided people for a solid year and now he's voluntarily catapulted himself into the middle of them.

'I'm fine.'

He is not fine. He is at a freaking party when he should be hiding. His brother is falling off the edge of the world because Sam's not there for him. He's about to lose everything. And there's a lump the size of the universe caught in his throat.

He is not fine.

Grady pats Sam's head and then his eyes light up at something behind them. 'Must run. Don't do anything illegal.' He speeds off in the direction of a girl with an airy pink dress.

'That's his girlfriend, Isla,' Moxie says. 'Don't worry, every time he mentions he has a girlfriend I get shocked all over again. She's super gorgeous too. Obviously has no standards. Anyway.' She nudges Sam with her hip. 'C'mon. I want you to meet someone.'

She tugs him into the crowd.

They circuit a large group of people by the bonfire and get away from the cars and the music that's set to level: 'make your ears bleed'. People shout Moxie's name and compliment her dress. She gives small waves and shouts a pleased 'Thank you!' now and then. Everyone else wears jeans and halter-necked dresses and collared shirts, everything in expensive cuts and glittering. Quite a few are barefoot. Quite a few are drunk.

Absolutely no one is dressed like Moxie and Sam.

Absolutely everyone keeps looking at them.

Then Moxie's hand tightens on his and she raises her free arm in the air. 'Kirby!'

There's a squeal from a group ahead of them and a girl breaks free and pelts across the sand. Sam has to – reluctantly – release Moxie so she can collide with this incoming comet of excitement. They exchange frenzied cries: 'I missed you!' and 'You look so beautiful!'

He stands back awkwardly.

Moxie twines her arms around her friend and spins her to face Sam. 'This is he.' She has the smugness of someone who's discussed Sam often. Behind his back.

Oh, great.

'Hi,' says Sam.

Kirby is frighteningly tall, with dozens of braids woven with rainbow ribbons and brown skin and the most delighted smile. Her wrists are covered in bangles that jingle every time she wildly throws her arms around – which is a lot – and Sam's so focused on their gleaming shine that he's not prepared for the moment when Kirby decides it's a great idea to hug him too.

He gets crushed and hopes he only whimpered in his head.

'It's confirmed,' Kirby says. 'He's adorable.'

Moxie looks pleased and reaches over to tug Sam's waistcoat. 'And he helped me sew. He did quite a lot actually.'

'Keep him,' Kirby says. 'Keep him for ever, Moxie.'

Moxie leans her head on Sam's shoulder for a second. 'I will.'

The circle Kirby was with now expands to devour Moxie. Girls from her class hug her and comment on the dress and she performs a small twirl on request. Her cheeks flush and she talks fifty miles a minute. This happy-Moxie is a sparkling explosion of life.

Sam steps back a little. It's all this: people, the noise, the close crush of bodies that smell of lilac perfume and coconut shampoo, the popping soft drink cans, the crash of the sea, and their loudly happy laughs. It scares him.

They're not marks and he's not stealing.

He doesn't fit here.

His fingers stray to his neck, to the key on a string, pressed warm against his chest. He imagines if he gets lost all he needs to do is pull out the key and say, *Proof I belong to the De Laineys. Take me home.*

A warm hand slips into his and he flinches before he sees Moxie peering up at him. Firelight dances in her eyes.

'Do you want to go?'

Sam glances over at the cars where Jeremy and Jack are snatches of spiky hair and a salmon shirt. They definitely don't look ready to go.

'I'm fine.' He tries to smile. He fails.

Kirby glides past with her eyes set on the boys in the cars. 'Is it all right if I use your incredible costumes as a conversation opener with anyone who's cute since you have Mister Sad-Eyed Gorgeous now and I'm alone in the world? Good, thanks, Moxie.'

'Hey!' Moxie sticks her tongue out at Kirby's fast disappearing back.

'Sad-eyed?' Sam says.

'In a sweet and adorable way.' Moxie turns and her fingers find his jaw, so light on his skin, and he shivers. Just a little. She smiles at that. 'Dance with me. Then we'll tell my brothers we need to go get ice cream, because I know you're an anxious wreck here.'

'I said I'm fine—'

'A considerate but very obvious lie.' She takes Sam's hand and drags him to the dancers.

The ocean whispers of seaweed and salt in the background while everyone dances. Music punches out of the speakers. Sand churns. Arms wave in the air as sweaty hair clings to foreheads.

Firelight heats Sam's back and the sea breeze strokes his face.

They dance.

Moxie is all twirling arms and spinning rainbow skirt. Most of her hair falls from the braid and little white flowers cling to the damp strands. She catches Sam's hands and he whirls her around. He can't dance. He's all elbows and knees.

He doesn't care.

Let him embarrass himself. Just so long as he's with Moxie.

The song ends and Moxie collapses against him. He puts his arms around her waist and they breathe raggedly together.

'Your hair is glittering.' Moxie runs her fingers across his scalp and shows him her speckled hand.

'Permanently,' he says. 'Thanks for that, by the way.'

'You're welcome. At least this way I'll always be able to find you.'

His smile is sad. It's like the entire night sings goodbye.

He runs his thumb over her bottom lip. 'Can we stop talking now?'

Her laugh is a burst of stardust.

He kisses her.

Maybe maybe *maybe* nothing matters past this party and this beach and this kiss. Moxie will be ablaze from all the praise of her sewing. Sam will hold her. He'll figure out a way to stay, to make Avery safe.

It'll all be fine.

Moxie sighs into his shoulder. She starts to say something, or maybe kiss him again, but a frown folds her face and she pulls away to look over his shoulder.

Sam turns.

Kirby is jogging towards them, face pinched.

A boy storms just ahead, fury in his jaw and eyes of murder.

'Hey!' he shouts. 'Is that Sammy Lou?'

Sam's hands drop away from Moxie.

The earth suddenly splits, a chasm caving downward like a fist just punched the world out from beneath him. The black hole takes everything – his heartbeat, his mind, the stars, his Moxie.

He's alone, he's just a shell, as the boy grabs the throat of his shirt. 'You tried to kill my cousin, *you piece of shit.*'

CHAPTER 31

Moxie shoves between the boy and Sam so fast they both stumble backwards.

The boy releases Sam's throat.

He still can't breathe.

'What the hell?' Moxie snaps. 'Don't touch him. Who are you?'

Kirby arrives, breathless. 'Um, OK, whoa. Let's calm down. Moxie, this is Griffin. Erm, Griffin ... Moxie. And Sam is ...'

Griffin's lips peel back in a snarl. 'You have some nerve showing up here, you twisted little freak.'

Blood rushes into Sam's ears. Or maybe it's the ocean. He can't quite hear through the roar. He can't quite see.

He needs to get out of here.

Run, Sammy.

Moxie's body coils beside him, smile gone as she stares daggers at Griffin. 'You want to explain yourself? Or do I just start yelling for my brothers? I have a *lot* of brothers.'

'Oh, I'll explain.' Griffin stabs a finger against Sam's chest so hard he flinches. 'Did you know this kid is wanted for assault?'

Moxie slaps his hand away since Sam hasn't moved a muscle to defend himself. 'I'm pretty sure,' she says coldly, 'you have the wrong person.'

'Yeah, sure I do. Sammy Lou? His brother is Avery and he's got some sort of spastic disease.' Griffin mimes one of Avery's hand-flapping stims, his eyes cruel.

Sam's stomach knots. 'He doesn't have a disease and there's nothing wrong with him.'

Griffin ignores him. 'They go to that public school on the south side. Well, *went*. They'd better be thrown out by now since he nearly beat my cousin to death.'

'He did not.' Moxie's fury rolls off her in waves. 'And don't talk like that about his brother. That's the most ableist crap I've ever heard.'

She's defending Avery.

She doesn't even know Avery.

This is the Moxie he loves.

Griffin barely glances at her. 'My cousin was in hospital for *days* after this bastard punched his face in. West is in so much therapy now. You know who this kid is? He's a raging psychopath.'

Sam looks at his hands.

They shake.

He curls them into fists and he can feel the blood again, slick through his knuckles as he knelt on the ground in the school yard, one hand around West's throat, the other coming down again and again and again

and again again again again againagainagain again—

There was blood.

Avery was screaming.

They'd slammed his arm in a door and broken it, those bullies. Those stupid, goddamn bullies.

That'll stop you twitching.

All because Avery thought they were his friends. Following them around, talking nonstop, flapping his hands in excitement as he tried to *fit in*.

They strung him along and then cut him down.

Sam was going to kill them.

He was going to kill them all.

The lights on the beach flare too brightly and slam him back to the sand where this boy Griffin is red-faced and yelling.

Moxie turns to Sam. Her face is closed, unreadable, eyes obsidian in the dark.

Kirby mumbles something like, 'Yeah, um, talking to this guy was a bad idea. I'll get your brothers, Moxie.' She runs off.

Moxie reaches out a hand, but Sam is so far away she can't possibly reach him. She would need a boat and a bridge made of moons to find him again.

'You should be in jail!' Griffin shouts.

People are gathering now. Griffin's friends flood around him, tall and muscular, eyes full of fury and hungry to punish.

Sam stares. His whole body pulses with the memory of blood on his hands.

'He tried to – h-h-h-hurt Avery.' Sam doesn't look at anyone. 'I was s-saving my brother.'

Griffin spits and turns to his friends. 'Call the cops.'

'No!' Moxie cries. 'What are you … how – Sam, talk to me?' Fear trips over her face.

'What else do I need to say?' Griffin snaps. 'He beat the shit out of my cousin and you're defending him. Get the hell away, girl.'

Then Griffin grabs the shoulder of Sam's waistcoat and smashes his fist into Sam's stomach.

Moxie screams.

Sam drops to his knees.

Air explodes out of his lungs and doesn't come back.

People shout and move around now, too close, too hot, too loud. Yells collide and someone calls out frantically for Moxie. The knot of people tightens.

Griffin towers over him, all coiled muscles and a watch that gleams gold in the flickering firelight.

Sam holds his stomach. He tastes tears.

Why didn't you *run*?

Griffin grabs Sam's hair and tips his head back, raising his fist again. For a second Sam just stares at those burning eyes—

And then Moxie shoves Griffin and knocks him off balance.

'Don't you *dare* hit him,' she shouts.

Griffin staggers a few steps and then spins on Moxie.

Hands shoot out. Snatch at shirts. *Stop* is whispered.

Griffin closes the distance between him and Moxie with a step and a roar and he twists, ramming his shoulder into Moxie.

She gives the smallest cry.

And falls.

Sam's world speeds up.

You do not touch Moxie. You do not ever ever ever touch Moxie.

He springs up in a churn of sand, his fingers curling to fists. To do what they know best.

And then he's on Griffin like a shot, knuckles on flesh, on bone.

Hit.

He kicks Griffin's legs out from under him and they fall, Griffin roaring, Sam deadly and silent. His fist comes down, his knees press into Griffin's chest to pin him. He doesn't think.

He hits.

In a very small corner of his mind he is dying.

The earth rushes around him, spinning fast, trying to throw him off into the stars.

Behind him a girl screams, her face a broken mirror of agony.

Stop.

He should. He has to stop. *Save Avery. Where's Avery?*

'*Sam.*'

He can't he can't he can't stop

stopstopstopstopstopstopstopstopstopstopstop
stopstopstopstopstopstopstopstopstopstopstop
stopstopstopstopstopstopstopstopstopstopstop
stopstopstopstopstopstopstopstopstopstopstop
stopstopstopstopstopstopstopstopstopstopstop
stopstopstopstopstopstopstopstopstopstopstop
stopstop—

Hands hook under the shoulders of Sam's waistcoat and yank him off. There are bodies everywhere, tall as mountains that block out the light. There's sand in his mouth, in his eyes. There's blood. Sam tries to breathe but he hasn't lungs any more.

'What's *wrong* with you?'

'Someone get help!'

'Sam, *what*—' The last is Jeremy, now clutching Sam's arm.

Sam jerks away.

Griffin holds his broken nose and roars.

Their faces blur and spin before him. They are red teeth and burned-out eyes. They are horror and disgust and rage.

Sam shoves through them and they back out of his way.

Scared of him.

Just like he was so scared of his father.

Only one girl doesn't move. Her dress is a flood of sunbeams and her mouth is a terrified twist.

He runs past her.

Run, just run. Just run for ever.

He scrabbles up the bank, his feet hitting the road so fast he trips and falls and rips his jeans. It hurts and he's glad. He's so glad. He wants to hurt. He wants someone to pin him down and beat the living daylights out of him.

He deserves it.

You despicable boy, his aunt said. She's right. They're all right. He's just like his father. He should be in prison.

He picks himself up and runs down the road. Runs until his undone shoelaces twist about his legs and he falls in the long seagrass by the highway. He pulls out Avery's phone. *Fix all your problems*. He's shaking so hard he has to hold it with two hands.

The sea wind whips his hair and he tastes blood and salt and ruin.

'Vin?' He's crying. 'Vin, let me talk to Avery. P-p-please, he has to come get me.'

The voice on the other end is smooth and calm as cold glass. 'Avery's busy right now.'

No.

No.

'P-please.' Sam's voice jumps so high it cracks and he can barely get the words out. 'Please, d-don't do this. I need him. *I need him.*'

'OK, OK, calm down, kid. I can barely understand you. What happened?'

'I h-h-hit ... I just h-hit—' Sam shatters. He's sobbing now, the phone slipping against his cheek.

'Tell me where you are. I'll come get you.'

'I want Avery. Please, I w-want Avery.'

'I'll get him for you, kid. Just hold on.'

It's an impossible command. Sam has nothing left to hold on to.

CHAPTER 32

A car pulls up in front of Sam and headlights blaze white-hot in his eyes. Sam covers his face.

The driver's door pops open and Vin gets out. She's crisp and fresh as always, hair neatly styled in waves over one shoulder. She wears high boots that crunch gravel as she strides towards Sam. Kneels down. Tips Sam's chin up.

There's blood on his hands.

'Is it yours?' she says.

Sam shakes his head. He's hollowed out.

Vin hauls Sam to his feet. Keeps soft hands on his neck, on his shoulders, and propels him into the car. Sam collapses on the passenger seat, draws his legs up, tucks his head down.

Vin gets in and revs the engine. She pulls a chocolate bar out of the console and slaps it in Sam's hand. 'Eat.'

Sam turns his head away.

'I'm not messing about, kid. You're in shock.' Vin snatches the chocolate back and rips the plastic. 'I won't take you to Avery until you eat it.'

Tears spill down Sam's cheeks. 'I'm going to be sick.'

'No, you're not. You're taking a bite. Right now. Go.' She revs the engine again. 'I don't want to hang around here. Do you?'

Sam takes a bite.

He tastes blood and no chocolate at all. But he takes another bite and another as Vin pulls the car back on to the highway and speeds into town. Vin only slows down for traffic lights and a cop car pulls past and drives off the way they came. She doesn't comment.

Chocolate melts and smears on Sam's fingers. He wipes it on his jeans. He looks at his waistcoat, Moxie's amazing, detailed work. Her pride.

Bloodstains stare back.

'So Avery's working,' Vin says finally.

Robbing houses. Armed burglary.

'Why aren't ... you working?' Sam's voice sounds numb and thin even to him.

'I organise.' Vin shifts gears and the car shoots through an intersection. 'I plan. I say jump and people jump and the job goes perfectly. Chocolate help?'

Sam didn't taste it. But he's not shaking any more. He's not sure if it was the sugar or having something to do that wasn't cycling the image of his fists coming down. He leans his head against the window.

'Good,' says Vin, voice elegant and easy,

'because I want you to do something for me.'

Sam's stomach flips. 'I can't ... *please*. I just want Avery.'

'You do this, and you get Avery. I'll put you both up in a motel so you can hide for a few days. I'll sort it all out, you hear me? It goes away when I want it to.'

It goes away.

The sob comes out unbidden. Sam presses his arm over his mouth.

How much goes away? Tonight?

The whole summer?

Moxie?

'You just have to climb through a window, flip off an alarm, and open a door. Nothing else.' Vin spins the steering wheel. Streetlights flash in Sam's eyes. 'Then you sit in the car, I do a bit of work, and we go pick up Avery.'

She flips off the headlights and slides the car into an empty underground car park. She pulls up and shuts off the engine.

'I can't,' Sam whispers. Can he even walk right now? He is an empty pit, the darkness drained to puddles of tears and despair and hate hate hate.

Vin turns on him, her face a blank hollow in the shadows except for perfect red lips. 'You do it, or I throw you to the cops. Help me and I fix everything. It's not a decision.'

Sam swallows.

'Get out of the car,' Vin says.

Sam gets out of the car.

They walk three blocks. Vin keeps them in the shadows, avoiding storefronts where there might be cameras. She has a black duffle bag slung over a shoulder. Sam has to admit – Vin knows what she's doing. There's a sense of safety in that. Comfort. If someone else points the way, says take this, sit here, keep your mouth shut now – you get to be safe.

This is why Avery keeps working for her, isn't it? He wants to be safe, same as Sam. But he found his *safe* among thorns and poison and Sam dug his out of warm earth and sunlight.

Part of Sam's brain shuts off, the part that reminds him that he would've kept hitting if Jeremy hadn't pulled him off. *He doesn't want to be like this*. He focuses on Vin's heeled boots. Follow. Step here. Keep quiet.

don't

think.

They climb a fence and drop into a small car park lined with banksias and lavender. A building looms up like a brick mountain, a single light at the back door. Sam has no idea what time it is. Midnight?

'What is this place?' His voice is low.

Vin keeps them in the dark mouth of the fence and then crouches to unzip the duffle. 'Art gallery.

They've got a piece I've wanted for months.' Vin pulls out a black jacket and shrugs it on. Obviously with her loose hair and heeled boots, she wasn't planning on a job tonight. 'I have a contact overseas. It's an easy ten grand.'

'Ten grand?' Sam stares.

Vin's red lips twitch. 'You get a cut, little angel. Avery says you're obsessed with having a house. We can work something out. If you stay on. Keep working for me.'

Sam shifts his gaze away. He wouldn't – he can't—

He doesn't want this.

He doesn't want to admit he would fit.

He wants to curl up in Moxie's arms and eat waffles that smell of cinnamon and sunshine. He wants to forget what he's good at. Fists and theft.

Vin points to a drainpipe at the corner of the building. 'See that window? Bathroom. It's the only one without a locked screen and it'll push out. I've checked.'

'You want me to climb a drainpipe?'

'Don't pretend you can't. Avery tells me everything, remember?'

About the days they spent as kids, scaling the walls of their aunt's house, using drainpipes and cracks in the bricks to get on to the roof so they could vault on to the trampoline? So they could fly. Avery shouldn't tell stuff like that. It belongs to him and Sam.

'I can.' Sam's mouth is dry.

Vin tells him which halls to take, which staircase, which door leads to the back entrance and the alarm. She gives him a pair of thin gloves.

While she talks, she pulls a knife sheath from her duffle and straps it on to her thigh.

Shivers arch up and down Sam's spine and he has to grit his jaw to stop his teeth chattering.

It's not cold.

He's scared.

'You just flip the off switch,' she says. 'It'll turn off the light and camera and the alarm too. Then unlock the back door. Use your phone for light. Easy, kid, so easy. I'll be waiting there, and you head to the car afterwards.' She frowns and reaches for her vibrating pocket. She tugs out her phone and frowns at the screen. 'I'll take this. You got it?'

Sam nods.

He tugs on the gloves while Vin leans against the fence and swears quietly but viciously into the phone. Even Sam winces. He doesn't catch the name, but part of him wonders if it might be Avery. Don't think about it now, Sammy.

Take a breath. Focus. The building is tall and the window looks impossibly tiny.

He glances back.

Vin makes an angry flicking motion.

Sam runs.

He keeps away from the light, from the cameras, and reaches the drainpipe. His fingers crawl across bricks.

He climbs.

The tips of his shoes dig into the space between bricks and he scrambles for the pipe. It shudders under his weight, but he just moves faster.

Fast, boy, go fast.

He gets to the top and wedges his knees against the pipe and the wall. One foot snakes out to rest on the tiny window ledge. His heart crashes hard in his chest.

Don't look down. Don't look for Vin.

His gloved fingers find the screen edge and pry it back.

After this, he gets Avery. He gets to hide. He gets to—

never see the De Lainey family again

The screen pops free and falls. It crashes to the floor inside. The sound is an explosion over the empty car park.

Sam risks a glance over his shoulder, his body trembling with the effort to cling up here. He can't see Vin.

He grabs the window ledge, sucks in his breath, and pulls himself in.

It's tight.

His shoulders only just wedge through. The buttons on his waistcoat catch and then one rips off, falling soundlessly to the cement below.

Don't think about falling.

Sam wriggles in, his hands reaching out for the toilet and then resting flat on it. His legs slide the rest of the way and then he's doing a handstand on the lid.

He flips down, silent as death.

Silent except for the pulse under his collar bones saying *don't do this don't do this don't you dare do this*.

He walks the halls. Avoids the cameras. Gets to the back door. His shoes give soft pats on the tiles and he breathes too loudly. He finds the small white box and uses the light of his phone to flip the lid and stare at the switches.

Off.

He shuts down the light, the camera, the alarms.

Once he unlocks that door, this place is Vin's. This isn't spare change from a wallet and fistfuls of silver pieces. This is real and it's big.

Sam looks down at his shaking hands and slowly, carefully, he peels off the gloves. His fingers are red, a poisoned stain.

Moxie screams '*Sam*' in his ears. Not angry – frightened, desperate. A scream like someone holding on to a cliff that crumbles beneath their fingertips.

He feels hot. Sick. He's going to throw up.

He slides down the wall, holding his face. Tears spill between his fingers.

If he does this, it's the beginning, not the end. Vin will find a way to trap him, because that's the kind of person she is – and if she threatens Avery, Sam will be a broken puppet in her fist and she *knows it*.

And he will never see Moxie again.

No. He did that himself.

Sam isn't sure how long he sits like this, knees up to his chin, face buried, waiting for the silent sobs to stop racking his shoulders. The doorknob jiggles and then there's an urgent hiss.

'Sammy.'

Sam hugs his legs tighter.

'*Sammy*. Open it. Are you there? Did something go wrong?'

Sam picks up his phone with trembling fingers.

'*Sammy*.'

He turns it on, his brain frozen over because if he stops to think, if he hesitates, he can't do it. Won't do it. *Can't can't can't—*

The doorknob rattles again and Vin swears. Feet scuffle and then Vin's voice comes under the door, low and venomous. 'Sammy, if you are in there and doing this on purpose, you can't even imagine what I will do to you. Open – this – door.'

Sam hits *dial*.

Emergency picks up.

'Please,' Sam whispers, giving the address of the art gallery. 'It's being robbed. The thief is armed.' He's hit with a flurry of questions, but his eyes slither back to the door and the scratching of lock picks. He's out of time. 'She's going to kill me.' He ends the call.

The lock picks break off their careful scratching

and then feet scuffle. More than one set. Sam's heart skips a beat.

Voices sift under the door, low and then rising with agony.

Vin's is acid. 'I told you to go back to the car.'

'You told me where you were. I had to come! You have my little brother in there!'

The voice is knives and panic.

Avery.

No. Avery can't be here. Sam just called *the goddamn police*. He crawls forward, his mind blank on what to do next. He isn't thinking. He's just trying to stay upright when what he most wants is to curl into a ball and stop. Cease. Just let there have never been a Sammy Lou.

He leans his cheek against the cold door. Which is how he hears the cracking slap and Avery's cry.

Then—

sirens.

He has to get Avery out of here.

Nothing else matters.

Shoes scrape the cement outside and their voices cut off as the sirens blare closer. Sam flips the lock.

Avery's voice is high and trembling. 'Who would know—'

'The kid,' Vin snaps. 'The kid has a phone. I'm going to kill him.'

Sam throws the door open and explodes forward, all broken buttons and bruised knuckles and panic pulsing through his veins. Avery has a hand cupped to his lip, blood dripping down his chin, and his eyes meet Sam's with shock.

Sam doesn't stop. He flies past him, feet eating up cement as he makes for the fence.

Blue and red lights flash on the street.

'Run!' Vin gasps and pelts after Sam.

There's a brief hesitation and then Avery takes off too.

Sam doesn't slow for the fence, he just leaps and catches hold of the edge, toppling over like a boneless rag doll. He hits the ground on all fours and then he's up again, streaking through a yard and then curving out on a parallel street.

He runs.

They pound after him.

Chasing him or just getting away?

His lungs scream.

Avery pulls ahead of Vin and gasps Sam's name, but the rest of his words are stolen by the crunch of gravel as they dive down an alley and climb over a gate wedged between a pub and a closed antique shop. Sam hits the ground and keeps running. But Avery trips.

And then Vin is on top of him.

Sam skids to a stop at the other end of the alley.

Vin has Avery's arm. She smashes her elbow into his face and then drags him towards Sam and the darker end of the alley. Dim streetlight illuminates them – Avery folding up to protect himself, Vin growing taller in the shadows, lips twisted with vengeance.

'You dropped the bag of money, didn't you?' Vin says. 'Our whole night's work.' She throws Avery on the ground.

Sam takes a step forward. Another. Another. Vin's lips peel back in a vicious smile.

'Come over here, Sammy.' She puts a boot on Avery's back, pressing down. 'Come here and let's talk about what happens when you *mess with me*.' And then before Sam can speak, can act, can think, Vin raises her boot and stomps down hard on the small of Avery's back.

Avery's cry cuts the numb walls around Sam.

Red heat pours into Sam's eyes.

'NO.' He springs forward, fists curved to swing, but Vin is ready.

She ducks and then catches Sam's arm, twisting it so sharply Sam trips and chokes on a cry. Vin slams Sam into the wall and his head cracks against bricks. He sags to his knees, hands to his head.

Vin picks something up from the piles of alley rubbish.

A broken piece of plywood spiked with bent rusted nails.

Sam tries to scream but the world tips sideways and his head throbs and he can't even see straight.

Avery scrabbles to get up. 'Vin, wait. Please. I-I-I—'

Vin cracks the pole across Avery's stomach.

He falls back down with a cry.

Sam struggles to get up, grabbing at the wall for support. He needs it to stop spinning, *please stop spinning*. Vin sees him trying to move and flips the wood from hand to hand. 'You're next, Sammy. But I think it'll hurt you more to watch this first.'

She swings the wood again. It catches Avery across the shoulder blades with sickening *thwack*. Avery lets out a sob, curling into a ball and covering his head. He never runs. Never fights.

No.

No.

Fear fades from Sam's chest and rage pours in, enough to level mountains and explode seas. Sam leaps forward.

Avery's sob is broken.

Sam's cry is blood.

He throws himself at Vin, fists and teeth and torn lungs and murderous eyes. His punches are quick and aimed perfectly – kidney, nose, throat. And before Vin can grab him, Sam hooks his leg around hers and sends them both smashing into the alley wall. She lands a punch on Sam's jaw. But they fall and he's atop her now, knee in her throat. He raises his fist to her face. Twice in one night his soul spills red.

But he can't

do

this.

Sam keeps his slashed knuckles raised, Vin pinned, her eyes on him like an ice storm. A sob ravages Sam's chest. He doesn't … he doesn't … want …

His arm shakes, frozen.

He doesn't want to do this any more.

Vin's fingers claw at Sam's waistcoat.

There's a snick of metal slipping from a sheath and a smile curls her bloody lips.

A sob racks Sam's lungs and he slowly lowers his fist. He's not going to hit any more. He's not. 'You're never going to touch my brother again or I'll—'

His words snap off unfinished, because there's a flash of silver and a punch to his stomach.

His world shudders. He looks down.

The knife slips out of his stomach, red as cherry syrup, black as a long kiss in the dark.

He opens his mouth. Chokes.

Pain.

One bright spear of pain.

Vin shoves Sam off and now he's on his knees in the alley, his hand straying to his stomach. He tries to get up, but his shoelaces tangle and his legs buckle.

Behind him, Avery wails. High-pitched and childish and terrified.

Vin drops into a crouch in front of Sam. The world spins, a carousel of broken stars and blood-streaked knives. Vin's face fills his whole vision.

'And just think, when you're dead, I'll come back for your brother and I will carve my name in his skin before I kill him. That's a promise, Sammy Lou.'

She puts four fingers on to Sam's forehead – and pushes.

Sam falls.

He falls for ever.

He

     is

            going

       to

   die.

Avery catches his head before he hits the cement. Avery's arms surround him, pulling Sam to his chest and thrusting his hands over the blood gushing out of his stomach. It runs thick and red. So much of it. It doesn't really hurt. Sam tries to tell Avery that.

Nothing hurts.

It's OK. Don't cry, Avery.

'S-s-stop.' Avery puts one hand to Sam's face, holding him, holding him tighter than anyone ever has. 'I n-n-need you. Sammy! You c-c-can't ...' His voice breaks.

'Avery.' Sam's fist curls in Avery's shirt. The alley is quiet. Vin is gone. 'It's not bad.'

'No, no, no, Sammy.' Avery tucks his chin over Sam's head, rocking violently now. His hands flap and spin and jerk, desperate to put pressure on Sam's stomach, desperate to move. His stims get tangled when he's upset.

Sam is so very good at making people upset.

'Stay awake, Sammy.' Avery looks over his shoulder and screams for help down the alley.

No one hears. No one comes.

Sam tries to cough but it hurts too much. The pain is here, finally. He's cold. He has turned to ice in Avery's arms and he's afraid if Avery holds him any tighter he'll shatter. He wants to say this is nice, how Avery's hugging him – but when he opens his mouth, he starts to cry.

'I'll buy you a house, Sammy.' Avery pushes

hair out of Sam's eyes, smearing blood over Sam's cheeks. 'I'll buy you a hundred houses. I swear, I'll do a-a-a-anything. I'll go – I'll go get help.'

Sam's fingers claw Avery's shirt. 'Don't leave.'

But Avery's already letting go. Curving Sam's body into a ball as he lays him down.

'I'll be back in just a second.' Avery's voice is hoarse. 'I'll – I'll be back.'

His feet pound the alley, his screams for help already hitting the walls.

Then it's quiet.

Sam tries to put the pieces of himself together. Tries, with cotton and screws and wishes. But doesn't he deserve this?

He pushes fingers to his stomach and his breath goes out in a wet, short gasp. His ribs folds inwards as everything inside him shudders.

The boy turns invisible.

As he should be.

CHAPTER 34

They try to pry his fingers open.

He's too weak to stop them.

But if they take it away, the threads will snap and he won't be able to get back up.

'No, wait!' Avery's voice is panicked, words tripping over themselves. 'Don't take it. You'll break him if you take it.'

'OK, son, calm down. We've got this. We're doing what's best for your brother.'

Avery's words catch between a scream and a roar, 'Then don't *take it off him*. He needs it! Listen to me, listen, just—'

They leave Sam's fingers alone.

'What's he holding anyway?'

'A key. Can you go see how the cop's doing with the brother? We might have to sedate him.'

Sam's lips part, but he can't dig words out of his pockets to arrange them in a pleasing display for people to understand.

They need to understand the key.

If lost, please return to the De Laineys.

BEFORE

Sammy is fourteen and full of broken pieces.

Rain slicks down his face, plasters his thin T-shirt to knobbly, shivering shoulders as he stands in front of Aunt Karen's house in the dark. He's been here for a long time.

If he goes in, she'll call the cops.

After what *he did* to those boys at school.

Her car is in the driveway and the TV flashes behind half-closed curtains. The thin smell of tuna bake curls out of the cracked windows and he thinks he hears crying.

Or maybe that's the wind.

Or maybe that's him.

He knots frozen fingers around his shoulders and shuts his eyes tight tight tight. If he wishes hard enough, time will stop and fold backwards and he won't run across the schoolyard to the group of jeering kids and throw them aside till he sees his brother. Being smashed to pieces.

Blood and broken bone and hollowed-out eyes.

And *the screaming*.

Two seconds later and a teacher would have

been there, would have saved them.

But Sammy didn't wait and he beat that boy unconscious because how could he how could he *how could he let his brother get hurt*?

When they catch Sammy, they'll take him away. Prison. He deserves it. He always goes too far.

He'll die in prison.

He'll die without Avery.

He tells himself, a thousand times a day, that he exists for Avery, to keep him safe and hug him and calm him down and love him. Avery can't exist without Sammy—

or is it the other way

around?

Mud squelches under his shoes as he slowly crosses the yard. He ducks until he's below the window of the bedroom they share. He taps on the glass, but the rain thunders so loud how could anyone hear?

The curtain rips back and Avery's there, eyes melting pools.

'C-c-can you get my jumper?' Sammy whispers.

The curtain falls and there's a brief scuffling. Sammy turns to the front door just as it crashes open and Avery tumbles out followed by a string of shouts from Aunt Karen.

'If Sammy's there, I'm calling the cops!' she shouts. 'Come back inside, Avery. *Right now.* You'll get your cast wet. Avery? Avery!'

Avery shoots across the lawn, Sammy's

favourite yellow jacket in his hands. He has an oversized jumper on to hide how lumpy one arm is – the cast on his broken arm. Sammy expects the jacket to be tossed at him while Avery spins into frantic tears.

But Avery slams into him in a desperate hug and buries his face against his brother.

'Sammy.' It's a sob.

'Hey.' Sam clutches him, a drowning boy. 'Hey – h-hey, you'll get your cast wet. You should go back inside.' He feels the fever raging on Avery's clammy skin and the bright, unfocused look in his eyes from the pain. He's only just out of hospital.

'Are you coming in?' Rain sticks Avery's fine hair to his cheeks.

'I can't.' Sam glances desperately at the door. Has she called the cops already? 'I don't – I can't go to jail, I just *can't*. I'm going to … I'm running away.'

'OK,' Avery says. 'OK. I'm coming too.'

Sammy pulls away and grabs Avery's face, not forcing eye contact because he knows Avery hates that, just holding him tight so he knows these next words are serious. 'I won't have anywhere to live. Or sleep. Or eat. I'll … I'll steal. I'll steal houses. It'll be different every day, and uncomfortable and – everything you hate, OK?' He's crying now. Tears and rain. 'You can't do this with me.'

Avery gently slips out of Sammy's grip and pulls

the already sodden jumper over Sammy's shivering shoulders. He zips it up for his little brother and then his fingers flutter for a minute in decision.

'You. And me,' he says. 'We.'

CHAPTER 35

He's too soft, they always said.

He shifts on the pillows, his eyelids swollen and sticky. He's too tired to make a proper effort anyway and if he moves too much, he feels the clenched tightness of his stomach where he's been punched.

Wait.

Stabbed.

A chair scrapes. Sheets rustle as elbows leans forward.

His cold hand is caught up in a warm one and a small metal object is pressed into Sam's palm.

His fingers fold over it automatically.

His key.

'They took it off you during surgery. But you have it back now. It's OK, Sammy.'

Sam drags his eyes open. His face feels stung and swollen, his throat flayed raw. He pushes past the haze of pain, the cotton, the aching behind his eyes – and sees Avery.

He looks terrible. His face is cleaned, but there are butterfly stitches on his cheek and his bottom lip is a mess of scabs. But it's his eyes, his storm-blue eyes that now look like a hurricane sucked them dry and filled them up with exhaustion and terror.

Sam's eyes droop to his arm, to the IV taped there. To the bed with the hospital blankets folded over his chest. His clothes are gone. Moxie's waistcoat is gone.

He ruined it.

All her work.

She'll yell at him for six days solid for—

Oh.

There is no more Moxie. There will be no more Moxie.

'This is a hospital.' The words scratch on the way out. He wants Avery to deny it.

'Yeah,' says Avery, voice thick.

'Do they ... do they know ...'

'Yeah.' Avery tugs the blankets up higher on Sam's chest. 'I'm sorry, Sammy. I-I-I had to tell them everything.'

Oh.

Sam waits for the fear to catch up, to pound into his chest with hot irons and hooks. But he just feels numb.

'You had stitches,' Avery says. 'But it went in deep so ... surgery. It took a while. I kind of passed out so I don't know how long.' Avery fusses with the blanket again, but Sam suspects it's to distract from his flicking fingers. 'I'm supposed to get the nurse when you wake up. For painkillers. Do you hurt? How bad?'

Bad.

'I'm OK.' Sam closes his eyes. 'Did they – get Vin?'

'No.'

'She ... stabbed me?'

'She ran. And no one knows who she really is and – I couldn't say too much or they'd know what I was doing for her but – shit, Sammy.'

He's crying.

Sam puts a hand on Avery's head. He's let his hair grow so it comes just past his ears, but it's flat and wispy, soft as sunlight and feathers.

'Do they know about what I did?'

Avery grabs Sam's hand and squeezes it. 'I don't think so. Just – just don't say anything till we get a lawyer.'

'Lawyer,' Sam repeats dumbly.

Avery scrubs his eyes with the hem of his T-shirt. 'You've got some asshat of a social worker already out there.'

Sam's lips tremble.

'Sammy, what was I supposed to do? I couldn't let you die.'

He's going to jail. He's spent a year of his life stealing into houses and trying trying trying to run away, and it's over.

A small part of his heart is glad.

He's so tired.

'I c-can't let them lock you up.' Avery's voice shreds with panic. 'I can't! Sammy – I can't. I *need* you. I n-n-n-need to be with you.' He scratches at his throat, a second away from spinning out, and Sam's in no shape to catch him. 'I lied when I said I didn't. You know that, right? I lied. I lied! I LIED—'

'Hey, hey, shh. I know.' Sam stretches out his fingers, brushing Avery's wrist. 'Have you slept?'

Avery shakes his head, whole body trembling.

'Are you staying here?'

'I'm not leaving you.'

Sam chews his lips for a moment. 'Can you fit on this bed?'

There's a pause and the sounds of the hospital filter in: hums of machines, squeaking of carts in the hall, a faint consistent *drip drip* past the curtains.

'My hands are going like a psycho,' Avery says. 'I don't want to hurt—'

'Don't talk like that about yourself. Hear me? You need to move. It's OK.'

Avery whimpers.

Sam scoots over on the bed, even though it feels like punching himself in the stomach all over again. Avery hesitates a moment and then scuffs his shoes off and climbs on. The bed really isn't big enough for two, but the Lou boys are small. Avery turns on his side and Sam tips his head so it rests against Avery's chest. Avery flicks his fingers by his ear, listening to his own calming beat.

'Is this OK?' Avery says. 'I can move.'

'Don't leave.'

'I'm not leaving. I just don't want to hurt you.'

'Avery.'

'Yeah?'

'Don't leave.'

Avery tucks into Sam, two broken pieces in a puzzle box.

'I'm not leaving,' Avery says.

CHAPTER 36

The trick is to keep quiet.

The trick is to hold on to Avery.

The trick is to only cry in the dark so you won't get pitying looks from the nurses who think it's the pain but it's not it's not it's not.

It's the falling.

Sam curls in a ball on his bed, hospital gown slipping off one shoulder, while he focuses on counting the strands of the cotton blanket. His stomach feels like every muscle has been cut open and stretched like taffy. Sometimes he can't take a deep enough breath. He won't eat. It's been twenty-four hours, and he's so, so sore.

The nurse has just finished with his bandage change, and hands him a paper cup and pills. 'Your social worker is coming in now.' She pulls the hospital gown up his shoulder. It just slips back down.

He's too small for an adult one and guesses they didn't want to give him one with kid patterns because he's a criminal. He's trouble. They don't want to see him as a child.

'Do you know where my brother is?'

'Sleeping in the waiting room around the corner. Do you want me to fetch him?'

'When is—'

There's a slight scuffle at the entrance to Sam's room and a jumble of tense whispers. The nurse frowns and pushes past the curtain around Sam's bed to see. He curls tighter into a ball. Every sound, every scrape, every crisp tap of shoe on the floor, makes him think they're coming for him. His lips move to ask the nurse to get Avery, but she's too far away and he's too hollowed out to do more than whisper.

'Excuse me, but you can't be in here.'

Sam tenses.

'But it says family, right? I'm family.'

'Uh. You look nothing like—'

'Oh, just five minutes. I've run across the entire city to find him. *Please.*'

Sam's fists clench around the blankets and he struggles upright, a cry on his lips – a desperate, pleading cry.

Let me see her.

A whimper escapes instead, but the curtain shoves back and Moxie De Lainey appears.

It's a fist to Sam's already pulverised stomach. He isn't sure if he wants to hide or fling his arms around her neck or sob his heart out.

'Thank God.' Moxie skids to a stop at the end of his bed. '*Sam.*'

His name is a sob, a prayer, an accusation all at once.

She looks frazzled, her hair loose and dishevelled, her shirt damp with sweat – like she truly did run across the world to find him. For a minute she just sucks in air and her eyes devour Sam and he thinks *maybe maybe maybe* he will keep it together.

But then she frowns and her mouth punches out words that tear him to pieces.

'How *could* you?'

He shrinks against the pillows.

'Was it all true?' Moxie's fingers tighten around the end of the bed frame. 'What you did? I figured out your parents are abusive assholes and you had to run away, but it's actually more than that. It's you—' She stops.

It's you who's the monster.

He wants to say sorry but he knows it's pitiful and nowhere near enough.

Slowly, like she doesn't want to, she sits on the very corner of his bed. An ocean away. 'We looked everywhere. We were out till dawn just driving up and down the coast. I was so scared.'

'Moxie.' His voice cracks on every letter.

She lays her hands in her lap. Doesn't look at him. 'I told my dad everything. I should've done that a long time ago.'

She thinks the whole summer was a mistake.

Sam pulls the blanket up to his chin and buries his face. He wants to curl under it completely, disappear. He grips this world with two fingertips and he's tired and he hurt everyone and he should just let go.

Her voice is tight. 'Dad said he could've helped.'

Too late now.

'He couldn't.' Sam's heart punches holes in his chest. 'The police have looked for me for a y-year and your dad would've had to hand me over—'

'What? And you don't deserve to be caught? Like because you beat someone up for a "good reason" that makes it all right?' She whips to face him, a blaze that scalds his soul. 'You need serious help.'

What he hears is,

You can never be forgiven for that.

He knows. Look what he did. Look at his hands. Look at his eyes, carved with lines of violence and crime.

She slips a phone from her pocket. 'I'm calling Dad and he can—'

'No.'

Moxie looks at him.

Sam's mouth is cotton and ash. 'I don't – I don't … you should just go.'

Her jaw trembles. 'Seriously? You're going to be like that?'

'I don't need your help,' Sam whispers, cutting his heart out in bloody strips. 'Just leave it, OK? My brother's here and you could get into a lot of trouble for … you know, sheltering a criminal.' He already has to bury mountains in his pockets to try and keep Avery's name clean in this.

Avery. Avery. Avery.

All waif and damp eyes and fluttering fingers.

'And your brother?' Moxie says, stiff now. 'I passed him sleeping in the waiting room when I came in. How is he going to help you? You said *he* needs help.'

He does.

'We'll be fine.' Sam rubs his knuckles over his eyes.

'You know Griffin's family is pressing charges, right?' Moxie folds her arms, phone tucked against the crook of her elbow. But at least she didn't call anyone. 'Not that I didn't feel like punching him too – but you were way, *way* overboard. And then … then *what even happened*?'

Sam feels sick. 'I got stabbed.'

Moxie's eyes widen. For a second she looks like she'll puncture the distance between them and take him in her arms. But she doesn't. '*What*? By who?'

Sam closes his eyes. He couldn't tell her, even if Avery hadn't already said to keep his mouth shut until they get a lawyer.

'Someone who hit Avery.' Sam rubs his eyes again. They keep filling up. He's so soft.

The trick is to not be so soft.

'I'm sorry,' he whispers. 'I'm so so sorry.'

Moxie backhands her eyes furiously. 'I know Griffin hit you first. But … Sam, you scare me.'

He scares Avery too. He scares himself.

I want to stop, he could scream. *I don't want this to be my forever.*

But instead, he tugs threads of the blanket and wishes there was a way to say sorry. It took golden thread and squares of cloth and a box of caramel chocolates last time. This is infinitely worse.

He'll need a ladder into space and a bucket to collect sunbeams so he can stitch her a dress with his bruised, broken fingers. And even then, would it be enough?

'I don't want you—' she begins, but cuts off as three adults stride into the room.

Sam knows she hadn't finished the sentence, but all that repeats in his brain with razor barbs is *I don't want you—*

I don't want you—

I don't want you—

Moxie stands quickly. There's a man and woman in suits, and a cop behind them in full uniform with weapon belt clanking. Sam's insides turn to ice.

'Hello, miss.' The man wears entire black – black shirt, smart jacket, impeccably shined shoes. 'I'm Sammy Lou's social worker and I'm going to have to ask you to leave.' He turns flint eyes on Sam.

Sam wonders if you have any chance in a court at all if your social worker looks like he hates you already.

Moxie pushes sweaty hair out of her eyes. 'I can get his brother—'

'Not necessary.' The woman's hair is a sea of silver. She sets a briefcase down, her eyes flicking over Moxie with suspicion. She turns to the social worker. 'No visitors for my client. Have the hospital staff notified. This could already be a problem.'

The social worker gives a tight nod and motions for Moxie to leave.

She turns to Sam one last time, her eyes pools of unshed tears. She bites her lip, the lemon and steel fading to this vulnerable, agonised look. She mouths, *Let me help*.

Sam gives the tiniest shake of his head.

And then they're ushering her out the door and he loses her.

Sam bunches his fists in the blankets. He needs Avery. They're not going to let him have Avery. Hot tears sting his eyes and he doesn't bother to rub them away.

The social worker holds out his hand to shake Sam's. 'Emery Evans,' he says. 'And this is your lawyer, Celia Polnik. She handles many of our kids' cases, so you're in good hands. Now, the police have some questions for you.'

Sam's throat is dry. He has no words. Can't they see? He dropped them when he ran, and now his mouth is full of splinters.

Just then Avery sprints into the room, half slamming against the wall in mussed, sleepy, sock-clad haste. He bolts over to Sam and throws himself to his side. His thin chest moves raggedly. Maybe a girl woke him on her way out.

'OK,' Avery says, 'OK, I'm here. You can talk to him now.'

Like they need Avery's permission to come anywhere near his little brother.

CHAPTER 37

Sam insists he can dress himself, but he underestimates how much it still hurts. He puts on black dress trousers and socks and then decides he needs a break. Possibly a nap.

Possibly he could never wake up.

His fingers brush over the bandages taped to his stomach. It's been a week and he should've been out of the hospital earlier except they have nowhere to put him. And the hospital psychiatrist isn't happy with how little Sam's eating. Or how often he screams himself awake at night. No one knows what to do with him.

That's great, because he doesn't know what to do with himself either.

Avery, so far, slips through the cracks of everyone's attention. But flint-eyed Evans has zoned in on him, and Sam knows it's only a matter of time before he deals with the panicked, flapping Avery too.

Sam starts to go back to bed and tackle the shirt and tie later, when Evans walks crisply in.

Sam pulls himself upright. 'You said you

weren't coming till four.'

'I said we're going to the courthouse at three.' Evans's dark eyes flit about the room. No Avery. He seems satisfied. 'Get your shirt. We leave now so we can start the paperwork before the judge is in. It's just a preliminary hearing and Polnik will do the talking.'

Sam's shoulders cave inward. He pulls on the white shirt, still creased from the packet, and slowly does the buttons. Evans brought the clothes in earlier. A vicious ache runs through Sam every time he thinks of the waistcoat. Ruined with blood and sliced by the knife. They threw it out.

Don't think of the waistcoat.

Or Moxie.

You're *not allowed*.

You don't deserve to.

'Avery isn't back yet,' Sam says. 'He went to get a clean shirt—'

Evans picks up the tie and impatiently gestures for Sam to stand. Sam feels like a speck of a boy next to Evans's towering limbs. The man is all spider-thin fingers and a disapproving mouth.

'He can meet us there.'

'He won't know where to go,' Sam says. 'He might not make it in time. We have to wait.'

Evans does the tie efficiently, sliding it too tight and then adjusting Sam's collar. 'We're not waiting.'

Sam understands.

Evans did this on purpose. He always brings

paperwork and lawyers and police in when Avery isn't there. When Avery's sleeping. When Avery's gone to try and find Aunt Karen. He despises Avery for skirting the system and being guilty but with not enough proof to nail him. From snippets Sam's picked up, he's waiting for Avery's case to be assigned to him. Then his spider fingers will be all over Sam's brother.

But he doesn't want Avery at the courthouse. Not Avery's loud tics or panicked outbursts or the way he freaks out when someone comes close to Sam.

But Sam can't go without him.

He's so empty. They tried to stitch him back together, but too much already fell out. Stars and buttons and caramel truffles.

'I need Avery.'

'What you need,' Evans says, 'is a very merciful judge and a perfectly respectful attitude. Cooperate, Samuel, or this is going to go worse for you.'

My name is just Sammy, he wants to say, but he just picks up the splinters of his soul that are left, and follows Evans out.

CHAPTER 38

Sam tests the car door handles as soon as Evans isn't looking. Locked from the outside. The car smells of ground coffee and paperwork and there's not a crumb to be seen. Sam has been around several social workers, but Evans is something else. Maybe when they get a case stamped with the words *assault* and *runaway* and *thief* and *invisible boy*, they pick the caseworkers who are made of black ink and hard lines.

Evans's car purrs smoothly through the city. He glances once in his rear-view mirror and Sam stares blankly back.

'Am I going to jail?' Sam says at last.

'I can't predict the judge.'

A non-answer. Sam should be used to those.

'When we go back to the hospital to get Avery—'

'We're not going back.'

Sam's eyes snatch to the driver's seat, but Evans just holds the wheel calmly like he didn't puncture Sam's thin web of calm.

'After this, I'm taking you to a youth detention facility and we'll move through your case from there.'

'Avery—'

'Yes, I'll look after Avery.'

no no no don't touch him

'But I need to see him again.' Sam's voice is panicked.

Evans doesn't notice. Or care. 'You will eventually. For now you need constant supervision and completion of your mental health assessment.'

Sam digs fingers into his hair. He's ripping apart. 'I need air,' he whispers. Then louder, 'I need the window down. I'm going to … I'm going to be sick.'

This gets Evans's attention fast. He pulls up at a red traffic light and twists in his seat to where Sam hunches in the back. Sam must look white enough that Evans flips the lock off in the front so Sam's window can zoom down.

Sam unbuckles his belt and puts his whole head out.

'Sit back down,' Evans commands. 'Put your belt on and—'

But Sam's already climbing out of the window.

Evans gives a startled exclamation and whips off his own seatbelt, but Sam's been running away for years and he knows how to be fast and light and unexpected.

He hits the road in a crouch and then springs forward. Pain instantly explodes through his guts, but he ignores it, running down the row of growling cars waiting for the lights to go green.

Evans yells at his back.

Horns blare.

Sam runs.

'You can't afford to do this!' Evan shouts.

Sam tucks his head and swerves amongst cars. His shoes hit the sidewalk. He's through an alley and climbing a fence and across someone's backyard before the pain slices, white and blinding, through his stomach. He buckles to his knees in the grass and grabs his stomach.

Get up. Keep running. You have to get out of here.

Sobs rip from his throat and he picks himself up, pushes on, climbs another fence, and falls flat on his face in stones and weeds. When he gets up this time, his shirt sticks to his side. Blood blooms across the white like spilt paint.

He's good at running away. Come on, he's good at this, he can still do it.

He loses himself in backyards and old roads and he walks and walks until his stomach can't take it any more and he throws up. It's like ripping stitches. It's like the knife going in again and again. He throws his tie away.

Keep walking.

His legs know the destination even before his mind does.

Walk, Sammy, just walk.

They said they would help.

But they lied, of course they lied, no one wants

to help Sammy Lou, the boy with fists full of cut glass and violent desperation.

The sun bathes the world in dusky blues and pinks. It hits the sprawling butter-yellow house and turns it into glittering gold – the only gold Sam couldn't quite properly steal. His muscles throb and his ribs splinter and all the hope left in him bleeds out.

He slumps into the gutter in front of the house.

And sits.

Just like old times, when he had a mouthful of apologies but none seemed good enough.

It's late enough that everyone will be home. Jeremy is probably cooking – it's his night, isn't it? – and Jack will be loitering uselessly about the kitchen because as much as they deny it, those two stick together.

Toby is probably drawing on a wall.

Grady is reading and bossing everyone around.

Dash will be jumping on the trampoline in the backyard with the neighbour kids, mud on their knees, while they practise speaking Elven.

Moxie is

Moxie is

Moxie is

Moxie hates him.

His brain shuts down, because thinking of her just spills him into reams of fabric and buttons and knotted threads while she laughs at him and snatches the needle away to do it herself. While they whisper for hours about everything and nothing and he learns her deepest fears and her best days and memorises every fleck of colour in her eyes.

Sam rests his face on his knees. He is an empty boy and when people see what he truly is, they hate it.

This house will never be his.

A rattling van pulls into the driveway and the engine shuts off with a crunch. A breeze brushes through the gnarly rosebushes and chills Sam's neck. It tastes of cooler days and the end of summer.

It had to end.

Boots hit the footpath behind him.

He keeps his face pressed in his knees.

'Sam.'

The voice is softness and sorrow.

Mr De Lainey drops down into the gutter beside Sam. He doesn't touch him. Sam tips his head sideways, just a little, to see Mr De Lainey's sawdust-covered work trousers and cement-splattered boots. He doesn't look at his face. Can't look. He never wanted those disappointed eyes on him.

Why did Sam come back?

'You're bleeding.'

'It's fine,' Sam whispers into his knees, arms still wrapping himself into a tight ball. 'It's not bad.' It hurts like his skin has been peeled off and stitched on inside out. But it doesn't hurt as much as being in front of the De Lainey house again.

'You're lying.'

Sam shrinks into himself a little further.

But Mr De Lainey's voice isn't angry. He stated a fact and now he stretches out his dusty legs on the road, like he's ready to sit for a good long while.

'I know you're looking for something, Sam,' he says. 'I know you found it here. And I want you to have it, you hear me, son? I want more than anything for you to have this.'

'This,' Sam repeats into his arms. 'A family.' His voice dries in his throat. 'A home. I really want a ... h-h-home.'

'But you can't steal it.'

'I know,' Sam whispers. *I know I know I know.*

'You have to build it.'

Sam peels his face away from his legs, his lashes wet and heavy. He meets Mr De Lainey's eyes, ready for that crushing wave of disappointment.

But the gaze before him is just sad and tired. Dirt stains Mr De Lainey's face, proof that he knows how to build what he wants.

'And I'm going to help you build it.' His voice is quiet, calm as summer. 'It'll be slow and we'll have to go backwards to set some things straight. You can't build a house in the sky, Sam, you have to have two feet on the ground. No more hiding and running. You need help, real help. And I can be here for you, every minute.'

'They'll take me away.'

'We'll get you back. The right way.'

337

Sam takes a deep breath and slowly, the last shreds of his stamina falling away, he leans sideways until his head rests on Mr De Lainey's shoulder.

The De Lainey father scoots closer and pulls Sam into his arms. He's all sawdust and sweat and he holds Sam like he knows how to keep boys who are slipping.

They stay like that for a minute or a year.

Then Mr De Lainey pushes to his feet and pulls Sam up, carefully checking the bloodstain on Sam's white shirt. 'We're going inside to get this cleaned up.' Not a question. 'And then you can let me know what we're doing. I won't stop you if you leave. But if you stay, we're building properly, starting with a phone call to your social worker. I confess I've been asking about you and already have his number.'

Sam nods, his words in knots.

He trails behind Mr De Lainey, past the rosebushes and the mess of toys in the front yard. Sam falters on the steps and Mr De Lainey quietly points to the tall front window, which throws golden sunlight all over Moxie's sewing table. The top of her head is visible, bent over cloth and needles.

'I don't want to go in,' Sam says.

'I'll bring the first aid kit out then.' Mr De Lainey gives Sam's shoulder a squeeze and goes inside.

A wave of hellos and the smell of pasta and

frying onions pour out. There's the squeak of Toby's tricycle and the slam of Grady closing a book. The sewing machine shuts off.

Sam takes a step towards the window. Another. Another. He raises a trembling hand and

taps the glass.

Moxie looks up.

She's wearing a striped yellow shirt and overalls, her long legs bare and streaked with coloured markers thanks to a day with Toby. Her hair is caught in a frizzy bun. A scowl fits over her lips, all vinegar and suspicion.

When she sees him, the scowl falters. Her lips part in surprise. He lets his forehead rest against the windowpane, wondering if he has anything to say after he told her to leave.

Then she slams down her handful of cottons and storms away.

He tips back from the window and looks at his fingers as they unravel like he's a boy of spun wool. He pushes away from the window. He deserves that. This. All of it.

He should just walk away now.

Steal another house.

Disappear.

But he

doesn't

doesn't

doesn't

want to.

Then suddenly Moxie is sweeping out the front door, rainbow strips of fabric falling out of her pockets. Her eyes burn and the vinegar frown is gone, replaced with something like longing. Something like fear. She doesn't walk to him, she flies.

Her hands are at his face, tracing his jaw, his cheekbone, his lips.

He expects a slap.

Instead she puts her arms around his neck – carefully, like she knows he's unravelling. And she hugs him.

His arms slip around her back. She is endlessly warm, like hugging waffles with honey.

'I'm angry,' she says fiercely. 'I'm angry at you but I also care so much. I told you that, didn't I? You're making me care when I said I was done with that.' She pulls away from him, her eyes bright. 'How dare you get stabbed?'

'I'm nothing,' he says. 'I'm nothing and I'm from nowhere and I don't want to hurt you.'

She shakes her head. 'Things hurt. People hurt. Life hurts. I don't want you to disappear, Sam.' Her hands slide away from his neck. 'I hate that you lied and I hate that you're running. But I *don't* want this to be the end.'

Sam takes a shuddering breath. 'I'm sorry.'

She glances down then and sees his shirt. She gives a sharp intake of breath. 'You stupid beautiful boy. Go sit on the steps. Right now.' Then she spins and runs inside.

Sam does as he's told.

She returns with a first aid kit and a clean shirt, which Sam thinks Mr De Lainey was probably fetching but got rapidly relieved of. She throws the lid open and rummages for clean bandages and tape. Then she unbuttons Sam's shirt. Blood soaks her fingertips.

He's so cold.

She peels off his old bandages, wiping it clean as best she can. 'I think you've busted a few stitches.'

'I kind of ran across the city.'

'Typical boy with a pea-sized brain.'

He nearly smiles.

She tapes a fresh bandage on and he tries not to think about her hands on his feverish skin and how fiercely tight her lips are as she concentrates. She bites the tape off and then hands him the T-shirt. He gets stuck lifting his arms high enough. She helps.

'You lose it when someone else is getting hurt,' she says suddenly.

Sam tugs the shirt down so the bandage and his sins are covered. It's Jeremy's shirt, a superhero emblazoned on the front. Ironic.

'I'm sor—'

'No, don't say sorry again. Tell me what you're going to do now.'

'I'm a bad person, Moxie.' His voice is stripped raw. 'I'm not Goldilocks. I'm the monster in the woods. I can't stop myself. I-I-I get so close to killing people whenever they touch Avery. And I

341

don't like it … I hate it. I *hate* it. I deserve jail. I deserve it if you never speak to me again.'

'You can do monstrous things and not be a monster.'

'I don't w-want to be this.'

'Then we'll help you not to be.'

'It's too late.'

'No, you listen here, Sam.' She sits down so close to him, her leg crushed to his. She takes his hands and their fingers fit together.

He aches.

'Life punched you to your knees when you were little, so you freaked out and fought back. None of this is right or good or – or *fair*. It's so, so unfair. But I won't stop forgiving you.'

'Everybody leaves.'

Her thumb brushes the bruise on his cheek. 'I'm not leaving.'

She pulls his chin down and their mouths meet. It's not the lit skin and wild beauty of their other kisses. It's salty tears and bloody memories and empty boxes. She tastes of longing, he of tears.

She stops kissing him and wipes his cheeks with her palm. Her eyes are wet when she smiles. 'You're going to make me cry again and then you'll be in trouble. I hate crying.' Her nose touches his and their lips brush again—

And then a body thumps into the gate and there's a disbelieving curse.

They look up.

Avery hangs over the front gate, his shirt soaked with sweat and chest heaving. His eyes are wild as explosions and wars and he grips the fence like it's the only thing keeping his exhausted legs upright.

'Sammy.' He gasps for breath. 'I ran all the – way – over here – to rescue – you—' He sucks in a ragged lungful of air. 'And you're *just kissing* – in the sunset? You little jerk.'

Moxie looks like she's holding back a laugh. 'Finally I get to meet Avery properly.'

Avery grabs his knees and wheezes. 'I'm going – to – puke – on you – Sammy. In just – a second.'

Several curious faces crowd the open De Lainey door. Clearly they were giving Sam and Moxie a moment but – the moment is officially over.

Jeremy squeezes past the others on to the veranda. 'Hey, the return of the second Sammy.' He nudges Jack. 'He looks like a wild sort of elf. No! A lost boy from *Peter Pan*.'

Jack snorts. 'I think he swam here.'

'I ran,' Avery growls. His eyes shift from one face to the other, not sure who's joking or who's the enemy.

Mr De Lainey appears, wearing worn jeans now with a baby on his hip. 'Reece De Lainey,' he says calmly like every day battered boys tumble into his yard.

Avery seems to have regained his breath. He attempts the gate, fumbles the latch, kicks it, and then just climbs over. He walks cautiously up the path, eyes like snake slits and fingers flicking his thighs. Typical Avery around new people: scared and wanting to curl in Sam's arms – but teeth bared to bite if it's not safe.

'Sammy,' he says, 'we need to—'

'We're about to have dinner,' Mr De Lainey says. 'And then Sam's deciding if he's going back or not. You can stay too.' He folds his arms and leans against the veranda rail. 'Do you want a job?'

'A w-w-what?' Avery looks like a frightened rabbit.

Sam snaps his gaze to Mr De Lainey. What is he doing?

'I work in construction,' Mr De Lainey says. 'I have my own business. I'll hire you as a paid apprentice and you can sleep here.'

Sam understands.

The De Lainey father gets it. He's seen Sam in tears with clenched, bloody fists and knows that the surest way to save him is to save his brother.

Avery just stares. He's abandoned trying to still his hands and they spin in circles by his sides. But he sets his jaw and doesn't shrink away. Like he's trying to make up for fifteen years of leaving Sam to look after himself.

'What about Sam?' Avery says. 'They'll take him away – they'll ... no-no-no—'

'Yes.' Mr De Lainey doesn't lie or manipulate. 'I'll go downtown first thing and get a lawyer and start things moving to get Sam's custody if I can.'

He rubs his jaw. 'That's if Sam chooses to go back to court. Either way, the job and bed are yours.'

Avery doesn't know how to respond. He looks at Sam and then back to the De Lainey father.

Finally he swears. 'You really mean it.' He swears again, confusion in every syllable.

Jack gives a low whistle. 'I cannot *wait* to see Dad handle this.'

Mr De Lainey just smiles and pushes away from the veranda. 'Dinner's in five minutes. Avery, come inside and get some water. Do you like pasta?'

The twins shove their way back inside, both talking at once about how about their dad can fire them if he's hiring Avery and then they can spend every afternoon swimming.

Judging it safer with everyone gone, Avery crosses the remaining ground between him and Sam. He turns fierce eyes on Moxie – like she's the one taking Sam away.

Well, she did. Just a little.

She matches his look, blade for blade. 'You better stay for dinner or my dad will transform into a mother hen and shed feathers everywhere.'

'*What?*' says Avery.

'It's a joke,' Sam says. 'You'll like their food. They don't always mix everything.'

Avery scuffs Sam's shoe and glares, his hardest punishment since they were kids. 'You shut up. You scared me to death, you know that? They've got cops out looking for you and that asshat

Evans nearly strangled me because he thought I abducted you.'

Sam takes a deep breath, the hollows in his chest filling in.

All his people are here.

Everything he loves.

'Would you?' he says. 'Would you stay? If I … if I had to go to prison for a while?'

The tightness around Avery's mouth loosens and his eyes bleed a sadness so deep. 'We could steal a car and drive away—' His words snap in half suddenly, like he gets it. Sam is tired. Sam can't do this any more. 'I'm going to get a drink of water.' He jogs up the remaining steps and walks into the butter-yellow house.

It folds over him.

Sam's shoulders sag a little, like he's held himself on high alert too long. He leans his head on Moxie's shoulder and they watch the sun steal the last golden rays and pin a thousand stars in the sky. Dishes and voices clash behind them.

Mr De Lainey comes back to the veranda and whispers in Moxie's ear. Then he sets a phone next to Sam. 'If you decide to call your social worker, the number's there and ready.' He brushes a palm over the top of Sam's head before he goes.

The phone might as well be another knife. If he calls, he's going back to court, back to face everything he's run from. There will be angry eyes, sentencing, juvie … and he'll have to bear it. Alone.

Except maybe he won't be alone for ever. Maybe, when it's over, he'll get out and a family will be waiting for him, a family who'll keep his brother safe until Sam can come—

home.

The veranda's quiet again, just him and Moxie and the stars. She kisses him, on the corner of his mouth, and then slips back into the house.

He can't be an invisible boy when she can see him. He can't steal houses or the girl inside them, but he can build a bridge of moons and caramel cakes to get back to her.

So Sammy Lou
      picks
            up
                  the phone.

ACKNOWLEDGEMENTS

This story is intensely special to me and I am caught in an eternally delirious smile as I hold the finished copy. It is constructed entirely out of wishes and hope and wouldn't be here without these incredible people:

Polly Nolan, my extraordinary agent! I can't thank you enough for all the belief and encouragement as we wrangle my books into acceptable shapes.

The whole team at Orchard Books! Special appreciation to my editors, Megan Larkin and Rosalind McIntosh, who turned *The Boy Who Steals Houses* into a book I am so proud of. And also many thanks to Sue Cook, Thy Bui, Alison Padley, Alice Duggan, Monika Exell, Georgina Russell, Naomi Berwin, Emily Finn and Sarah Jeffcoate.

I owe so much (more than an entire cake by this point) to my magical friends. Maraia, you are incredible and keep me sane and have read this book so many times. Thank you for shouting encouragement while I run about like a headless chicken. To Maria Kuzniar, Miriam "Finn" Longman and Daley Downing: you are brilliant authors who I'm proud to know as we tackle the woes and wonders of writing. Thank you for your advice and flails!

To the bloggers and readers who, after they finished yelling at me through tears, proclaimed their love for *A Thousand Perfect Notes*. You have been a mountain of encouragement. (Where would I be without you?!)

I also owe a moment to my parents who raised me on ink and books. And to my odd pile of siblings: no, you didn't inspire the De Lainey family. Except you, Jemima. Remember that time I cracked an egg on your head when we were kids? I may have stolen the occasional wisp of inspiration from you for the sibling shenanigans in this book.

And to anyone reading this book who is searching for something like family or a home or friends who will wrap you up tight and keep you close: I hope you find what you're looking for.

Read on for a peek at
A Thousand Perfect Notes
by C.G. Drews

CHAPTER 1

What he wants most in the world is to cut off his own hands.

At the wrist would be best. That hollow tiredness that stretches from fingertips to elbow would be gone for ever. How sick is that? There must be something seriously – dangerously – wrong if he can lie on his rock-solid mattress at night and think about lopping off limbs and using bloodied stumps to write 'HA!' on the walls. He'd be a scene out of a horror movie.

And he'd be free. Because, without hands, he's worthless to her.

To the Maestro.

His mother.

But the entire handless daydream would require *action* instead of *fantasising*, and he's not so good at that. Even stupid small stuff – like spontaneously detouring by an ice creamery on the way home from school and treating his little sister to a double whipped fudge cone instead of keeping the strict time schedule the Maestro demands – is impossible. He won't even try something like that. Why? A taste of fudge and freedom isn't worth it?

No.

He's just not made for rebellion or risks.

Fantasising is all he's good for. Sick dreams of mutilation, apparently. Which hand would he even cut off? Right? Or left?

It scares Beck Keverich – the way he thinks sometimes.

His digital clock reads 5:12. Still dark. Still cold. It's always easier to batter his way out of bed in summer, but now that autumn has wrapped bare, twiggy fingers around the universe, his alarm clock feels like it's shrieking in the middle of the night. And he should've been up twelve minutes ago.

It's surprising the Maestro hasn't rattled his door to roar at his laziness.

Beck peels his head off the pillows. He wishes he could dissolve into them. Did he even sleep last night? His wrists ache like he's been juggling blocks of cement. Did he quit at eleven? Midnight?

His fingers moan, *it was midnight, you fool.* They also say *get us warm* and *let us rest this morning* and even *we're going to curl into a fist and punch the wall until we shatter*. His fingers are cantankerous like that.

Beck rubs his hands together, blows on his numb fingers and curses broadly to the universe – because it's quicker than being specific about the depths of his loathing of the Maestro right now. Then he approaches the object of his doom, his life, his worth.

He slams the piano lid open.

The Steinway upright is the sole glory of his room. Not that there's much else *in* the room. He has a bed that feels like snuggling rocks, broken blinds on the windows, a wardrobe of second-hand clothes and shoes held together with duct tape and hope – and a twenty-thousand-dollar piano.

As the Maestro says, 'A good piano is all the hope I have that *mein Sohn* will improve his *schreckliche* music.'

Beck only spent his toddler years in Germany, but stayed bilingual by necessity – he needs to know when his mother is sprinkling burning insults over his head. Although her curled lips and glares also speak volumes.

Schreckliche means *terrible*. Awful.

It's a summary of Beck.

You are an awful pianist. Your music has no future. You have no talent. Why don't you play faster, better, clearer? Why do you hit the wrong notes all the time? Are you doing it on purpose areyouplayingbadlyonpurposeyouworthlesslittle—

'You suck, kid,' Beck says calmly to himself. 'So work.'

It's his routine pep talk to get motivated in the cold pre-dawn darkness. Now for staccato notes. Double fifth scales. Diminished seventh exercises. Fumbled notes. Trills for his iced fingers to fall across.

He'll wake the Maestro – although she's probably already awake and seething that he started late – and his little sister. He'll wake the neighbours, who hate him, and he'll start the local dogs howling. He'll shake the sleep from the weeds strangling the footpath, and the broken glass from some drunken brawl, and the homeless who lurk in the dank non-kid-friendly neighbourhood playground.

By 8 a.m. Beck's fingers will feel like flattened noodles and his eyelids will be coated in cement.

And all the time, he dreams of sawing off his hands or even his ears.

Of walking out and never coming back.

He dreams of utter silence – so then the tiny kernel of music inside him could be coaxed to life. It's unbelievably noisy in his head, noisy with songs of his own creation. But since the Maestro will have none of it, it stays locked away.

Play the music on the paper. No one cares about the songs in your head.

His bedroom door crashes open and his little sister appears with a howl like a wildcat.

Joey is a tumbleweed of wire and jam stains, set on maximum speed and highest volume. She's exhausting just to *look* at.

'IT'S FIFTEEN MINUTES TILL WE GO,' Joey bellows. She solemnly believes Beck can't hear anything else when he's on the piano. He *can* hear, he just can't multitask and answer.

His cyclone of music fades and silence pours over Beck's fingers. Relief. By this point, if Chopin walked into the room, Beck would throttle him with a shoelace. He hates these pieces the Maestro demands he learn.

It's past eight. He's not even dressed or had breakfast.

'I hate Mondays,' he mutters and reaches for his school shirt. At least when one lives in a room the size of a broom closet everything is in easy reach.

Joey's face puckers. 'It's not Monday.'

'Every day is Monday.' A perpetual string of Mondays – he does belong in a horror film.

It takes his aching fingers two tries to get the buttons.

'I made you lunch,' Joey says, spider-climbing up his doorframe. 'A surprise lunch. A *scrumptious* surprise lunch.'

'That sounds … terrifying.' Beck balls his holey pyjama shirt and throws it at her face. She gives an indignant squeak and drops from the walls.

To prove his point – OK, fine, because Joey loves a good show of theatrics – Beck drops to his knees, clasps his hands together, and wails like an impaled porpoise. She's giggling before he even starts to beg.

'Don't *punish me*. Please. What have I *done* to deserve this torment?'

'It's not torment!' Joey says, indignant. 'I'm a scrumptious cook. Even if you're a *bad brother* for being late yesterday.'

That would be on account of his English teacher, Mr Boyne, having a flare up of *I-care-about-your-horrible-grades-so-I'm-going-to-bawl-you-out-to-prove-it*, which included a demanded display of Beck's comprehension of the text. The 'comprehension' was, of course, non-existent. Hence Beck was late to pick up Joey.

The preschool teacher, whose face reminded him of a king crab, snapped at him about 'responsibilities', too.

'If I was a witch, I'd turn you into a toad,' Joey says, confidentially, ''cause everyone gets mad when we gotta go to the city for you, and Mama says we're going again soon.'

Beck cringes. There's a state championship coming up to obligingly stress everyone. Oh joy. And failure, with the Maestro hanging over his shoulder, is *not* an option.

'But I'd turn you back into a boy *someday*,' Joey says, warming up. ''Cause I like you, even if you always play the same notes over and over and over, because Mama says you're a *Schwachkopf*—'

Beck covers her mouth. 'OK, calm down. My delicate self-worth can only take so much. Is the Maestro already foaming at the mouth?'

Joey glares from behind his hand.

He removes it. 'I'm sorry I play the same

song so much. I'm – practising. For that big concert.' *Practise, or the Maestro's fury will know no bounds.*

'Lean close,' Joey says, 'and I'll whisper *I forgive you* in your ear.'

Beck does without thinking. But she jumps on him, yowling like a kitten made of cacti, and Beck goes down in a tangle of shirtsleeves and mismatched buttons.

She's only his half-sister – the Maestro has an affinity for short relationships that end in screaming fits and neither he nor Joey knew their fathers – but Joey's a pocketful of light in his gloomy existence. He has to love her twice as hard to make up for the sin of hating his mother.

Predictably, breakfast is cornflakes with a side dish of disapproval.

Has there ever been a time when the Maestro didn't greet him with a glare?

She sits in a corner of their tiny kitchen with squash-coloured décor that probably looked trendy thirty years ago. Who is Beck kidding? That shade of yellow *never* looked good. A single piece of burnt buttered toast sits next to her mug of coffee. The table can seat three, if no one minds bumping elbows, but as usual it's flooded with the Maestro's sheets of music. She tutors musicianship and theory at the university. Beck wonders how often her students cry.

Beck slinks past, telling himself he did everything

right. She has nothing to erupt about. It'll be OK – totally OK.

He reaches for two bowls as Joey bangs around his legs, prattling about how she's going to be a chef when she grows up.

'And I'm gonna call my restaurant –' she sucks in a deep breath to yell '– JOEY'S GOODEST GRUB.' She jabs her spoon into Beck's ribs to get his attention. 'That's a great name, right?'

'Yow – *yes*.' He snatches the spoon off her.

He fills Joey's bowl with cornflakes first, which leaves him with the mostly smashed flake dust. With milk, it'll become sludge. Brilliant. He sets Joey's bowl on her pink plastic kiddie table in the corner, and eats his while leaning on the fridge.

Joey launches into a detailed description of what her chef apron will look like – something about it being shaped like a unicorn – which exactly no one listens to.

Beck watches the Maestro's red pen whip over the music. The students' work looks like something has been murdered over it.

Beck checks the plastic bag with his squashed sandwich. Joey has a thing about making his lunch. He sniffs it and detects peanut butter, tomato sauce and – are those raw pasta shells? Maybe he'd rather not know.

'You'll be late.' The Maestro's voice is deep and raspy. Even if she didn't have the temperament of a bull, she's an intimidating-looking woman.

Broad-shouldered, six foot, with a crop of wiry black hair like a bristle brush – and she has long, spider-like fingers born for the piano.

Beck shovels the last globs of cornflake sludge into his mouth and then runs for the school bags. He crams in his untouched homework and sandwich, but takes more time with Joey's – checking that she has a clean change of clothes in there, that her gumboots are dry, and her rainbow jacket isn't too filthy. A finger-comb through his curly hair and duct-taped shoes on his feet, and he's ready.

Joey pops out of her bedroom dressed in overalls with a pink beanie over her brush-resistant black curls. She snatches her jacket off Beck and dances towards the door. Preschool is blissfully free of dress regulations.

Beck has worn the same uniform shirt for so long it looks more pink than red.

They're about to run for the front door when the Maestro shuffles papers and says, 'A word, *mein Sohn.*'

Really? They have to do this now? She couldn't just let them skid out of the door, out of her hair, without raking him over the hot coals for once?

Joey kicks the front door open with her glittered gumboots. 'I'm gonna beat you there!' she yells.

Beck slinks back into the kitchen, slowly, his eyes on the ugly tiled floor. If he doesn't make eye contact with the tiger, it won't eat him, right? One of these days he'll just bolt out the door, defy her, just once. Instead of acting the obedient puppy, resigned to its next kick.

'*Ja, Mutter?*' He uses German as a tentative appeasement.

The Maestro lays down the red pen and kneads her knotted fingers. The tremors have already started for the day – the tremors that destroyed her career and turned her into a tornado over Beck's.

Painfully slow seconds tick by like swats against Beck's face.

He has to get out.

Needs

to

leave.

'You woke late,' the Maestro says. 'I don't permit *Faulheit* in my house.'

'I didn't mean to be lazy.' Yeah, he slept in all of twelve minutes. 'I'm sorry.' Suck up. It's the only way to get out alive.

The Maestro snorts. 'Why are you inept at dedication and commitment? Do you want your progress to stagnate?' She picks up her mug. It trembles violently and coffee sloshes over the side. 'Or is this your streak of *teenage* rebellion?' She sneers the word 'teenage', like she never was one. Which is highly likely. Beck always imagines she strode into the world as a bitter giant, ready to clobber everyone with a piano.

'I'm sorry.' Beck resists a glance at the front

door to see how far Joey's gone. He doesn't like her to cross the road alone.

'*Ja*, of course you are sorry. A little parrot with only one phrase to say. A lazy parrot who – *look at me* when I speak to you.' Her crunchy voice rises, and she hauls herself upright, more coffee escaping her mug and dripping down her wrist.

He doesn't want to do this again. He's going to be *late*.

'*Mutter*, please, I've got school.' Beck snatches a glance at the clock.

Her hand flashes out of nowhere and slaps his face. The shock of it sends him a step backwards. He always forgets how fast she can move.

'Do not disrespect me!' she snaps. 'School is not important. I am speaking to you. *That* is important.'

Beck does nothing.

'The only important thing in your life is the piano.' Her voice shakes the ceiling plaster. 'The piano *is* life. And every time you laze instead of practising, you shame me. You shame my name. You'll amount to nothing, *Sohn*, nothing! Are you listening?'

'Yes, *Mutter*.' Beck speaks to his shoes.

'Is my advice a joke to you? LOOK AT ME WHEN I SPEAK.'